MW00979898

THE CHILDREN OF ELI

A Novel By Mike Cranny

National Library of Canada Cataloguing In Publication Data

Cranny, Michael
     Children of Eli

     ISBN 978-0-9920349-0-0

     I. Title

© Michael Cranny 2013

A Cranberry Ridge Communications Publication:

Michael Cranny
mcranny@shaw.ca

For Valerie

CHAPTER 1

A rchie Stevens didn't like it. Cal Fricke wasn't going to give him a case. That was obvious. Archie figured that Fricke was sending him a message — Archie was supposed to take the hint and quit. He thought about it, seriously considered it. Then he happened on an open file in Cold Cases and took it on — all on his own. It was something to do while he made a final decision about his future. The case concerned abalone poaching. Fricke laughed when Archie told him about it, and gave his okay. That was a signal too.

The file didn't contain much on the surface: abalone poaching, a midnight beating and death threats, a suspected gang link — no names on the report sheets in the folder. Archie called Fisheries and learned nothing new — besides the fact that abalone poaching was a problem in the area. It was one of those cases that should have been followed up at the time. Now, it was a phantom of a case, retrieved by a phantom detective, himself. Even the original investigating officer was dead. Detective Robert Wilkins, aged thirty-eight, Archie's age, died too young — killed when he lost control of his vehicle on the Bastion Highway.

Archie learned as much as he could about abalone. He visited seafood restaurants and seafood suppliers. He asked lots of questions. Then he moved on to marine supply shops, marinas and boat yards, and did the same. He got nothing. His case was fading away. His last hope was Nick Donaldson. Donaldson had a dive shop outside of Harsley. The Harsley Police Department, Archie's own, had arrested him for fishing infractions over the years — some poaching too. No surprise there. Nick was an old, out-of-work, cold-water diver who needed to make a living. Likely, he was still poaching or knew who was. Archie finished reading the old reports he had been studying. It was almost dark when he left the station and headed for Nick's.

Archie wondered how he would open the conversation with a man he'd once been on friendly terms with. Nick might even pick a fight. Archie had no idea what he would do if that happened. He wasn't particularly good at holding his temper. Then again neither was Nick.

Archie slowed his 4Runner so that he wouldn't miss the overgrown access. The road-marker reflectors showed suddenly — high up in the screen of old-growth hemlock. He braked, took the tight right, eased his car over the culvert and started down twinned tracks that passed for a road, saw that the pivot log gate was up indicating that Nick might be home. The forest pressed in close on both sides, giving Archie a sense of oppressive desolation, and of the death of the Nick's hopes and dreams.

A quarter of a mile in, he saw something lying beside the road and stopped the car. A deer lay on the verge, broken and still. Archie got out and shone his light. The eyes were flat and unseeing; fresh blood still dripped from the nostrils and pooled on slick, brown, fallen leaves. Sad — the driver of the car that had killed the deer hadn't even stopped. Archie returned to his vehicle, tossed the Maglite beside him. He touched the accelerator and continued on, fighting the wheel as the 4Runner slipped in and out of deep, muddy ruts.

At last, he emerged from the dense forest. The road turned to smooth hardpan, curled down over the shingle drift and ran in a straight line along the beach towards the little cliff-backed harbour where Nick had his dive shop. Archie passed the painted board with its red diver flag. Ahead, he made out the outline of the dark shapes of the low, barn-like buildings that were Nick's shop, his sheds and boathouse plunked out in the treeless no man's land, unchanged and unimproved.

A line of stored fish boats, the fleet high and dry, with the same faded "For Sale" signs on each, formed a wall of wood and fiberglass hulls going nowhere. Nick likely never went anywhere near them; he'd just let them rot on their trunions.

To Archie the boats represented dreams gone sour. He had tried that life, back when he needed a lifeline, when he needed a direction. He had fished on his Uncle Tony's boat "Wasko". Archie had tried hard to see a future in fishing. But he didn't want to end up like the owners of these boats with their long-expired licenses still fixed to the flaking walls of their pilothouses.

He parked a short distance from the shop, his headlights resting on a four by eight plywood sign decorated with amateurish pictures of wolf eels, octopus, starfish and awkwardly waving kelp. The faded sign announced Dive Adventures' offerings; package deals, wreck dives, big animal dives, deep adventure and catered lunches.

No lights showed in the shop or the attached house. Archie figured Nick was away, but it was hard to tell. He remembered that some rooms didn't have windows.

He hesitated and then shut off the engine. He leaned back in his seat and tried to relax, trying to suppress the feeling of aloneness that seemed to be his default state of mind. He reminded himself that he had nothing to lose; the Abalone Case would be officially dead in the morning. He opened his door; he felt the cold damp air. He listened, hearing the muted hum from the highway more than half a mile away, the wind in the hemlocks, and the chattering of beach stones as the surf rattled through them in the darkness.

He tried to imagine what might happen if he caught Nick red-handed and had to make an arrest. Not that that was likely to happen. More likely he'd finish up with his little, nothing case and put the final nails in the coffin of his unlikely career.

With his Maglite in hand he began to walk towards the shop. As he walked he glimpsed Nick's Jeep parked back of the refill station.

Archie sensed that something wasn't right. It occurred to him that Nick hadn't turned on the lot lights. With all the vandalism that was happening out that way, a motion-sensor setup would have been prudent; but Archie's arrival hadn't triggered any response.

He shifted his SIG Sauer from its holster to his jacket pocket as he strode across the gravel to the shop.

His foot slid as he tried to quickly climb the four broad steps to the low-roofed porch. When he regained his footing and started up the stairs again, broken glass crunched under his foot. He turned on his Maglite and hooded it with his hand and saw that the front window was smashed. The front door was open too, the lock displaced and the sash splintered around the striker plate. He realized he'd been holding his breath and exhaled.

He took his pistol from his pocket, eased back the slide and released it slowly. He felt the jacketed bullet nose softly into the chamber. Then he took a position to the left of the door and listened for sounds. Procedure required that he call in and wait for backup, and he thought about it. But Archie Stevens had a hard time calling for help even when he should. There was no guarantee that he would get any anyway.

He made spit to moisten his dry mouth. Then he slipped his long body through the doorway. He put his back to the wall, held the Maglite away from him and snapped the beam inside.

The shop was deserted, but somebody had hit the place hard. Display stands were turned over, dive gear scattered, air tanks rolled across the floor and into corners, and there was more broken glass — a lot of destruction that seemed to have no purpose, as if somebody had targeted Nick for some special and punitive vandalism. The smell of wet neoprene, of oxidizing metal and damp canvas, lingered.

He let the beam of his light wander as he tried to make sense of what lay before him. He saw long, wet, black streaks on the linoleum and his heart leapt in his chest.

Again he thought about backing out and calling in, but he didn't. He had to see for himself, out of pride, or friendship, or something. Pistol at the ready, he followed the blood trail down the narrow hallway towards the back. His thoughts were focussed and clear. His movements were purposeful. He passed a freshwater tank filled with dive gear, passed the pay showers and stopped at the door of the change room at the rear of the building. He caught himself holding his breath again. But the palm that gripped the SIG Sauer was dry.

Nick's body was bunked up against a row of lockers. Archie stared at it for a long time. Profound sadness threatened to envelope him but he pushed it down. The body didn't look like a person at all, more like a bundle of discarded clothes, with the skin shining linen white in the beam of the Maglite and the blood pooling black and gleaming on the scuffed plywood floor.

Archie angled around until he could see the face, the body so curled up that the head was almost under the shoulder, the throat cut right through and gaping. The face was older than he expected. He coughed against sudden nausea. To fight the squeamishness, he busied himself with procedure — checking rooms, making mental notes, taking care as he moved, preparing the scene for forensics. When he had done enough, he went outside and called the station. He couldn't shake the image of the corpse. He felt faint, walked to the edge of the parking lot and threw up.

CHAPTER 2

The conference room was off square. At some point a contractor had used swamp green paint on the walls. This had a tendency to pick up grease and smudges; it now resembled botched camouflage. People meeting in the conference room wanted to get out as quickly as they could. Cal Fricke, who hated meetings, hadn't done much to improve the décor. Not a damn thing hung on the walls. It was close to midnight, an hour and a half since Archie had left the murder scene in the care of two patrol officers and he was still wired.

Cal Fricke rumbled in at last. He sat down heavily, laid a thin file folder on a work surface marked by boot heels, pens, burins made of paper clips or other fragments of metal, and cup rings. Archie wasn't sure who'd actually organized the meeting on Nick's murder but it likely wasn't Fricke who had been at a card game somewhere downtown and seemed none too pleased to be chairing a midnight briefing.

Archie waited to be called on. He was supposed to go over his impressions of the murder scene with whichever detectives Delia John had been able to contact late in the evening. He had no idea whom among them would lead the investigation, just that it wouldn't be him. That being the situation, he wanted to give his report and go home to bed. He was suddenly profoundly tired — shock likely. Fricke ignored him and everybody else, leafed through the file folder and made notes on a yellow legal pad. Ray Jameson shambled in five minutes later. The set of his long face told nothing but then it never did. Jameson seldom smiled. Jason Humber and Chad Reddin, two detectives who dealt mostly with robbery, followed close behind. Humber was Jameson's buddy and often seconded him. He grinned constantly no matter what the conversation. Body-builder Reddin was relatively new and had transferred from some other force. Archie had a limited read on him. None of them acknowledged Archie nor did he offer them any greeting.

Fricke grunted something. Archie, who had been sitting on the edge of the table, picked a vinyl-seated chair at the far end and dropped into it. He had hoped that Thomas Lee, one of the few cops who had been at least half friendly to him, would be there. Lee would be senior enough to take over the investigation and probably would be amenable to Archie being on the team. That wasn't likely to happen with any of the others, particularly with Jameson. But Lee hadn't shown yet; most likely, the case would go to another.

For a few minutes, the other detectives chatted about nothing important. Archie was wondering what they were waiting for when Fricke suddenly alerted him to the fact that that they were waiting on Archie, that he was supposed to be briefing the room on what had happened and that he'd better get on with it.

Archie's mouth went suddenly dry. He nodded and stood up like a school boy making a presentation. To his surprise, everyone, including Jameson, stopped talking and made to listen.

"I'll start with time of death," he said. "The coroner hasn't been at the scene and won't be for a few hours because she's attending elsewhere at the moment. Personally, I figure it was about 4:30 in the afternoon, give or take a half hour."

"So, you figure it was still light out when he died?" Fricke asked.

"It's definitely possible and I think it's likely."

"How so?"

This was from Jameson sitting at the end of the table closest to Cal Fricke.

Archie paused. "The shop lights weren't turned on."

"The killer could have turned them off," Jameson said. "You think about that possibility?"

"Yes, I thought of it. It's possible that whoever killed the victim could have turned the lights off, but I doubt it. Anyway, there are other factors."

"No kidding. Like what?" Jameson asked.

"Blood and other things," Archie said.

Jameson shook his head. Archie knew his attempt at exposition must have sounded lame. Still, it didn't make any sense that the killer, or killers, would turn the lights out, not out in the sticks where Nick's shop was located. Why bother? Also, he had discovered that the lot lights and their remote sensor were controlled from a panel in the back that didn't look at all like what it was supposed to be. It had been closed, and Archie had had a hard time finding it.

He was too nervous to defend his position further. He struggled through a description of what he had seen, about the position of Nick's body, about why he'd been at Nick's in the first place, and his immediate observations. Going through the straight observation part, the facts, somewhat settled his nervousness. He finished off by saying that the site was secure, ready for whoever would lead the investigation, but Jameson wasn't finished with him.

"I admire the way you figured out the time of death. I just wanted to tell you that. Nobody left the lights on. Cute."

He laughed and looked at Humber and Reddin who chuckled in agreement. If he'd had more confidence, Archie would have said that he had figured time of death mostly because the blood on the floor had lightly skinned over and that he knew from hunting how long that took. Or he would have told them about the dead deer and when he figured a vehicle leaving Donaldson's had hit the animal, and when it had died. But he didn't care to get into more discussion with Jameson, so he just sat down and looked straight ahead.

Fricke grunted something like "thanks for the roundup", and then hummed and hawed for a time about budgets and manpower. Archie half-listened, trying to stay focussed on the details. He was anxious to leave. He thought again about quitting the force, wondering if there was much point in staying. The earlier exhilaration he had felt had gone and now he felt drained. He hadn't eaten for many hours, which further complicated his mood. It still seemed unreal that Nick was truly dead. He would have left the room if he could have done it without losing face.

As he thought about Nick he lost track of what people were saying until he heard his name repeated with swearing following it.

"You can't be fucking serious, Cal!"

Ray Jameson was not happy.

Fricke was on his feet now, thick arms folded on the curve of his belly. He looked amused, like he'd just pulled a prank.

"You'd normally be the lead on this Ray, but you've got your plate full. Gorton is on extended leave. Humber's going on holiday in a few weeks and Reddin's got no experience with this kind of thing. Stevens has the courses and the training"

"I don't give a shit. I can handle this," Jameson said. "This is goddam politics, Cal, and you know it."

Fricke's face reddened.

"Don't give me any of that crap, Ray. You got complaints you can see me private. We're going to let the kid have a chance on this one. It isn't a high-profile case — dead-beat murdered out in the boonies, end of story. The media's going to forget about it in a day or two; there's no glory attached to it. Why would you even want it?"

Jameson didn't say anything. Instead he stood up and stalked out. Humber watched apparently amused, his grin unchanged.

"Doesn't sound like I'm needed," he said.

"You can go," Fricke said. "And take Reddin with you."

The words were barely out of Fricke's mouth when Reddin was on his feet and gone too. Humber followed him, laughing. Archie could hear them talking all the way down the hall. He had never felt so uncomfortable, or so trapped by circumstances. Fricke sat back down and looked intently across the table at him. Archie couldn't read anything in the gaze.

"There's truth in what Ray says," Fricke said. "There's always politics in my job. The thing is that it don't change nothing. Thomas Lee has some personal issues so he can't really take the lead right now. Ray is busy; Reddin's busy; Humber's Humber. There isn't anyone else but you unless I bring in somebody from Rochville and I may have to do that anyway. I don't want to do it, but I will if I have to. Clear?"

Not exactly a vote of confidence, Archie thought. The old Archie would have known what to do, which would have been to tell Fricke to go fuck himself and then quit. But he was tired of that road; tired of letting pride and resentment torpedo any chance he might have of success. Anyway, he didn't have any cause to get prickly. Fricke was being frank and was giving him an opportunity that wouldn't come again. Straight talk was always good. He watched Fricke rub his eyes with his short, thick fingers. Then Fricke looked right at him.

"You want this, Arch," he said. "Or should I call Rochville?"

"So long as you're not going to be breathing over my shoulder every five minutes, I'm good with it."

"Within reason, you can handle it how you want. I need results pretty damn quickly. I'll decide who helps you on this and let you know. I contacted Rochville about getting their forensic team; apparently they'll arrive pretty quickly. Coroner won't make it until eight or nine in the morning maybe. Beyond that it's all yours, the warrants, interviews, expense forms, the whole deal. It's a big job for a greenhorn."

"I don't want Reddin."

"You won't get Reddin. He doesn't want to work with you anyway, which should be obvious. Lee is a possibility to assist, but I'll let you know. What I want you to do is go home. Get a couple of hours sleep and be at the murder scene first thing in the morning. Plan things out and get back to me."

"I'm going to Donaldson's now."

"No you fucking won't. I want you there with a clear head. There's a lot to do."

"If I'm in charge, I'm going back now. If not, screw it."

Fricke shook his head but it wasn't his way to load up an assignment with conditions. He looked hard at Archie and shook his boulder-sized head.

"Get your ass out there then. I'm going home and I don't want to hear nothing about nobody screwing up no assignment — pisses me off. "

And then the meeting was over. Archie left the room. He had things he figured he'd need from his office and headed in that direction. A few cops from the night shift were at their desks. Most were preoccupied with what was happening on their computer screens. One or two were chatting, drinking coffee. None of them acknowledged him as he passed.

He stopped at his desk and looked at the area around it. The small space seemed inadequate now. He would have a team working with him. He'd need to hold meetings, put up white boards; he'd need more room. He remembered that there was an empty office nearby. He grabbed stuff off his desk and went down the hall to claim it. When he had finished establishing a presence, he headed for the door, stopping at Delia John's desk to leave a note asking her to have his phone number moved in the morning.

Outside, the night was clear, but clouds threatened to obliterate the gibbous moon. The 4Runner was covered in dew, even though it had only been sitting there for an hour. As he got into his car he saw a note under his wiper. He pulled it out and looked at it. Somebody had drawn a picture of an Indian with a feather headdress and a tomahawk, with the words "Watch your scalp, Stevens — Ha-Ha!" printed in crude, oversized letters.

He looked around to see if anyone was lurking, watching for his reaction. He regretted doing so. But he neither saw nor heard anyone. He wanted to get mad, but instead he shook his head, balled up the note, and tossed it.

CHAPTER 3

B right emergency lights lit the scene. Archie watched as a sky-blue BMW manoeuvred past the wall of boats, the driver carefully avoiding the road's many potholes. The car stopped next to the far end of the caution tape where the parking lot was smoother and looked somewhat more graded. For more than a minute, the car sat idling, the wipers slapping drizzle off the windshield at long intervals. Then the engine was shut off, the door opened and Thomas Lee stepped out onto the gravel. He rearranged a very fine overcoat and a mauve scarf, stood and peered out at the sea a hundred yards away before he looked for Archie. The case could easily have gone to Lee; Archie wondered what the man would think about having to take orders from someone less experienced.

He liked Lee. Lee had been on the force for years and was one of the few officers that Archie hadn't tried to make look foolish, back when Archie was raising hell and testing the Harsley police department every way he could think of. No wonder some of the cops couldn't see him for what he was now. Strange the way life turned out. But Lee was okay, no problem then and, hopefully, no problem now.

Lee navigated the puddle-strewn parking lot and crossed to the berm where Archie was standing.

"They've got tape running all over the place," Lee said. "There's a big gap at the west end. It's untidy."

He pointed to the string of caution tape that ended in the middle of nowhere. Archie stiffened, called to an older, uniformed cop named Jim Stone who was walking back to one of the vans.

"Stoney?"

"Uh-huh?"

"The tape's stopped over there. Get another roll and make sure the whole crime scene is enclosed."

Stoney hesitated, then shrugged and lumbered away to rearrange the tape. Archie realized he'd given his first real order and noted that Stone, maybe the oldest officer on the force, seemed to accept his authority — more or less. It was a start.

Lee looked towards the low building housing the dive shop.

"The body inside?" he asked. He stayed on the gravel below where Archie was standing so that Archie had to look down at him. Lee obviously didn't want to risk his loafers and immaculate trousers on the muddy side of the berm, which was still wet and slippery from the previous night's rain.

Archie started to walk the berm towards the path to the shop. Lee paralleled him, trying the impossible, which was to preserve the shine on his shoes.

"He's still lying in the back part of his shop," Archie said. "You and I are going to be working on this case together at least for the next two weeks."

Lee's face remained expressionless; it was hard to figure out if he was happy with the situation or not.

He was quite a bit shorter than Archie and had to walk faster in order to keep up. Archie realized he'd been striding and slowed down. The berm eased away and soon they were walking side by side towards the broad steps leading up to the porch, although Archie still stood a head taller.

"Did Fricke brief you this morning?" Archie asked.

"He said you'd fill me in with all the details." Lee took off his gloves, layered them one on the other, folded them, slid them into the pocket on his Burberry Mac and waited for Archie to continue.

"Beyond the fact that you found Nick Donaldson with his throat cut and that there was a break-in, I don't know a thing."

"The first part is right anyway."

"So you haven't got everything figured out?"

The words were peevish but the tone was... Lee changed the subject before Archie could think too much about it.

"Heard they did a number on him."

"Surprised the hell out of me, for sure. I came out to ask him about abalone poaching and found him in the back. Not pretty."

"This is your first murder, right?"

Archie didn't confirm or deny it.

"Why don't you just follow me and see for yourself."

Lee followed Archie up the steps. There was an open box of booties near the door and they both paused and slid some on over their shoes. Lee looked at the broken glass and seemed interested in how it was scattered around. Then he squatted and looked through the lower part of the door into the shop after which he stood up and straightened his trouser knees.

"Strange," he said.

"That's what I thought."

They were both looking at the pattern of the broken glass, how it lay. They followed a marked path into the shop. The forensics team had only just arrived and hadn't left much evidence of their presence beyond some yellow location markers within. That helped. As much as possible, Archie didn't want to see the scene as others saw it, to be prejudiced by too many markers and labels.

Archie led the way further inside, through the shop and down the row of lockers where people stored their clothes while diving, to the back where Nick's body lay and stopped. Lee whistled through his teeth and moved around to get a better look. Archie hadn't looked at the corpse for a few hours. Now, it almost demanded attention. Nick's skin was stark white, the face strangely serene. The position of the body seemed even stranger to Archie than it had when he had first seen it. On the other hand, his state of mind had shifted. He was now more clinical, more detached.

Lee walked around to the other side, being careful not to step in the blood. He shook his head.

"Phew! What do you think?"

"That they rolled him over after they cut his throat and searched him," Archie said. "The left arm got pulled out of its socket; they must've really wanted something."

Lee took some shots with his phone camera of the area.

A .32 Smith and Wesson lay near the splayed right leg. The hammer was still cocked. It was an old pistol, the bluing gone in places so that the bare metal showed through.

"I'm guessing the pistol belonged to Donaldson," Archie said. "He must've shot somebody with it."

He indicated the pattern of blood spatters high on the wall.

"Blood everywhere. Are these pistols single or double action?" Lee asked.

"So far as I know, they're single action, which might mean that he was just about to shoot again.

"There are two empty cartridge cases over there. I don't think that's Nick's blood on the wall either but we'll know after it's tested. I'd guess the wound it came from wouldn't be too serious, just hurt a lot. To me, it isn't lung blood or gut blood. Appreciate it if you'd look into that. Check the hospital, every clinic too," he continued.

"Spatter analysis will help here. I can do that," Lee said.

Archie watched as Lee took an electronic tablet out of his jacket pocket. He turned it on and then entered something using the touch screen.

"Did you find any footprints?" Lee asked.

Archie shook his head. There was a wide swirl of streaked, smeared blood now dry on the floor and he pointed it out to Lee.

"They used a mop in here."

"Outside? It's pretty muddy."

"No tracks in the mud. There weren't any prints anywhere, not that anyone has found yet anyway."

"What do you make of that?"

"My guess is that they took off their boots and walked away in their sock feet — maybe. There's a lot of gravel back there that wouldn't show tracks. Forensics will be going through the living quarters and out buildings but it looks like everything happened here. Check with them later."

"Donaldson usually worked with John Robbie," Lee said. "We have a file on Robbie. I guess you've thought of pulling him in for questioning?"

Archie looked past him towards the front room and its repair bay.

Lee repeated his question. Archie refocussed.

"There's no indication that Robbie had anything to do with this," Archie said. "But yes, I want him questioned. If nothing else, he may be able to give us some ideas about Nick's recent activities. I'd like you to talk to him as soon as you can."

"I've already got him on my list. I know Robbie and Nick worked some stuff together and they both drank at Moffat's quite a bit."

"I can't really figure the motive for this. Not with Robbie anyway. He was Nick's buddy."

"I saw them together two days ago," Lee said. "They were downtown and they both looked drunk. Maybe they got into a fight here and it got nasty."

Archie shook his head.

"With the level of violence and destruction here, I don't see a scrap being at the bottom of it."

Archie crouched down and examined the body again. Two forensics people were bustling about in the next room, working their way towards them. They had already examined the body *in situ*. The awkward way Nick lay bothered him. He couldn't quite figure out why at first but then it became obvious.

"You think you're missing something?" Lee asked.

"I've got a hunch."

He tugged the shoulder back and looked at the dislocated arm, saw the bruises on it, missed because of the body's position. Then he stood up, cocked his head and peered down the hallway in the direction of the door. He looked up at the blood smear and then again towards the smashed front door pane. He walked to a pony wall and examined it intently.

A local Harsley tech came in carrying a fingerprint kit. Lee, watching, reached into his top pocket, pulled out a package of gum, popped a piece out through the foil; put the packet back into the pocket of his Mac.

"You got it all figured out now?" Lee said. "The whole thing from A to Z? Seriously, what do you think?"

"I'm going under the assumption that it was probably still light out when Nick died, which would make it no later than five like I said in the briefing notes. I haven't changed my mind about that. I think he had just come back from a dive and somebody was waiting for him when he got home. To me that means that he knew whoever it was who killed him and he probably even let them in. After that it got nasty. His arm was dislocated because somebody pulled something off him, likely a wetsuit. What I can't figure out is why. Plus where is the suit?"

Lee nodded. He scratched his chin with well-manicured nails.

"They got him out front but how'd they take him? He would presumably be in control of the situation if he knew the killers. He was a big guy so he wouldn't be easy to beat. Did somebody he knew pull a gun on him? Or get round behind him and knock him down maybe?" he said.

Archie pinched the bridge of his nose, trying to shake an incipient headache that was certainly the result of sleep deprivation

"I've asked myself the same questions. It's not completely clear to me yet."

"He must have dragged himself back here before they finished him."

"You're sure it's more than one?"

"Look at him. He's a big guy. It would take more than one and likely as many as three. I think that one of them was a big guy as well, maybe even bigger than Nick."

Lee looked puzzled. Archie wondered why people found it so hard to see what was obvious.

"Look," he said. "Nick weighed, what, maybe two-fifty and he was taller than me, standing six two or so. One attacker doesn't seem likely. Plus somebody strong enough was able to pull his arm out its socket.

"You're right. That'd take a lot of strength."

"I think three men, maybe four. But not together. One man came first. Then the others came and finished him off."

"What do you base this theory on?"

"Common sense and a hunch."

"Great."

Archie was reluctant to put out a theory until he had more to support it. He had hunches but nothing more. He was too new to this to lay them out. Plus the last thing he wanted was to be contradicted, or shown to be an idiot because he had overlooked something. Besides, he wasn't sure about Lee yet and he knew Lee wasn't sure about him. Anyway, the scenario he pictured had two men doing the killing and a third watching, standing at the pony wall.

"I want to get your thoughts on something else," Archie said.

They left the body and went back into the shop. Archie pointed to the little alcove hung with regulators. There was a messy workbench there, strewn with tools, O-rings, regulator parts. Looking past the mess they could see the signs of a scuffle, containers knocked over and a coffee cup lying on the floor beside its spilled contents.

"That's Nick's, I guess," Lee said. He was looking at a bloody handprint on the wall close to the alcove.

"I think so. Stoney found an abalone iron with blood on it out back. That's probably the weapon that knocked him down. Forensics will probably have it bagged up now but you'd better take a look at it."

Lee nodded. Archie waited while Lee entered something else on his tablet and then aimed it at the workbench and took some shots with its camera. When he finished, they followed the blood trail back to the body, trying not to get in the way of the forensics techs who now seemed to be everywhere. Donaldson's Dive Adventures was getting crowded.

"You figure that maybe he got something out of his safe, he went over to his workbench, he got hit, came to, he shot somebody, somebody twisted his arm out of its socket and then cut his throat to finish him?" Lee said.

"Something like that."

"Why didn't they stop him from going into the back?"

"That's a good question."

Lee hiked up his pants and squatted down to look at the gaping wound under Nick's chin.

"Almost took his head off. Pretty dramatic."

Archie had to look away. He glanced at the ceiling, his clinical distance suddenly gone. He knew Lee had figured it out — that he, Archie, was squeamish, something he didn't want spread around.

"What about an ordinary break-in and robbery gone bad?" Lee asked.

"I don't think so," he said. "It was made to look like it, but the dive computers are still here, other valuable stuff too. Not much missing that I can see. And you saw what I saw at the door."

"That the glass was smashed out not in."

"Exactly."

"So, what do you want me to do, Archie?"

"What do you mean?"

"I appreciate the grand tour but I'm not sure how I fit in here."

Archie raised his chin in the direction of the corpse.

"There's a lot to do. You got experience in murder cases. By rights I should be working for you, but that's not the way it is. All I can say is that you drew the assignment and I'm glad you're here."

"You know why Fricke won't give me the responsibility, I guess."

"I think so. It isn't right."

"It has to do with the death of Bob Wilkins."

"All I heard was that he drove off the road."

"And how I pulled my weapon and said something to Jameson?"

Archie didn't want to get side-tracked.

"I guess. What about Wilkins's death? What bothered you?"

"That didn't make sense then and it doesn't now. Bob was too careful and too competent."

"Car accident could happen to anyone."

"Bob and I were close."

Archie wondered what he should say to that.

"Did you know about Wilkins investigating abalone poaching?"

"Not really."

"How long do you think Fricke is going to wait before you're back running investigations?"

Lee shrugged, sat down in a chair close to the wall, thoughtful.

"I really couldn't say."

Archie scanned the corridor, looked to the back door and waited. The events of the previous evening were starting to take shape and he hoped Lee would come on board. Lee preened his eyebrows with the little finger of his left hand.

"Who else do you have? Who's the team?"

Archie grinned.

"So far just you and Patsy Kydd."

Lee harrumphed, said, "Amazing."

"Considering who else is down at the station, the fewer the better. Know anything about her?"

"She's a forensic anthropologist. She dropped out of a PhD program and ended a long term relationship."

Archie said, "Great," without sincerity.

"She's got every guy's attention at the station."

"No comment."

"Not mine," Lee said.

"No, I guess not."

"You got a lot of information out of her even so."

"Women like to tell me things."

Jim Stone appeared in the doorway. He shot Lee a glance, looked at Archie and raised his eyebrows.

"What is it, Stoney?" Archie said.

"The coroner is on her way. Cal Fricke called and told me to tell you that he wants you to keep Ray Jameson informed."

Archie said, "Shit," just as Ray Jameson came in, heavy boots loud on the wood floor. He was a long lean whip of a man with a grim, dark face. Like always, he acted like he was in charge, or ought to be. He scarcely looked at Donaldson's body. He turned to his partner, Chad Reddin.

"This is a big case for a new detective," he said

Jameson's voice grated more than usual. Reddin nodded.

"Like you say, Ray."

Archie said nothing, letting Jameson say what he had to say, and then hopefully he would tire of the sport and go someplace else.

"Want us to look around for you there, *Detective* Stevens?" Jameson pushed the needle in a little deeper, hoping for a reaction. "Me and Reddin can get things set up right for you. You could even go home, or to the bar. You can take numb nuts here with you." That was directed at Lee. "I got some time. I can wait for the coroner. I'll do you the favour."

Archie pretended to look off in the distance. He turned back and looked at Jameson.

"Were you saying something, Ray? I wasn't paying attention."

He noted the change in Jameson who was not relaxed now, not dominating like when he first came in, pissed off.

"Fuck you, Stevens. I try to be nice and what do I get. I should've been harder on you when you were a kid, should have run your sorry ass up to juvie. People like you don't appreciate nothing."

Archie grinned, shook his head — nothing else to do.

"Whatever you say, Ray."

If he was going to let Jameson get to him he might as well go home now. They had a long history. A lot of people figured Ray had let Archie's father die in the accident that killed him. Archie had once wondered that too but he doubted it had happened that way. Billy Stevens had to take responsibility for his own death. Archie had decided long ago that he had no attachment to his old man and his death had never really been an issue for him. He and Jameson just didn't like each other, and that wasn't going to change. Besides, it rankled him the way Jameson treated Lee who was a far better cop than Jameson would ever be.

The coroner's van arrived and, a moment later, Priscilla Ito bustled in tailed by her young assistant. She congratulated Archie on his assignment, greeted Thomas Lee warmly, ignored Jameson, and went to the body, pushing aside the fingerprint guy enroute.

Jameson lingered, his attention on Ito and her assistant, watching them as they worked. When they had finished, Archie gave his okay and Ito removed the body. Jameson went out then, following Ito with questions. Reddin took a quick look around and then followed. But the tension Jameson generated lingered. Ito returned with forms that needed to be filled out and signed. Lee took them from her.

"I can do these."

Archie nodded.

"We'd better talk to John Robbie, sooner rather than later."

"I'll get a patrol car to go to his place, see if we can pick him up this morning."

"Get Delia to put out a bulletin on him right away."

"Okay."

"If Robbie's involved, that could mean Bill Tran is worth talking to as well."

Lee shot him a look. Bill Tran meant big trouble. Archie hoped his face didn't give anything away. Lee probably knew that Archie knew both John Robbie and Bill Tran from the old days. Thankfully, Lee didn't pursue it. He sighed, took the paperwork to Donaldson's old desk and sat down to work through it.

Archie left him to it. He went back and watched as the body was loaded onto the gurney.

With the body gone, he had a few more things to check out before he went in to town to get the results of the autopsy. He'd looked for hard copy nautical charts at the dive shop; Nick should have had a stack of them but there wasn't a single chart in the shop and he wasn't sure why that would be the case.

It bothered him that Jameson's visit had affected him — in spite of his best efforts. He tried to refocus, to get his mind off the sense he had of being where he shouldn't be, of being an interloper.

It was something he had struggled with for most of his life and accounted for much of his bravado — and the chip on his shoulder. And it fed the deep, deep anger that followed him like a cloud.

CHAPTER 4

Archie pulled himself out of bed and stumbled through his borrowed apartment to a designer kitchen that was light years from what he was used to. He needed coffee but had forgotten to buy it, again. In fact, there wasn't much of anything in the kitchen to eat or drink, no food in the fine birch cupboards, nothing in the fancy two-door fridge, nothing. Not that there was much point to stocking the place, or getting used to it. He'd be gone in a few months when the lease expired.

He picked up a glass that looked cleaner than the others on the counter and filled it with cold water from the spout in the fridge door. As he drank, he looked over the rim at his reflection in the black mirror of the kitchen window and mentally interrogated the image.

In the night he had woken wishing Streya Wainright was still with him but she wasn't, and

wasn't going to be. It was unusual for him to regret, especially where women were concerned,
and he wondered if it was because he was getting
older. He put the glass down, gave his reflection
the finger and turned away. Then he walked
down the hall, went into the bathroom with its
heated floor and started the shower.

An hour later, he was back on Nick's side
road. He finished the egg bun he'd bought at
Avril's Donut House, tossed the crumpled
wrapper over his shoulder, and gulped the last
of his coffee. The empty cup joined the garbage
piling up behind the passenger seat.

The ongoing drizzle irritated him more than
usual. He growled against the fact that he still
needed his headlights at eight in the morning.
His people had lived in this one place forever
and some adaptation to the grayness, to the cold
and wet, should be in his genes. Instead, he
stayed moody from November to April. Hell, he
didn't even like seafood that much.

Soon he was out of the trees and into the
open. He drove down the bank and into the
parking lot at Donaldson's Dive Adventures for
the third time in twenty-four hours. He parked
outside the now complete perimeter of caution
tape.

Patsy Kydd walked towards him smiling. He
put his hands into his jacket pockets, hunched

his shoulders against the drizzle and looked past her to the horizon. She stood waiting for him to say something, her smile fading away.

"I thought Thomas would be here by now," he said.

"He took some more tire impressions and then he decided to go get coffee. He's been up most of the night."

Archie couldn't think of anything to say so he gave her something to do.

"Take a walk around. Look for anything that seems out of place."

"What do you think I've been doing since six this morning?"

"Did you move anything?"

That made her flush.

"I'm either on this case or I'm not."

"You're new."

He was aware of the irony of that statement even before it was out of his mouth.

"I know I'm new, but I'm not stupid," she said.

She touched the brim of her ball cap in mock salute and stalked away, hands deep in her pockets, shoulders back. He watched her until she disappeared behind the boathouse and drove the idea that she had a nice ass out of his mind.

He focussed now on the case and thoughts of motive and means. He'd learned that Donaldson's laptop computer was missing and wondered if it might be significant. He walked past a scud of white plaster where Lee had taken tire impressions and continued on.

The drizzle switched to rain as he wandered — big, bitter-cold, November drops. He took a short-cut over a low, grassy bank that gave him a different view of the shop and the property it sat on. He hadn't gone ten feet when he saw the dark shape under a knot of blackberry canes, a diving glove that somebody had dropped. He walked to the brambles, took out the forceps he carried in his jacket pocket, hunkered down, stretched, reached past the canes, squeezed, and drew the thing back. He stood up with it just as Lee pulled into the lot.

He waited, rain streaming off the peak of his hat, while Lee got out of his car, tight in his buttoned up Burberry with his natty fedora clamped on his head. Lee walked quickly. He handed Archie the cup of coffee he'd been carrying. Archie took it and held up the glove by his fingertips.

"This get missed?"

Lee shrugged, the rain rapidly darkening the shoulders of his coat.

"It happens. Patsy should see this too."

Lee called Patsy on the walkie-talkie and then mumbled something about going inside. They walked through the rain, up the steps and into the shop.

Inside, Archie placed the glove on a counter-top. It lay like a dead thing on the dirty glass. The two men waited, not speaking. Patsy, dripping wet, joined them moments later. She looked at Archie, somewhat accusingly he guessed, which made him think about how much more comfortable he was at doing things alone.

Lee put on violet-framed reading glasses, leaned forward and peered at the glove like a casino box-man examining suspect dice. He put his own small hand near the big glove.

"Big hands like the victim's," he said.

Archie nodded.

"It could be Nick's glove. Probably is."

He watched Patsy study the glove. Suddenly she reached out and squeezed the neoprene.

"There's something in here," she said. "It's flat — like a medallion or a coin. If nobody has any objections, I'm going to turn this thing inside out."

She picked up the glove and turned back the cuff. The rolled edge of something metallic appeared. She slid a slender finger and thumb into the little pocket sewn into the gauntlet, pulled out a thick gold coin and held it up to the light.

"This might be important."

She grinned at him as she handed it to him. He held it by its edges, turned it over and looked at the markings on both sides. The coin was unlike anything he had seen, more like a commemorative piece than real currency. It had stars and astrological symbols on one side and a single big star and foreign writing on the obverse.

"Doesn't look like any coin I've ever seen," Lee said.

"What's the writing?"

"A Scandinavian language, I'd say," Patsy said. "Not German or Dutch — I know what they look like."

"Bag it up and take it to the lab. Find out everything you can about it."

"It might be nothing in terms of the murder," Lee said.

"Let's keep this to ourselves for the moment," Archie said.

"Why do I have to keep it secret," Patsy said.

"Because I asked you to."

"You want me to break with procedure just because you…"

Lee intervened, trying to break the tension before it had a chance to build any further.

"It's early. I don't think it's unusual to pick and choose at this stage."

"Exactly," Archie said.

Patsy shook her head. She fished a plastic bag from her jacket pocket, put the glove in and labelled it with a Sharpie she'd taken from her pocket. Then she put the coin in another bag, and labelled it.

"Okay?" she said.

Before he could answer, she spun on her heel and walked past him out into the rain. As she was leaving, Stoney appeared in the doorway, his poncho streaming water.

"We found a computer in a ditch up the highway," he said. "Might be the one you're looking for."

"Good if it is."

Exactly where a stolen computer fit in wasn't at all clear to Archie, but he hoped he'd find out. In the meantime, he had to get the results of the autopsy that should have started already. He left Lee and Stone to their work and walked back out to his car, thankful it had stopped raining.

He drove past where the deer carcass lay. It looked like coyotes had been there; a lot of it was gone. By the time he got to the highway, he needed his sunglasses. The brighter light made him feel better and less pessimistic. He was hungry again. The Satsuma Café was on his way to the morgue where the autopsy was being held, so he'd have enough time to stop and get a bite. There was a chance he might run into Streya but he'd take it. The food at the Satsuma Café was much better than any other place en-route. He drove down the hill, took a left on Admiral and pulled into the parking lot.

He picked a table on the outdoor terrace, close enough to one of the propane heaters to feel the warmth and sat down facing the boat basin. A waitress in a down vest showed up a minute later with a menu. She looked surprised to see Archie. He knew her, one of the Linde-man girls from Beecher Bay.

"How're things, Natalie?" he asked.

"Streya isn't here today, Archie."

"I just want lunch."

He wondered why his love life should be everybody's business.

"Lunch I can do."

She took his order for coffee and a clubhouse sandwich and went back through the swinging door into the restaurant. When she was gone, he took out his notebook. He still liked the old-fashioned notebook better than the devices most of his colleagues seemed to carry these days, which was funny because he was younger than most of them. Soon, he was making notes, deep in thought. He didn't hear the person come up behind him and was surprised when the seat opposite him was suddenly occupied.

Arnie Bulkwetter was the manager of the larger of the two marinas in town. Archie had worked for Bulkwetter for a while; back when Archie was a teenager. He figured Bulkwetter probably still owed him pay from those days, but the man's way of accounting had been more like Three-card Monte than anything else and Bulkwetter always came out ahead. Like always, Bulkwetter started talking right off, oblivious to the fact that Archie was busy.

"That's some deal about Nick Donaldson," he said.

"What do you mean, Arn?"

"You know — the slashed throat and all."

So far as Archie knew, nobody had even notified Nick's next-of-kin. Certainly, the details of the murder were not supposed to be out for public consumption. He asked Bulkwetter how and what he'd heard, but Bulkwetter just laughed.

"For Christ sake, Archie, this is Harsley. There are no secrets here."

Archie said that while that was likely true, he wasn't about to talk about any ongoing cases.

"Sure, sure," Bulkwetter said.

The Lindeman girl brought Archie's order. She shot Bulkwetter a distasteful glance. Archie picked up the sandwich and ate; then he sipped his coffee, studied the other man. Bulkwetter also seemed to be studying him.

"He was supposed to call me," he said.

Archie put the sandwich down on the plate. The gas heater hissed loudly in his ear.

"Who was?"

"Nick. We were going to do some fishing together."

Archie picked up his sandwich again. He was listening.

"When was that?"

"A few days back."

"And you didn't hear from him?"

"No, but there was nothing unusual there."

"So you and him fish together much? I didn't know that."

"I'm usually too busy but, yeah, sometimes."

"Once in a while you do or more often than that?"

"Marina stuff keeps me occupied, so not often."

"So why are you telling me about a fishing trip that never happened?"

"No reason."

Bulkwetter was a talker but there was more to it than that.

"Anything else you can tell me about Nick, about who he was hanging with? What he was up to?"

"Nah. You know Nick. Not overly talkative."

"You see John Robbie around anywhere?"

"No, but I know what you're thinking," Bulkwetter said.

"What's that?"

"That maybe he killed Nick. That he's always short of money. That he's got connections with Bill Tran through Bonnie. Tran's a son of a bitch — as we all know."

"I just asked if you'd seen him. I don't suspect him of anything, but I would like to talk to him."

"I bet you would."

Archie took another bite of his sandwich.

"Why do you say that?"

"He'd be the guy."

Archie said nothing. Bulkwetter stirred in his seat.

"Weather stinks," Bulkwetter said. "Ho hum."

He looked past Archie towards the harbour.

Archie was too tired to play games with Arnie Bulkwetter, but he had an idea that the man might know something useful. Playing hard to get might be the only way.

"I'm trying to eat my lunch, Arn. I got work to do myself."

Bulkwetter raised his eyebrows in mock surprise.

"I'm not going to talk about police business, Arn, so forget it."

Bulkwetter shrugged. He shifted the conversation to nothing in particular, talked about how he'd seen Archie drive in from his office window, about how he didn't like to stay cooped up in his office.

The Lindeman girl came back and Archie asked for his cheque. Bulkwetter didn't seem to want to leave, but he wasn't forthcoming either. He rambled on some more about the weather, boats, the town, and then shifted to questions about the Wainright sisters, Streya in particular. Archie said nothing on the subject. He was tired of listening and getting nothing. When the bill came, he got out his wallet, peeled out a ten and a five and stuck them under the sugar container.

"I got to go Arnie."

He stood up. Bulkwetter extricated himself from his chair as if to follow. He grinned at Archie.

"You get Robbie and you've got this thing solved," he said. "I'll bet you money on that."

"If you say so, Arnie."

Bulkwetter laughed and turned for the stairs. Then he ambled off in the direction of the Marina. Archie watched him until he saw the man go through the back door of the two story marina office. A department ghost car pulled up and Chad Reddin got out. He tossed his still-smoking cigarette into the gravel and climbed the steps and walked towards where Archie was sitting. He nodded a greeting.

"You staying, Stevens?"

"No, I'm on my way."

"I'll take your table then."

"You're welcome to it."

Archie gathered his stuff. Reddin eased into a chair, unbuttoned his jacket, revealing the black-handled butt of the nickel-plated .45 automatic he always carried, nestled in its under-arm holster. He took out a pack of cigarettes and placed them on the table. The pistol and holster seemed like a clumsy rig to Archie — showy too. Reddin slapped his lighter on the table's glass-top.

"You making any progress on your little case there?"

"We're going to trial on Monday."

"Ha. Ha. I'm serious."

"So am I."

"Asshole."

"Like you say, Reddin."

"You know what you can do, Stevens."

Archie laughed, turned and walked down the steps to his car. He had nothing personal against Reddin who seemed to be good enough at his job. Maybe it was the association with

Jameson. And the show-off pistol and other stuff too. He looked up over the dash, saw Reddin was now standing, talking on his cellphone, animated in conversation. Archie watched a moment. Reddin looked angry, walked out of sight towards the far end of the deck. Archie turned the key, started the 4Runner and drove away.

CHAPTER 5

John Robbie parked out of sight of the highway. He never came near when anybody else was around, which was better for her anyway, him glaring at any guy that spoke nice to her — which still happened. Bonnie Tran saw him when he needed a meal, or when he was lonely. He was edgy and unpredictable, and she liked that in a man or needed it. She contemplated refreshing her lipstick, thought better of it, got rid of her apron and straightened her hair. Time had sifted out her life and left her with John Robbie — suffit!

He came in all at once, wet and dishevelled and shut the door quickly behind him. He'd brought a packsack with him that he kept close. She watched him look out the windows as if he was afraid he'd been followed. She leaned back against the counter, lit a cigarette and waited for him to settle.

"Nobody else around?"

"Who were you expecting, John?"

"Don't get smart."

There was suspicion in his voice, more than usual.

"You're wet."

"I showered — for you."

She laughed.

"That'd be a first."

He glanced at her, an odd look she couldn't read, and then looked out the window into the parking lot again. When he turned back he seemed to be different — easier, as if he had put on a mask.

"If you're looking for a meal, you're out of luck. Day's over and I'm not firing up the burners just because you showed up."

"I didn't think you would."

"So — are you hungry?"

"Starving."

He unzipped his jacket and tossed it on the back of a chair. The leather smelled damp.

"Be nice if you'd call once in a while."

"Been busy. Meant to."

He shot her a sideways glance, a look too broad to misinterpret. She gave his ass a tentative slap as he bent down to retie a boot lace, saw the old burn scars on his neck and shoulders. Something from his time in prison, she knew. He stood up, unexpectedly grabbed her around the waist and squeezed her into him. She didn't pretend to squirm away this time. If she did that, he'd hold her too hard and she wasn't sure she was in the mood. She leaned against him, and he growled into the nape of her neck.

"I'm hungry."

"Later."

"Make something."

He loosened his hold on her. She lingered; he pushed her towards the kitchen. She laughed, told him to go fuck himself. Then she said, "I'll cook something for you. Because you're like a lost boy and I feel sorry for you."

She went to the fridge for the steak, flipped the burners on as she passed the stove. From behind the slide, she watched as he slouched into his favourite booth. He dug around in his packsack until he found what he was looking for. He sensed she was watching and turned so she couldn't see.

She fried onions and mushrooms, reheated some country potatoes from breakfast. She brought the meal and beer to the table, turned up the radio in passing, a slow tune, an old Rodney Crowell — "Till I gain control again." She sighed, settled back into the seat opposite him, took a pull on her beer, and watched him closely. He gobbled his food, hardly chewing it.

"You going to get mad if I ask you something?"

He put down his knife and fork too slowly, too carefully. He focussed on her, his small eyes jet-hard.

"What?"

His voice was as flat as the top of the table. She was used to dealing with suspicious and dangerous men. She had, after all, two ex-husbands not too different in temperament from the man sitting across from her — experience, no substitute for it. She kept things light.

"I didn't see anything, Johnny boy. I just know you got something more than steak and Bonnie on your mind tonight."

When she saw him relax a little, she said, "I keep my mouth shut. You know you can trust me. I never ask usually."

"Damn right."

"You piss me off sometimes."

"I know."

That was as close to an apology as she'd ever got from him. He cut up more steak, put down the knife, stabbed the meat and loaded up his fork.

"I got to get in touch with Bill. There's something I want to talk to him about."

"I thought you worked for him."

"With him sometimes, not for him — and not lately."

He talked with his mouth full. She waited, knowing she'd probably wish he hadn't wanted to confide in her, but needing something beyond her café — the Zuider Zee. Finally, he said,

"There's weird shit happening."

"I don't want anything to do with my brother, if that's what you're getting at."

He looked at her like a poker player searching for an opponent's tell.

"You got no choice."

"I always got a choice, Johnny boy."

He laughed, shook his head. He reached past her, took one of her cigarettes from the pack she'd left on the table and lit it. He stared at their reflections in the black mirror of the window awhile. She looked too. She saw him and her — a wiry little man, hunkered down, framed by the backwards lettering and herself, a worn out Vietnamese immigrant with red-dyed hair who still looked good if the light was right, which it sure as hell wasn't right then. She fussed her hair back with her hand, waited for him to say something. The wind pushed at the birches at the edge of the parking lot; the rain slashed hard against the windows.

He reached out and grabbed her arm. He was surprisingly strong for a small man and his fingers bit hard into her flesh. She tried to pull away and he squeezed harder.

"So?" he said.

"Why do you have to be this way? I always do what you want."

He eased up a little, and she wriggled her arm away.

"You get hold of Bill. I need to talk to him soon. Tell him it's to his benefit."

That worried her too. Going to Bill meant trouble, especially if it was to his benefit.

"I wish we could stay away from that bastard."

"Not this time, Bon."

She nodded, agreed to make the call and he relaxed a little. She looked at her arm, saw that he'd left marks. She shook her head angrily, said, "Shit," turned her arm and showed him.

"You asshole — look what you've done."

He didn't seem to notice, just went on with the line he'd started.

"This is important."

"So — what is it then?"

He put up a hand, cocked his head like he was listening for something. Then he got up and checked to make sure the front door was locked. When he came back to his seat, he pulled the packsack to him and opened it. He pulled out an old purple Crown Royal sack and rooted around inside it, finally producing two gold coins the size of silver dollars. He set them down on the table, one beside the other, coins but not coins, more like medallions with stars on them. He anticipated her question.

"They're Brother Eli coins," he said.

She looked at the coins and then at him, like she was expecting him to tell her that he was joking. He didn't.

"Did you steal them?"

He shook his head, pushed the coins with the tip of his finger and then dropped the empty whisky bag over them.

"Nick found them when he was diving. At least, I figure he did. I was up in the boat all day and he was below working abalone. He left one of his gloves in my boat and I found it when I was home cleaning up. The coins were in this little pocket he had sewn into the gauntlet cuff."

"Did you ask Nick about them?"

"Nobody's asking Nick about nothing anymore."

"How do you mean?"

"He's back at his shop with his throat cut."

She took a few minutes to let that sink in, said, "Fuck", and slumped back in her seat.

She looked across at him, saw something in his face, sorrow maybe, or pain.

"Jesus, John. How did that happen?"

"I don't know."

They sat quiet for a minute or two, him looking out to the window, out somewhere beyond the sound of wind and rain, her looking at him, wondering. He read the suspicion in her eyes before she could hide it.

"I didn't kill Nick, Bonnie."

No anger in the voice like she would have expected.

"I don't know if I believe you."

He nodded, said, "Your prerogative."

"Did Bill do it?"

"I don't know."

That worried her.

"What do you mean?"

"I've got to talk to him."

"Jesus."

"You going to help me on this?"

She nodded.

"What about the cops? Won't they be thinking that maybe you killed Nick?"

"Likely."

She picked at the label on an empty beer bottle with a long fingernail, its red varnish chipped and broken. He watched her, waiting. She looked him in the eye.

"How much do you think?"

"Who knows — a lot. This is big."

She stopped picking at the label, sat back and folded her arms across her chest.

"Jesus."

"The cops will come to talk to you for sure."

"What'll I say?"

"Nothing beyond the fact that you never seen me. That's the point — you can't let on you seen me, Bonnie. Not to anybody."

"I understand, John."

"I don't want you to get hurt."

He put his hand to his forehead and leaned into it. She waited for him to make a move, watching him, feeling something for him. He got up, pulled his shoulders back, walked towards the hallway that led to her bungalow. Whatever the danger, he had put the thought of it out of his head. She took the plates to the slide. He looked back at her; shot her a lost little boy half-smile. She 'tcched' through her teeth, massaged her upper arm until the circulation returned and then she followed him into the bedroom.

CHAPTER 6

Archie watched as the pathologist finished the autopsy on Nick's body, now laid out on a stainless steel table. Archie's questions resulted in explanations more detailed, more long-winded than they needed to be and he wondered if Roger Chu was giving him the gears. And he hated that Roger probably sensed his squeamishness. He had had to fight nausea and the weird light-headed feeling that threatened to embarrass him. When it had passed, he took in and evaluated what the examiner was telling him. Chu was an old-timer, but he seemed fascinated with his work and seemed to take a childlike delight in it.

It was no surprise that Nick hadn't survived his throat being cut. He also had been hit twice on the head with a weapon with a thick, dull edge, hard enough to incapacitate him. He had a 9mm bullet lodged in his chest. Also somebody had mashed two of his fingers, his left arm had multiple bruises and the left shoulder had been dislocated. Archie noted each of these things as they were pointed out to him. He said nothing about what he had already observed at the crime scene. He needed to know the order of events. That was what was important.

The gunshot wound was new to him. The 9mm parabellum bullet had made a small hole underneath Nick's arm. There were no powder burns. No one had had seen the bullet hole before because of clotted blood on the torso from the neck wound and densely matted hair.

When Archie asked, Chu pointed out the exit wound. The bullet had ripped through the skin of the throat, the damage obscured by the greater wound. Archie tried to imagine the position of the shooter, below Nick, arm straight out — then the shot. Nick had knocked the person down — Nick with his arm raised to strike. Maybe. He hadn't gone easily. That was certain. Archie had other questions.

"How long between when he got hit and when he got shot?"

"That's the interesting thing," Chu said. "I'd guess probably an hour or two."

"Was he hit twice — like once and then, sometime later, hit again?

"The crusty blood near the eyebrow where the skin was torn back from the parietal bone." Chu said. "That will tell you."

Chu glanced at Archie maybe hoping for a reaction. He seemed slightly disappointed that none of what he said or did seemed to make Archie faint or retreat from the autopsy theater but Archie was past the point where that could happen. All he saw now were facts, objects, parts of the puzzle he needed to solve.

"The blood on the head had started to scab," Archie said. "So there was a time lag."

"You got it."

"It looks like he tried to wipe it away at some point."

"You're very observant, detective. He did, or somebody else did."

"He was hit again but how long after?"

"The second time was, maybe, twenty minutes. The blow probably knocked him out."

"Why do you say that?"

"The location of the blow and its severity — he would have seen stars, certainly, and likely lost consciousness."

Chu had stopped playing around, stopped trying to get Archie to pass out. He was completely serious now and he got right to the point.

"You see the mashed fingers?"

"I see them."

"I'd say that that happened while he was still alive. Somebody smashed them with a blunt instrument, maybe the same weapon that killed him, but you'll have to figure out that part. This man was tortured, detective."

Archie nodded. It was obvious now that Nick had been punished or interrogated, or maybe both. He asked about Nick's dislocated shoulder. What Chu said had at least partially confirmed what he'd been thinking. He would need to know what forensics had found and, maybe, ask them to look again at the safe. He also had to find the wetsuit Nick had been wearing. A drysuit was hanging in the locker room, but it wasn't damp and, anyway, Archie had found a tear in the skin of it that made the suit unusable. He was certain that Nick had used a wetsuit on the day he died and that was missing. He wondered if Nick had told the killers what they had wanted to know.

He thanked Chu, asked for a copy of the report to be delivered to him. Then he left the lab and drove to the station. He parked in his usual spot and went in the back door. He avoided the coffee room and anywhere else he might run into people and have to talk. He had asked Thomas Lee to meet him at his office and he knew Lee would be punctual. He fell into his desk chair, not bothering to take off his jacket.

He threw his cap on his desk, leaned back, and tried to rub out the knot that had been building above his eyes. The nub of his problem was that he had, as yet, no motive for the torture and murder of Nick Donaldson. He had nothing really, beyond some wild guesses.

CHAPTER 7

Thomas Lee walked into Archie's office, brushed off the seat of the chair and sat down. Archie had sent him to interview some of Robbie's associates and had hopes that Lee had learned something, maybe even found something that might pass for the missing motive. Lee read the question in his expression and shook his head.

"No certainty about where Robbie is or what he's been up to but we do have something to go on. I took a black and white with me out to his place on the Premier Forest cut block. His boat and trailer weren't there and there was no sign that he had been home — if in fact he had, so I contacted the ferries and the airport to check their CC cameras and their parking lots. Eventually we found Robbie's pickup, boat, and trailer in a ferry long-term parking lot run by the Salish out on the peninsula. It's been there awhile so he could have been on the nine o'clock ferry yesterday, or even Monday night. He's likely on the mainland somewhere."

"When are you going out there?"

"I was going to go right after our meeting. We'll need a search warrant."

"I'll see what I can do but it's pretty short notice. I think I'll come out there with you. You said his trailer was there too?"

"And the boat."

"That's strange. Why take the boat?"

"I haven't any idea. Maybe he was too lazy to unhook the trailer."

Archie called Delia John and gave her the particulars. She would contact a judge and look after getting the warrant. Then he pushed himself away from the desk, uncoiled his legs, and stood up, wishing he had a window to look out. He told Lee about the autopsy. Lee shook his head sadly. Archie asked how the forensics work was coming along. Lee put his computer tablet on the desktop, pulled up a fingerprint image and a file photo mug shot of John Robbie. Archie almost laughed. Robbie had a smirk on his face that made him look like he'd been photographed because he'd wanted to be.

Lee brushed his fingers across the screen to shrink the image. A rap sheet appeared beside it.

"Not all the results are in," he said. "We pulled a thumb print off the abalone iron that matched John Robbie's. Other than that, some of the blood that had splattered on the wall near the body wasn't Donaldson's, so he did hit his attacker when he fired his gun like you figured. We got some of Donaldson's diving stuff from the freshwater tank, but we haven't found the other glove we were looking for. The pockets on the dive vest were open but there weren't any more coins in them, nothing at all in fact. Lots of fingerprints in the shop but nothing that helps. No prints on the coin, of course. So far, it looks like Robbie's the guy we're looking for."

"How'd we happen to have Robbie's prints on file?"

"He did time for some biker-related stuff years back. And he worked for Bill Tran a few times moving stolen goods but we didn't have enough evidence to hold him. There was a drunk and disorderly."

Lee tapped the screen of his tablet, looked something up.

"There's the possibility that he killed a guy when he was in prison, but no charges were laid."

"Was there anything on Nick's computer that would help?" Archie asked.

"Not that we've found. The hard drive has had a complete scrub, and there are no prints on the machine."

"Except for Nick's?"

"Not even his. The machine's been wiped clean."

Archie swore under his breath — Nick would have had had maps and charts bookmarked on his computer. Had they been there, he might have been able to track Nick's movements on the days before he died.

"Let's go. We'll take my vehicle"

He grabbed his cap from his desk. Lee followed.

Their route took them through busy hallways. It was shift change and officers and detectives were coming and going. Reddin and Jameson came out of the coffee room. Jameson planted himself firmly in Archie's way.

"You're supposed to keep me posted, young man. How come I don't have a typed update on my desk?"

Archie shot Jameson a look and then pushed past him. Reddin tried to block Lee's passage; Lee sidestepped, grunted something, carried on. Out in the parking lot, Archie let himself relax. Jameson was an irritation and Reddin was a jerk, but Archie had too much on his mind to worry about either. He waited as Lee arranged

his coat and together they went to Archie's
4Runner at the far end of the lot. Lee climbed in
beside him after shoving a pile of books and papers to one side so that he had room to sit.

"What a mess."

"Yeah, well..."

They picked up coffee at Avril's and then
took the highway out to the ferry terminal at
Saturn Bay. The long-term lot was a private operation on the Cheslat Reservation. The lot attendant was a Salish named Williams. Williams
looked at Archie's identification and gave him
an "I don't believe it" look. Then he pointed out
Robbie's pickup and trailer parked near a ditch
at the edge of the lot.

"Did you see him when he dropped it off?"
Archie asked.

Williams shook his head.

"There's no attendant here after seven. Yesterday's when the rig was first noticed, when I
took down the license number. Including today,
he owes for three days right now. I figure he put
it here night before last."

"So you don't really know when he arrived."

"It'd be about ten at night I guess. I happened to come through at nine and it wasn't
here and then at eleven when it was. Like I say,
there's three days owing."

Lee thanked Williams. Archie led the way to the truck and boat trailer. The rig was badly parked, one wheel of the trailer rested on a rocky outcrop, tilting the frame.

"He parked in a hurry," Lee said. "I'd say he must have been running to catch the ferry, except that there isn't one at that time of night."

"He didn't leave the Island. I'm not even sure he's still alive," Archie said.

He looked inside and pointed to the blood on the seats.

"The warrant is superfluous now," Lee said.

Archie had brought a Slim Jim from his vehicle and he used it to open the passenger side door of the pickup. The smell of blood was strong, that and the pungent reek of wet neoprene. He snapped on latex gloves, placed the heel of his hand on the edge of the bench seat, reached over and opened the driver side door. Thomas Lee looked in, craning his neck around. He'd smelled the blood too. He pointed to the roof liner.

"It's up here," he said.

Archie knelt down and looked up at the smeared blood on the faded cloth.

"I wasn't expecting this," he said

"You think it's Donaldson's blood then?"

"We'll find out."

Archie leaned in and looked over into the space in back of the seat.

"There's a wetsuit here," he said. "It didn't get dried the night Nick got killed. I'm almost certain there'll be a bullet hole in it under the arm. So much mess — whoever dropped this off was in a hurry. Better get forensics out here right away. You'll have to stay here until they come. I've got to get back. Patsy's going to update me on the coin we found in the glove. I'll get Stoney out here with a burger for you. Wait in the toll shack until the tow truck comes."

Lee nodded but looked irritated. Archie knew Lee was tired and ready to go home, but dinner and relaxation would have to wait. Archie pulled off his gloves, dropped them on the ground, and headed back to his vehicle. He stopped before he got in. Lee was close by, walking toward the shack.

"Don't let that truck out of your sight," he said. "And be careful."

Lee nodded, tapped his coat and under it the Berretta he carried. Archie called in, gave the message to Stoney and then drove out of the lot.

CHAPTER 8

When Archie got back to the station, he went directly to the basement lab to meet Patsy. She led him to the counter where she had Nick's glove on a tray and next to it, like a museum exhibit, the gold coin she'd pulled from it. She told him what she'd been able to learn.

"The language on the coin is a kind of Finnish dialect, highly idiosyncratic. I haven't been able to figure out what it means but I've got somebody on the way to do that. There is a word in English. See, it says <u>Eli</u>. No shop or collector has reported a coin like this missing so far as I can determine."

The name, Eli, registered with Archie, but he saw that it didn't seem to mean anything to Patsy. No reason it should, he thought. She hadn't been in Harsley long enough.

"I called Streya Wainright and asked her to come have a look," Patsy said. "She's of Finnish descent, so I thought she might be able to translate."

Archie stiffened. Streya was a complication he didn't need. Even now, the mention of her name raised mixed feelings within him.

"There must be somebody else in this town that can speak Finn."

"Maybe, but I saw Streya at the Satsuma and I figured she could help."

"You mentioned that we had this coin and that it had the word, Eli, on it?"

Patsy nodded.

"Jesus."

"When I did, she said she'd come over."

She picked up on Archie's discomfort right away — women seemed good at that in his experience. She had figured out what it was all about too — he could see that in her face — that she'd put the sequence together, that he and Streya had had something going, that Streya had left him, that he was still hurting. She'd be partly right if that's how she had it. He must have sworn again under his breath because, to his surprise, she reacted like she wanted to protect him and said, "I can interview her, you know. You don't have to be here."

Archie shook his head.

"It's not a problem."

She opened her mouth to say something else but the back door buzzer sounded and she stopped herself. Then she looked into his face like she was assessing his temper. Apparently satisfied, she went to answer the door.

He waited, having no choice in the matter now. She came back with Streya, tightly bundled up in leather against the wind and rain. Streya took off her woollen cap, released a cascade of red hair, pushed it back behind her ears and nodded a greeting at Archie. Her smile seemed warm and her blue eyes were big and bright. His own greeting came out more like 'huh' than 'hi', all he could manage under the circumstances. And then he saw Ray Jameson in the far doorway, watching, curious. Jameson leered, said "Chief," laughed, and walked on.

Streya moved closer to Archie, close enough that he could smell the herbal shampoo scent of her hair. Like always, she demanded his attention and, when she had it, she went on with the show. She unzipped her jacket slowly, took it off and tossed it over the back of a chair.

She wore a form-fitting, low-cut V-neck sweater of soft white wool that displayed just the right amount of décolletage, the little mole on the white swelling curve of her right breast visible, the creamy flesh slightly dimpled by the violet lace edge of her bra cup. His eyes went there. Her eyes tracked his and he knew, by the certainty in them, that the effect she had had on him had been intended. She smiled like a satisfied cat, "Nice to see you again, hon."

Her voice was husky, the tones rich and shadowed. He couldn't think of anything to say so he nodded. She seemed to enjoy his discomfort, waiting and watching his face until he said, "You too."

Then Patsy moved in, business-like, breaking the spell, asking Streya if she would look at the coin and then leading her away to the lab.

Archie lingered, happy that Patsy had been there to remind him, somehow, that he shouldn't let Streya manipulate him — which he wasn't going to do anyway. She'd taken him by surprise. Nothing more to it than that. Patsy took the lead, showed Streya the coin and asked her about it. Streya glanced at Archie, lifted her chin, smiled. Patsy was brusque.

"Can you read the lettering, Streya?"

Streya ignored her, looked to Archie again, glanced at the coin, and nodded her answer to him.

"It says that Brother Eli is the prophet and saviour of the Children."

"You mean the Children of Eli and their leader — that Brother Eli?"

Archie hadn't known that Patsy had even heard of the Children. Streya seemed distracted suddenly, or puzzled. She kept her eyes on the coin.

"There was only one. Where did you get this?"

"We found it at Nick Donaldson's," Patsy said.

Archie shot Patsy a look. She caught it, looked back at him defiantly, not embarrassed like she ought to be for giving out information. He picked up the questioning.

"Have you seen a coin like this before?"

Streya didn't hesitate, obviously expecting the question. Her 'no' was emphatic.

"I heard Nick Donaldson was broke," she said. "Everybody says that that marina of his was bankrupt. He must have stolen that coin from somebody. Likely his partner, John Robbie, killed him."

She looked to Archie to agree with her. When they'd been together, he usually had. This time he kept his mouth shut.

"Don't you think?"

"We'll check"

Now he was aware that Patsy was focussing on him — female curiosity perhaps. Suddenly, Patsy said, "If he stole it, why would he have it stuck in his diving glove?"

Archie, startled, glared at her. She had brought him back to focus and, momentarily, he forgot Streya. But he couldn't believe what he had just heard, nor could he imagine why Patsy would volunteer such information. He asked Streya to wait out in the hallway. She tossed a smile back at him over her shoulder and went out. When he figured Streya was out of hearing, Archie leaned in close to Patsy; he kept his voice low.

"Try to remember that this is a police investigation, detective. We're looking for information; we're not giving it out."

He heard the harshness in his voice, but then she ought to know better. She crossed her arms on her chest, looked straight ahead, jaw set, deep-brown eyes bright with umbrage, said, "She wasn't going to tell us anything and you know it. My guess is that she already knows it came from Donaldson's. She's got something riding on this."

"How do you know that?"

"I can just tell."

He'd have to be satisfied with that. Anyway, she might have something.

"Maybe you're right," he said. "Even so…"

"You can see it, can't you? I'm glad. She knows a lot more than she's saying, but you're so gaga over her that you can't see it."

A denial wasn't going to work so he called Streya back into the room. Streya's demeanour had changed; the look in her eyes was different too. She seemed agitated, impatient.

"I've got work to do," she said. "I'd better go. If you need anything else translated, let me know."

Patsy's "Thanks for coming," was sisterly. She left the room before Archie could stop her, which left him alone with Streya — Patsy's retaliation against being told off maybe.

Streya seemed to have been waiting for the chance. She moved closer immediately. Only inches from him now, she breathed his name. That husky quality there again just for him, the sound of a rainstick turning. But, for some reason, he wasn't having it, not this time. He got business-like, thanked her, led her to the back door — a policeman dismissing a cooperative but useless witness. Piqued, she retrieved her jacket and put it on, zipped it up, keeping her back to him.

Outside it was cold. A few bright winter stars were visible high overhead. He tried to close the door behind her, to leave her, to go back to his office but she hesitated in the doorway, waiting for him. She turned, looked up into his face, her eyes inviting, her red hair wind tossed, errant strands catching against the gloss of her lipstick. He stuffed his hands into his jacket pocket and grunted that he would walk her to her car.

She seemed satisfied with that and led the way. Then she stopped there, leaned back against the fender. She looked up into his eyes again, a question there. He knew it was best if he was out of there.

"Forget it, Streya. This isn't going to work."

"I don't know what you mean."

She looked hurt.

"Okay, you don't know what I mean. How about this? You lied about that coin."

"Everything I said about it is true."

"Bad choice of words. You kept something back."

"There's nothing else."

"Suit yourself." He turned away. "I've got work to do."

"Then you'd better do it."

She was angry now, the old Streya coming out. She dragged a bundle of keys and baubles out of her pocket, searched for the right key, avoided looking at him, climbed into the car and started it. She stared straight ahead, him standing near the Beetle's open window unsure of what to do

She said something he couldn't quite hear over the whistle of the resonators. He moved close to the window to catch her words, put a hand on the roof of the car and leaned in. She turned, looked up.

"I made a mistake, Archie." Her breath was hot and sweet. "I want to see you again."

She turned her face away, the beginning of tears in her eyes now. That brought him back to reality.

"No crying, Streya. It's not going to work this time."

"I miss you."

"You say whatever you think will work."

"That's not true. I said I missed you and I meant it."

"I don't know what you want me to do about it."

"Just don't say no."

"Dammit."

He turned and walked away because he had to. She slammed the shifter into gear, revved the engine and turned the radio on loud. The sound followed her as she drove out of the lot. Tears and then rage — that was Streya, plus the lies, nothing changed. He remembered a line from a Steely Dan song his uncle used to play, something about "loving a wild one." Wild and dangerous too, he thought. He lingered at the edge of the half-empty parking lot, breathed deeply, reset his thoughts and then went back into the building. Delia John, working nights doing dispatch, stopped him as he passed her station.

"Fricke called. Said he needs to talk to you about your progress. That'd be tomorrow morning at eight. Unless you want me to say that I didn't see you?"

Archie nodded.

"That'd be better."

Then he had a thought, something he wanted to check out.

"Also I'd like to look more closely at the file on John Robbie."

He waited until she found it and then he walked it back to his office.

CHAPTER 9

Archie got out on the road early, turned down the volume on his scanner so that he couldn't hear any calls from the station and put his cellphone on *silent*. The Zuider Zee, Bonnie Tran's restaurant, was on the northern edge of Harsley, backed by forest. She was John Robbie's girlfriend and might know where he was, and there was an off chance that she might even know something more about what Nick and his sometime partner had been up to lately. She was sorting through an order of bread and buns when he arrived, checking things off against a waybill. She didn't seem surprised to see him and she wasn't particularly friendly. He sat down at the counter, unzipped his jacket, and reached for a newspaper like he'd just dropped in for coffee. She hardly looked up. He opened with the weather.

"Stopped raining for a bit," he said.

"A news flash from the cops. Perfect. What can I get for you?"

"Just coffee, Bonnie — if you don't mind."

She flipped over a mug and set it on the counter, filled it with dark stale coffee. He dumped a stream of sugar in, followed that with three creams, and watched the liquid change from black-brown to the colour of concrete.

"Lots of work with the restaurant, I guess."

She grunted, "Uh-huh," continued with the waybill, said, "I'm used to it."

"Not much time for a social life."

"Not going to answer that one, officer."

He looked at the reflection of the dining room in the long, horizontal mirror that hung on the back wall where the blue and white ornaments left by the original Dutch owners still hung. He wasn't used to employing this kind of questioning, the polite kind, and he was afraid it showed. He had hoped that because he had known her in the old days that she might be more cooperative.

"My dad had a café up in Taggart Bay when I was a little kid. Couldn't seem to make a go of it. The old man didn't have a head for business, they say. He had to take a job up at the mill and worked there until the accident."

"That Taggart Bay place has gone under more times than a deep sea diver. The location is wrong. Too far from the mill for the guys that work there, too close to the mill for the tourists. An idiot can see it."

She caught herself. "No disrespect to your old man."

Even so, his old man would have had more pull with Bonnie and the kind of people she hung with. She was editing herself too — not normal for Bonnie Tran.

"You got some problem, Bonnie? Something you want to talk about?"

"No."

She was too emphatic.

"Are you sure?"

"I said no, for fuck's sake."

She turned away, made it obvious that she wanted him gone. The conversational approach wasn't working, so he went at it directly.

"You know I came to ask you about John Robbie?"

"It'll have to wait." She held up the waybill as proof that she had work to do. "I'm way too busy. Come back tomorrow."

He wondered if she really expected that he would leave just because she asked him to, said, "Stop what you're doing so I can talk to you," added, "please," as an afterthought.

She put down the bill, set her hands on her hips, and did her best to hold her temper. He saw that she was struggling with something, kept his eyes on her.

"You're going to have to make the time to talk to me, here or at my office."

He looked at the bruise on her arm.

"Somebody grab you?"

She glared at him, but the eyes had fear in them.

"My sweater was too tight. What do you want me to say? And just so you know, I've got nobody for the next shift and I got lots of things to get ready."

"When'd you last see John Robbie?"

"I haven't seen John for weeks."

He watched her eyes.

"You're sure?"

"Positive. I'd know if I saw somebody."

"Exactly when did you see him? When was the last time?"

"I can't remember. I'm getting sick and tired of being harassed by you guys?"

"What do you mean by that? Has somebody else been here?"

She shook her head, looked away. He tried a few more angles, but she stubbornly refused to give him any information. He decided he'd give her a chance to stew a little, and then maybe have Stone bring her in for questioning. Not that that would work any better.

"If I don't hear from you soon, I'll send someone."

He took a business card out of his top pocket and pushed it across the counter in her direction.

She looked at it.

"Detective — sheeit!"

"I'd appreciate a call. Or John can call me himself."

She lifted her shoulders and dropped them, an exaggerated shrug like a schoolgirl asked about some boy she wasn't supposed to be seeing.

"He does what he wants. Anyway, I got work to do."

"Don't wait too long, Bonnie."

When he was almost out the door, she picked up his card, crumpled it, and threw it on the floor — she made sure he saw it. He shrugged, grinned. Then something occurred to him.

"Your brother Bill, in Empire City…"

"What about him?"

"I was wondering if he'd been up here lately. I thought you might have seen him."

He saw surprise in her face. She wasn't as good at keeping her thoughts to herself as she used to be.

"What would he want here?"

"I don't know but I'd hate to think that you'd go to jail as an accessory."

He had no business saying that to her but he did it anyway.

"Accessory to what?"

"We're investigating a murder, Bonnie. It's got a kind of Bill feel to it."

She shuffled a sugar shaker, lifted it up, put it down.

"I don't know nothing and I haven't seen him or John and I'm tired of talking to you."

She turned her back to him and went into her kitchen. He finished, dropped a five on the counter. He called out, "See you, Bonnie," but all he got in response was the muted slamming of a freezer door.

He left the restaurant and walked out to his car, turned the volume up on his police radio, checked his cellphone for missed calls and got the result he expected, which was that Cal Fricke wanted to hold an update meeting. He decided he wasn't ready yet to listen to Fricke or Jameson or somebody else whining about zero results and inexperienced detectives. Fricke would have to wait.

At the highway, he had a thought. He headed in the direction of his home village at Kokishilah. The road took him over the river where he used to fish when he was a kid, past side roads leading into old logging shows, past the cut block where John Robbie lived — the use of an old house trailer for staying there as a sort of unpaid custodian. Lee had been there but Archie wanted to have a look for himself. But that would have to be later when he had time to be thorough.

CHAPTER 10

The village spread along the river for almost a mile, the houses mostly close to the road. The Kokishilah Tribal Office occupied a field across the road from the huge tribal longhouse, both buildings fronted by totem poles. Archie stopped first at the office, a non-descript, brown-sided, flat-roofed building, asked for the Chief, Pete Wilson. Pete generally knew what was going on the water: Archie was directed across the road to the longhouse. He found Pete busy with wires; he was trying to set up a sound system for some upcoming event, all the time arguing with Councillor Walter George who obviously had different ideas about how to do the job. They didn't stop working when Archie walked in, pointedly ignoring him. Both had been good friends of Archie's once, not so anymore, certainly.

"Hide the bingo chips," Walter said. "The cops are here."

"You're a funny man, Walt," Archie said.

"Who's being funny?"

Pete Wilson looked up from the cables he was trying to sort out, nodded but didn't smile.

"You got time to talk?" Archie asked.

"Sure — if I keep at this I'm going to screw something up."

He dropped the cables he'd been holding, motioned Archie to the cedar benches along the wall of the longhouse. They sat down almost side-by-side, stared off into the rafters; Pete waiting for Archie to say whatever it was he had on his mind, it not being polite to press. Archie breathed in the smell of stamped earth, of salmon, charcoal, and wood smoke — intensely familiar.

"You know about Nick Donaldson, I guess?" He said that to his right knee. Pete spoke to his left hand, which he turned over and over as if looking for splinters.

"Somebody cut his throat."

"How'd you know that? We're not releasing details."

"Maybe not but everybody knows it. Word gets around."

"You've got a boat at Nick's in storage."

"I got three boats at Nick's — if you count the two the tribal council owns. They're all gillnetters and there aren't enough salmon to put them in the water."

"You ever hang with him or work with him or anything?"

"Not really. I played baseball against him. Why?"

"I was hoping you'd know where he poached abalone, where he might go when he was out on the water."

"You should ask John Robbie."

"I'm having a hard time tracking him down right now."

"Try the Zuider Zee."

"I could do that, I guess."

Pete grinned.

"Already thought of that move, I guess. There aren't many abalone left anymore but poachers still harvest them. Look Arch, we tried to nail the bastards ourselves but we couldn't pin them down. Somebody from your station tips them off."

"You're kidding?"

"I'm not kidding. There's a lot goes on around here that people don't know."

Walter George brought three mugs of coffee; one so battered and dirty that at first Archie didn't recognize the old Vancouver Canucks logo. Walter kept the dirty mug and handed the others to Pete and Archie. Walter saw Archie staring at his cup.

"It's a lucky cup, okay? I won't wash it until the Canucks win the Stanley Cup. I'd jinx the team."

Pete raised an eyebrow.

Walter shrugged, sat down so that he lined up with them, all three staring at the far wall. After five minutes, Walter spoke.

"What's the topic?"

"Nick Donaldson and abalone poaching."

"Too bad about Nick," Walter said. "He was diving near Cat's Cradle Island."

Pete turned so that he could eyeball Walter.

"How'd you know that?" Archie said.

His question was too abrupt, and he felt the quick shift in Walter's mood.

"I was out setting crab pots a couple of weeks ago and I seen him and John Robbie at the west end of the island. I doubt if they seen me. It was pissing down, and they were concentrating on what was in the water."

"Where was that exactly, if you don't mind me asking?"

Walter didn't answer. He shook his head like he was exasperated, went to the office, and came back with a chart. He spread it across his knees and pointed to the east shore of Cat's Cradle Island where the chart showed a long, shallow reef.

"Right there, near where the Children of Eli used to have their settlement."

He took a Sharpie from his pocket and marked the location with an 'X'. He handed the chart to Archie, struggling to let go of the fact that he was still angry with Archie about something. Archie had an idea what it was.

"You can borrow this," Walter said.

Archie let the chart lay where it was, not ready to accept whatever it was Walter had offered.

"What do you mean, Walt, about the Children of Eli?"

"Don't you know about them? Jeez, Archie, where you been? You ought to talk to your granny. She can tell you all about Cat's Cradle Island. The Children were a big deal in her day."

Archie didn't have an answer for that.

"I saw Nick heading there a week or so ago too," Walter continued. "I think he went ashore — spent some time there maybe."

"How come you see so much?" Pete said. "Most of the time you're in bed."

"How'd you ever get to be chief? You can't even put up a sound system. I have to take naps because I get up so early, smart ass. I'm on the water by first light most days."

Pete raised an eyebrow in pretended disbelief.

"What's it like over there?" Archie asked.

"You go to Monkey Beach," Walter said. "That's where the old settlement is, and the dock — such as it is."

"Monkey Beach?"

"It's called Jutilainen Cove on the charts. It used to be a place where the Sasquatch visited — the Bigfoot — back in the old days. That's how it got to be called Monkey Beach."

Archie shook his head, "Sasquatch, Jesus."

"There are such things, Archie. You cut yourself off too much. You got yourself a big head…"

Pete shot Walter a look. He caught it, looked into his cup, said, "That's all I got to say on the subject."

Archie didn't have a reply for that. It cut too close to the bone, thought but didn't say, "Hell with you, Walter."

Pete picked up the threads and carried on like nothing had happened.

"The Finns who first settled there laid out the town of New Jerusalem. They wanted to make a paradise on earth but that idea fell through. There were still some of them there when Brother Eli came with his Children of Eli cult. The Children took over, rebuilt the town, and built Eli a temple. They did a lot of criminal stuff to raise money, I heard. Most of the buildings have fallen down now. Their temple is still in pretty good shape though. And the old wharf is solid enough."

"So nobody lives there now?"

"Not that I know of. It's a weird place. I've been ashore once or twice. We've got a land claim there but that's likely to take years before it gets settled."

Archie stood, drained his cup slowly and then put it down. He was thinking it was time he took off out of there and stood up to go. Walter kept his eyes on his own cup, "You should come out here more often, Archie."

"He's got a point," Pete said.

"It's your goddam home," Walter said.

Archie couldn't think of anything to say to that except, "Yeah, I know."

Archie hesitated, thought he needed to say something more but instead he thanked them for the information, too formally he realized. As he walked out into the pale, late autumn sunshine, he heard Pete and Walter pick up their argument. He heard his name and figured that they were probably talking about him becoming a cop. Screw them. He wanted to be gone, but he had one more stop to make before he left Kokishilah.

His grandmother lived in a faded, yellow bungalow at the edge of the village. She was old and her memory was almost gone but she might remember the Children of Eli and what they were all about. He almost missed seeing her, a tiny woman hunched over in her garden, hardly moving. She was picking the last of the dahlias — very slowly. She wore the old Cowichan sweater she had always worn, grey on grey. She looked up at the sound of the car door. She didn't seem to recognize him.

"You come looking to buy salmon?"

Archie smiled and shook his head.

"Not today, Gran. I just came to say hello."

She peered at him through half-shuttered old eyes, lifted a bony finger, tapped the air with it. He knew she was searching her memory.

"I know you. You're Darlene's boy. You're the boy who joined the cops. The one who started off bad and then wizened up."

"That's me, Gran." He walked up the gravelled walk so that she could see him better. "I'm Darlene's boy, Archie."

She straightened up as best she could, dropped the dahlias into her basket and waited until he was no more than a few feet away. Then she held up her hand and commanded him to stop.

"You're at exactly the right distance for me to see you clear."

He waited while she studied him, looking at him this way and that, like she was trying to decide if he really had 'wizened up'. He dared not laugh.

She finished her inspection. "You've grown up real fine, Archie. You're a good-looking boy. How come you don't have a uniform and a real cop car?"

"I'm a detective now. I've got a uniform but I don't need to wear it since I got my promotion. And this is a real police car, just not marked like one. Those are for patrol."

"It looks like a Jeep to me. You're Darlene's boy, right?"

She looked confused, and Archie wondered for a moment if he was doing the right thing. Then he saw the joke. She was playing with him. He had forgotten about her sense of humour. It was always a mystery to him how she could be so good-natured, what with all heartache she'd had in her time — to which he'd contributed. He was sorry for that now, was sorry for it then too, except that the wildness and hurt in him was something that just took over until he felt that his skin wouldn't hold it. He forced himself out of that line of thinking and followed her, picking his way down the narrow path, dodging flowerpots and lawn furniture, as she hobbled on ahead.

Inside, she made him sit down in a huge old chair covered with brightly coloured crochet work. She gave him milky tea and stale biscuits, and watched him like an old hawk while he ate. Sometimes she shifted to the language of their people and he had to struggle to keep up. He was surprised by her memories of things long, long ago, but her forgetfulness of the immediate past worried him. She asked him about people he'd never heard of and he had to cobble together answers that made sense. She told him that her husband Moise would be back from cutting railroad ties soon and would be able to tell him what he wanted to know. Except that Moise had been dead for twenty years.

He turned down the renewed offer of tea and biscuits four times, when she forgot that she had already given them to him. When she made signs that she was anxious to go back out into her garden, he brought the conversation around to Cat's Cradle Island. She seemed reluctant to talk and he had to coax her. She settled back into her chair, her eyes shone like polished jet.

"It's part of my heritage, Gran."

She drew a long breath.

"That island had many fish camps on it once. Our family owned the rights to a big chunk of the west side, villages too, mostly deserted when the settlers came. The smallpox had killed so many back then that we had too few people to use all our old places. The villages there got abandoned. Then the settlers came pretty quick after that. The first ones weren't so bad — those Finlanders."

"And the others?"

"The others — you mean the Brother Eli bunch?" She pursed her withered lips as if the words had a bitter taste. "The Divine Spirits was one name they had but they called themselves the Children of Eli. They took over from the Finns. Made people think they were holy, but they were evil people. Nothing divine about them. They posted the land and shot at our people. They ran booze through the islands and other stuff too. Moise and the other elders think they killed two of our fishermen. They ran things in that town too, in Harsley — booze, drugs, everything. You can ask Moise about that yourself."

"Moise won't be back for awhile."

She stopped talking suddenly, her eyes focussed on something he couldn't see. Some dark remembrance moved across her features — great pain or fear. That happened with old people sometimes.

He wanted her to start talking again, about Moise and the good past, but then it seemed as if the dark memory had gone. She started to chatter, to talk about blackberry jam recipes, bingo, and the way young people were "going to the dogs these days." Suddenly, she stopped, reached out her arm, pointed fiercely with a bony finger — he guessed in the direction of the Cat's Cradle Island. She was very angry.

"The old days were a lot different than now," she said, her voice strong again. "We had no power back then. If the white man did something to us, it was hard to get justice. That Brother Eli was a bad one. He put machine guns over there on that island. They even chased white fishermen away. They killed people there, beat them up, tortured them. They did terrible things over at Monkey Beach. I know that from personal experience. The cops didn't do nothing."

He waited for her to finish but she seemed to want to change the subject.

"Why was that, Gran?"

"I won't tell about that."

He wanted to know what she meant. He tried to probe deeper, to try to catch the slippery eel of her thought, before she had drifted on to other things.

"I thought that Brother Eli thing ended when the police arrested him?"

"He disappeared." She almost spat out the words. "But his people are still around. You have the Norgard family for one thing — that sneaky kid, young Lars. He'd be a little older than you."

"I know Lars. One more question, Gran, if you're okay with me talking so much."

He waited until she looked at him.

"I'm glad you're here."

"I heard Brother Eli had these gold coins. What happened to them, does anyone know?"

The look in her eyes was soft as eagle down. She thought a minute and then she said, "Moise gets back soon, grandson — he'll tell you."

And he saw that she had gone somewhere else. The anger, or fear, that he had seen in her eyes had gone too. The shutters had closed. He let the conversation ramble wherever she wanted it to go. At last, she began to tire and then without warning she fell asleep in her chair. He stood, got her quilt and put it over her to keep her warm. He tidied up the dishes, cleaned off the counter and put the biscuits away. His hand was on the doorknob, ready to leave, when he heard her stir. He looked back at her. She smiled at him; the look on her face warmed him.

"You watch out for yourself, grandson. Stay out of those caves."

He turned to look back. He hadn't known about any caves. He was about to ask her about them until he caught the look in her eyes that said she wasn't going to say anything else on the subject.

"I'll be careful, grandmother."

"Go see your uncle Tony. He'll give you a sweat. A sweat will help you. You always got along well with Tony."

She closed her eyes again. He waited until he heard her snoring, and then he closed the door quietly behind him. He figured he'd send Lee up to Rochville. The city's police archives likely had something on the Children and the trial of Brother Eli and his close associates. Not that anyone on his team had time to look for gold coins or go on wild goose chases. Not with Fricke breathing down his neck. But what he knew for sure was that, sooner or later, he would have to go to Monkey Beach to try to recreate Nick's final day.

CHAPTER 11

Archie had hoped to go directly to his briefing room but Cal Fricke, leaving Jameson's office, spotted him right away. He moved out to block Archie's passage, easy enough for a man of Fricke's size. Fricke, chawing vigorously on nicotine gum, jerked a thumb in the direction of his office. Archie fell in behind the moving wall of tweed jacket that was Fricke's back, knew every cop in the station was watching him as he passed. Most of them had experienced a Cal Fricke rage at one time or another, and now they were hoping to witness the tornado again for its entertainment value.

Archie had an idea that Fricke wasn't likely to disappoint them. At his office, Fricke banged the door shut and then demanded to know 'why the fuck' John Robbie wasn't in custody. Archie shrugged. Maybe, he said, they would have Robbie by the beginning of the week but he wasn't sure if their suspect was even still alive. He told Fricke about the pickup and the blood but decided not to mention the wetsuit.

Fricke paused to take in that news. He was all wound up for a blowout and changing course was not an option, but he toned it down. He grumbled that finding the pickup was good but it wasn't enough. Archie had, he growled, better find and arrest John Robbie "damn fucking soon." Then he talked about Ray Jameson's success rate on serious crimes and how hard it ought to be for anyone to avoid capture on an island, even one as large as the one they were on. His meaning seemed clear enough; Archie needed to come up with a bone fide arrest or Jameson would take over. Archie said that he was still trying to work out a motive and making an arrest seemed even less likely than it had a day ago.

"I'll make an arrest when it's time."

"Don't give me that shit," Fricke said.

"You want me to tell you straight or not?" Archie said.

Fricke made a sound like an old grizzly, a thundering growl that started deep in his gut. Archie watched his face go through its moods, finally settling on something like acceptance of what Archie was saying. Archie knew that Fricke, for some reason, was getting pressure from the mayor and the media to wrap things up. The need to get results soon and to deal with the public was building. It was a part of the job Archie hadn't thought much about when he took over the case, but he would have to hold a press conference and he had precious little to say to reporters.

Finished with what he had to say, Fricke abruptly waved Archie out of his office and slammed the door hard enough to rattle the glass. Archie, under the gaze of a dozen or more officers and detectives walked, head high, to the dispatch desk. He stood at the counter until Delia John deigned to acknowledge him. She leaned on the triangle made by her hands and elbows. Her many bracelets rattled down her forearms. She looked up at him sideways, past a long, raven-black bang.

"You survived?" she said.

"Was there any doubt?"

"Oh, yeah. There sure was."

It took him five minutes of talking to find out from her what he wanted to know. Then he left the station and headed down to Old Town to look for Lars Norgard — sneaky little Lars, his granny had called him.

Norgard sometimes hung out with John Robbie and might know something that would help. After talking to Pete, Walter, and his grandmother, Archie was very curious about the Children of Eli. Norgard half-lived at Moffat's Bar, the kind of place you could call a dump without insulting anyone, including Moffat. Archie drove there to find Norgard.

The tavern was a low-slung building with a moss-covered, cedar-shingled roof. It sat on a gravelly bench at the edge of the boat basin and had a view worth a lot more than the business. The barmaid, Laci Laitenen, looked up as Archie pushed in through the storm door. Something from Robert Service, "how ghastly somebody looked in her rouge," popped into Archie's head and stayed there. Laci wore a miniskirt and a low-cut top, pretending she was twenty-one, which she wasn't by a long shot.

He nodded to her as he walked past where she was standing, and went deeper into the low-slung reek of spilled beer and stale smoke. The furniture was old, really old — retro on retro, and it was dark inside even though it was mid-afternoon. The few men drinking there likely didn't care if it was day or night.

He almost missed Norgard sitting in the shadows at a table near the dartboards with his back to the wall. Norgard supposedly made his living fishing a C-License but Archie knew his boat hardly ever left the dock. Mostly, Lars captained his table at Moffat's. When he saw

Archie, he made a move like he was ready to go, but then he settled back, tilted his chair against the wall like an old gunfighter, even nodded a half-hearted greeting. Archie slid into the chair opposite. Lars, waiting for Archie to open, spread his hands in the interrogative.

"You want something, Arch? Cops short of work or something?"

"Always got lots of work, Lars, but maybe I want to go fishing."

"Like — for what?"

"You tell me. You're the guy that does it."

"My boat motor's broke. So I'm not fishing these days, not that that would be your business."

"That depends."

Norgard fidgeted, fingers mowing the stubble on his lantern jaw.

"What are you really here for, Archie?"

"Maybe I was just making conversation."

"Hell, Archie. This ain't just conversation."

Archie kept his eyes fixed on Norgard and tried his damnedest to keep his cool.

"I'm looking for John Robbie. I need to talk to him."

Norgard shrugged.

"I haven't seen him."

Archie looked past Norgard towards the dartboard; saw the name at the top of a chalked list.

"You're a good dart player, Lars."

"You got that right. But I still ain't seen Robbie."

Friendly wasn't going to cut it.

"Your home-grow doing well?"

He had surprised Norgard with that. He could see it in Norgard's body language. Before Nick's murder, he'd heard that the Rochville cops were following up a lead on a big marijuana operation. Norgard's name had come up. They didn't have much, but Norgard probably wouldn't know that.

"Robbie ain't been around, Arch. I'd tell you if I knew anything, just to get you out of my space."

"Let's forget Robbie for now then."

"Then what will we have to talk about, you and me?"

"Are you still doing business with Bill Tran?"

Norgard looked over at the bar and then picked at a dirty, cracked fingernail. Archie knew that he was weighing his options, uncertain. He was on his guard for some other reason.

"I never see Bill these days."

"Okay. I got something else to talk to you about. Your mom and dad were with the Brother Eli bunch. They called themselves the Children of Eli, right?"

"That's no secret. So what? If we're talking family, we could talk about your white, rock and roller, old man and your old lady, a princess of the Salish people they say. Match made in heaven, that was."

"Nobody's perfect. But I'm more interested in your folks. Mine weren't involved in criminal cults."

Norgard's laugh was a kind of machine-gun stutter that had no humour in it. He tilted his head like an old heron and looked at Archie from under his brows.

"You asked about John Robbie. I remember now. I saw him on the road to the ferry, couple of nights back."

Laci Laitenen materialized at Norgard's elbow. Archie had been aware of her, watching them, maybe trying to listen in. She had a six-pack of beer and she dropped it on the table between the two men.

"Your takeout, Lars. You said you had to be going."

"He'll go when he's ready, Laci — and he's not ready."

Her thin lips compressed into a razor-thin line; her hard face was not at all flattered by the cold light from the window.

"This police business?"

"Fishing advice," Archie said. "Don't let us keep you."

She went. Archie leaned back in his chair, tried to decide how best to get what he needed from Norgard, and elected for the direct approach. He'd say what was on his mind and see what happened.

"I hear Bill Tran and John Robbie do business together sometimes."

The other man's hands wandered the tabletop. Then he slapped his hand hard on the table top, like he was angry or fed up.

"I got no time for this," he said.

He stood up abruptly as if he was about to leave, which took Archie by surprise. Archie leaned back in his chair and crossed his arms.

"I'd prefer you talk to me now, Lars. It'll be more convenient for you."

Norgard looked hard at Archie. Then he sat down again, rapped the tips of his fingers on the table and looked over toward the bar where Laci Laitenen had put her back towards them, pretending she was washing out glasses.

"I don't know about what Robbie does, nor Tran neither. If you got something on me and dope, Archie, you got to prove it. End of story."

Archie kept his voice low.

"Maybe this isn't the best place to talk. I'm thinking that I'll have to have you come down to the station for an interview, Lars. I know you're holding out on me. I got lots of questions, even some about the Children."

Norgard's eyes shifted. He rocked back in his seat, lit another cigarette and blew a smoke ring. When he spoke, his voice was almost inaudible. Archie leaned in to listen.

"I don't know nothing about them anymore."

Mention of the Children seemed to register with Norgard.

"If it's some sort of dope operation and you've got information we can use, I can give you protection."

Norgard laughed again, as if Archie had said something very funny.

"You haven't a clue, Archie."

"In two seconds, I'm going to formally arrest you for withholding information. You'll go to jail for obstructing justice."

That was a lie.

"Go ahead. You got nothing and we both know it."

Archie made a mental note about idle threats, wondered if there was more than one way to skin a cat. He shrugged.

"I took a shot, Lars. You can't blame me for that."

Norgard harrumphed. Archie didn't change his position. He hoped the expression on his face hadn't changed either. Then he was sure from reading Norgard's eyes that it hadn't.

"I figured it would go like this, Lars. If I don't have to pay for information I won't. We have a budget for informants but I've got to account for every dime."

Norgard's eyes narrowed. The corners of his mouth lifted in a foxlike smile.

"How much we talking?"

His eyes darted between Archie and the bar where Laci was still fussing around.

"I'll need enough to get the hell out of here. Plus this has to be kept between you and me."

"We can negotiate." Archie heard himself and thought that he sounded too much like a TV detective. "There's money but the amount depends on the quality of the information."

Norgard scratched his forehead. He waited until Laci had turned away again.

"As I say, I ain't personally involved. I might know something and I might not. Meet me at the Old Chinese Cemetery in two hours and I'll tell you more. Don't tell nobody you was talking to me and don't leave me hanging out there long."

"You have my word."

Norgard downed his beer and stood up suddenly, making out like he was angry.

"I told you that I don't know nothing, Archie. You got no right to harass me."

He almost shouted it. He picked up his six-pack and made a show of storming out. When he had gone, Laci rapped a beer glass down on the counter and shot Archie a peculiar look.

Archie, standing now, touched the brim of his ball cap and walked out. The predicted rain hadn't started, which was good. He felt positive about his talk with Norgard, although he also wondered if he was spinning his wheels. Robbie was still the key so far as he could see.

He had some time to kill before he went to the meet so he stopped and bought some protein bars and a diet soda from a gas station. Then he drove to a nearby park to think. The predicted rain still hadn't come yet and the rocks on the outlook were dry, so he picked one and sat down to look at the view. As he munched on a bar, his mind drifted to Streya Wainright. He wondered if he'd made a mistake with her, if he'd read her wrong. After all, she'd just acted like any normal person would have who had been called to the police station and asked for information. But then Streya was not a normal person.

The wind dropped a bit. He heard an eagle somewhere off down in the forest. From the outlook he could see what he had hoped to see, the places within a half day by boat from Donaldson's Dive Shop, the places where Nick might have been on the day he died. The sun, peeking briefly through the clouds, hit the windows of a boat heading out in the strait, crossing beneath his perch on the ridge, heading for the islands.

When he started on the abalone poaching investigation, he had asked someone at Fisheries to send over a nautical chart. He went back to his 4Runner to get it. When he sat back down on the rock, he unfolded the chart and checked it against what he could see in front of him. He remembered his conversation when he'd called Fisheries, apparently they'd been trying to nail Nick for abalone poaching and the Harsley police already knew that. The chart was marked with their best guesses about where the poaching might have happened.

The map was crammed with a skein of comments — <u>Doubt It</u>, <u>Too Visible</u>, <u>Polluted</u>, <u>Nope</u>. There were also lots of <u>PO's</u> for <u>Poached Out</u>. Red question marks were around Cat's Cradle Island, and there was a circled area on the west coast and marked with the words <u>Perfect Habitat</u>. It was right at the spot that Walter had shown him on the chart back at Kokishilah. Archie folded the chart and put it away. When he looked again, the boat he'd seen earlier had vanished.

He went back down the trail to his car and picked up the highway and headed south. The Chinese Cemetery was only five miles away but, once off the highway, he'd have to go down a long stretch of half-washed out road to get there.

A few minutes before three in the afternoon, he drove out onto a low sandstone bluff that overlooked the Strait. He pulled off to the left and backed the 4Runner into a flat space behind some cedars, a place where he could see without being seen. Backing in gave him the option of chasing after Norgard if that became necessary, even though that was unlikely.

His was the only vehicle in the parking lot, which suited him fine. He let his mind wander as he watched Harlequin ducks work the edge of the rocks. Then he mentally catalogued cloud formations over the mountains, and waited.

The half-abandoned cemetery was a popular spot in better weather, mostly because it got more sun than many places around Harsley. It was a good place for picnics, for watching birds in the winter, but not well visited when it was raining or threatening. After an hour had passed and Norgard had failed to appear, Archie gave up on him. He was angry now, mostly at himself for being strung along. A non-descript SUV drove past with two men in it, neither of whom he recognized. He started the 4Runner, made a wide circuit of the parking lot, and headed down the road.

He thought back to his conversation with Norgard at Moffat's and remembered the inter-action between him and the barmaid. They'd been leading him on all along, having a joke at his expense. He swore and stabbed the accelera-tor with his foot. The 4Runner lurched across a hummock in the road and almost bounced into the trees. Fighting to control the vehicle, he didn't have time to regret losing his temper.

The 4Runner lurched one more time, a big bounce off an exposed chunk of bedrock. Archie spun the wheel hard to correct and overcom-pensated, sending the vehicle bouncing hard the other way. That movement saved his life. Bullets smashed through the windshield, knocked out the driver side window and pattered into the metal of the 4Runner's body.

Archie stepped on the accelerator and held on, barely; he gripped the wheel with his left hand while he pulled at the SIG in its holster with his right. He hooked the gun out of the leather only to feel it slip from his fingers as the 4Runner lurched. The pistol hit the passenger seat before it skipped away and disappeared towards the floor.

He cursed again, held the wheel loosely enough to compensate for its wild gyrations, and drove on. Almost on level ground, he checked the rear-view mirror just in time, saw two men wearing camo and balaclavas running up the road after him. The taller of the two raised a weapon and fired. Archie ducked down and spun the wheel, throwing the 4Runner sideways. Bullets whumped into the tailgate and shattered the back window, covering him with diamonds of glass.

And then he was on the highway. He accelerated until he was out of range, did a high-speed spin-around so that the 4Runner's nose was pointed at the egress, braked, and caught his breath. He calmed himself, unclipped his seatbelt, ducked down and found the SIG in the passenger footwell. He sat up, leaned forward on the wheel and looked back in the direction he had come. Then he got out of the cab and stood on the highway ready to meet his attackers, his gun in hand. After a few minutes, he started to walk back in the direction from which he had just come.

CHAPTER 12

Archie bent down and picked a 9mm parabellum cartridge case from the hardpack on
which it was lying, examined it in gloved fingers. He placed the cartridge back down and
pegged in a yellow location marker beside it.
The men who had attacked him, plus their vehicle, an SUV from the tracks, were long gone. The
SWAT team that had come down from Rochville
in response to his emergency had left, leaving
Archie and his team to continue the investigation. Archie, still pissed at being fooled, plugged
into a simmering resentment that was never far
below the surface for him. He wished he had
had time to at least shoot back. But he had not.
He looked down the road to where Lee and Patsy were searching for additional evidence. Patsy
stopped, picked up something, called Archie
over. She held up a business card — English on

one side and Vietnamese on the other. She passed it to Archie.

"Bill Tran, Imports and Exports," he read. He passed the card back to her. "That's for the legitimate part of his business."

"It's looking like gang stuff, isn't it?" she said.

"Right now it is anyway."

Things were slightly easier between them. She was trying hard, again, to be collegial. He was keenly aware of the social distance between them. She was a university professor's daughter, or something like that; she came from money — the opposite of him.

Once they had done all they could at the ambush site, Archie gave the order to pack it up. It was late in the afternoon and there was little more that they could do in daylight. As they got into their cars, Stoney arrived in a patrol car with another uniformed cop and work lights. They would have a final look around, with fresh eyes — to complete the report. They would also wait for the tow truck that had been called to come and pick up Archie's bullet-riddled 4Runner, which had taken a slug through the block and was now useless.

Archie briefed Stoney and then went to where Lee was waiting in his BMW. Lee opened the door. Without a word, Archie got in, hunkered into the passenger seat and motioned Lee to go. Patsy stopped them before the car began to move, leaned in to the driver's side window and suggested they meet later over supper at the Satsuma Café to discuss what had happened. Lee seconded the motion. Archie didn't object, although he wanted to; he was feeling strange and would much rather have gone home.

Archie was still thinking through what had happened when Lee dropped him off in the elaborate Porte Cochere of the condo tower at four thirty. It was getting dark. Fricke told him that he would have a man watching the place in case there was another attack; no protest from Archie seemed to change his mind.

Archie looked for a patrol car, was relieved when there wasn't one, then saw a cruiser pull up and park in plain view halfway down the block. He walked over to it. A young officer, Tracy Gillot, rolled down his window and greeted him. When Archie tried to send him on his way, Gillot grinned and shook his head.

"Fricke said you'd try something like this. He also said that if I left my post he would can my ass. So, upshot, I'm staying."

Archie shook his head, turned on his heel and headed for his building. He heard the whine as the window on the cruiser went up. He walked back to the front door to let himself in.

He did not look back. The presence of a fresh-faced young rookie in a patrol car didn't reassure him one bit.

In the lobby, he passed an older couple who regarded his dishevelled clothes and dirt-covered cowboy boots with some disgust. He'd seen that same look before, when people saw him somewhere that they didn't expect to see someone like him. His transformation had only gone so far. At that moment, he probably looked like a street person looking for the opportunity to steal something

He checked his mailbox, chucked the offers for credit cards in the junk mail bin, found a letter from the woman whose apartment he was borrowing, and took it with him to add to the pile that was building on the table in the vestibule.

He had been surprised that the ambush hadn't affected him the way he expected but, as he went up to his floor in the elevator, the emotional distance he'd created suddenly wore off. Just inside his door, the light-headedness hit. He slammed the door shut, put his back against it, slid down until he was sitting with his legs straight out, helpless. Visions almost overwhelmed him — aggressive, punishing — scenes of flowing blood, of shattered glass, of the horror of Nick's slashed throat. He took his head into his hands and pressed his fingers into his temples, tried to stop the flow. He felt nauseous and his head felt heavy. Suddenly, he lost consciousness.

When he opened his eyes, he knew that he had blacked out and that some time had passed. It bothered him that he had lost control of himself but, he reasoned, he hadn't had more than half a dozen hours of sleep over the past three nights and a couple of serious shocks. It was a poor excuse but he'd take it. He certainly felt better, more refreshed. His head was clearer and the sleep-deprived spacey feeling he'd had for the past day or more had passed. He got to his feet, went to the settee, pulled his boots off, dropped them on the polished tile and then kicked them out of his way. Then he padded to the fridge in his sock feet, got the last of the diet soda he'd recently stocked, and went out onto the darkened balcony to think.

The condo had a great view in daylight but at night the lights of the city thrilled him. He would miss that view when he had to give the place up. The wind from the sea was cutting but it further revived him. He thought about the incriminating business card left at the ambush scene. That seemed too convenient. There were lots of oddities in the investigation.

The oppressive feeling that he was missing some key element and that there was a whole dimension to the case that he didn't understand returned. He remembered a Swaixwe mask he had seen once, an old one from a hundred years ago. It was skillfully carved, with the usual peg eyes and bird crests. It was the nose that was remarkable — a water bird tugged back the upper lip as if it was a skin. It was what the Swaixwe was all about — pulling back the skin of one world to open up the world beneath the obvious reality. Certainly, Nick's murder was one layer of reality but there was another one below it. He knew that, absolutely.

CHAPTER 13

Lisa Wainright was working the evening shift when he arrived at the Satsuma. She had never made a secret of the fact that she didn't like Archie, especially after his and Streya's breakup. Now she seemed more welcoming than usual, which was ironic because she'd been a significant factor in that breakup happening in the first place. In any case, he didn't go to the Satsuma much anymore, except when the urge for a good steak got too powerful. Then, he lingered, enjoying the satisfaction he got from the knowledge that his being there got under Lisa's skin. This time, however, she waved and smiled.

He had expected that either Lee or Patsy would be there ahead of him but neither had showed. There was always the chance they'd had some insight, or that one, or the other, had some new piece of information that might help confirm the theory he was developing. That was unlikely. He almost wished he'd cancelled. Having to wait irritated him intensely. At least he didn't have to worry about the upcoming press conference he'd been supposed to run. Fricke had taken that off his hands after the ambush on Chinese Cemetery Road.

He looked for and found the booth he had in mind, empty and isolated on the far side of the room and started for it. He glimpsed Wes Means sitting on the opposite side of the room. Means had been a public prosecutor and was now a private practice lawyer. He had an antagonistic manner and Archie's experience with him as a prosecutor had not been good.

Means spotted him and grinned, expecting, perhaps, that Archie would join him. Archie acknowledged him with a nod in his direction and carried on, hoping he'd be far enough away from Means that Means wouldn't be able to table-talk. But Means came towards him, carrying his coffee. He pulled around a chair from a nearby table, sat down, turned towards Archie. Archie noticed that he grimaced as if in pain when he did so.

"Hurt yourself, Wes?"

"Did something at the gym, I guess."

It could be true.

"Heard you almost bought the farm today, Archie."

"Where'd you hear that?"

"Where wouldn't I hear it? Everybody in the business knows."

"I guess."

"You're a lucky man."

"Not so much now that you're here."

Means shook his head.

"Not a scratch — too bad," he said. "Maybe you should stick to traffic or whatever it is you're good at. Stay away from things that don't concern you."

Archie resisted the urge to jam his fist into Means' face.

"What do you mean about things that don't concern me, Wes? Do you know something about this?"

"Not me — just wouldn't like to see you get hurt. I'm concerned that's all."

Archie was finding it more and more difficult to avoid being drawn into a situation that could do him nothing but professional harm.

But at that point, Lisa Wainright arrived with a full coffee pot in one beefy hand and a menu in the other. She looked at Means, who lifted his shoulders in a kind of shrug, and squinted his eyes as if some hurt had returned. Then, unexpectedly, he got to his feet.

"Take care, Detective Stevens."

Means went back to his seat across the room, retrieved his coat and then he was gone. But something about the exchange with Means bothered Archie. He just wasn't sure exactly what it was.

Lisa rubbed her free hand through short, stiff, red hair and grunted something that sounded vaguely like 'hello there'. Then she dropped a menu on the table and stood waiting for Archie's order. He took his time, but then ordered steak and coffee. She didn't even bother to write it down — he never ordered anything else. She went back into the kitchen. She definitely seemed less hostile than usual, but Archie figured that might be his imagination overworking itself.

He noticed with some satisfaction that his irritation had dissipated more quickly than usual — maybe he was making progress after all. The slight interaction between Lisa and Wes Means had also picked up his interest. It was like questions had been asked and answered, a silent, secret conversation. It occurred to him that they might be lovers. If they were, they had been pretty good at keeping it a secret. Harsley was a small town and word got around fast.

Lee arrived at last. He entered briskly, walked across the room and sat down on the bench seat opposite Archie. He apologized for being late, carefully arranged his coat, and took off his mauve silk scarf. Lisa arrived with Archie's meal, watched Lee settle in, raised an eyebrow, took his order, and left.

"So nice," Lee said sarcastically.

"Lisa is never what you'd call friendly."

"Not that I've ever noticed in the years I've been coming here."

"She sure as hell doesn't like me either."

Lee looked askance at Archie, like he wanted to ask questions, to probe deeper but Archie's look scotched that possibility. Lee took out his tablet and touched it into life.

"You want me to wait for Patsy before I start?"

Archie shook his head.

"You can start."

Lee turned the tablet so that Archie could see the screen. The data had been organized into a highlighted table.

"Very pretty. Got anything new?"

"I like things organized," Lee said. "The blood tests for Robbie's truck aren't in so nothing conclusive there."

Archie had heard that bit of news already.

"I'm sure it's Nick's," he said.

Lee nodded.

"We found a bag of immature abalone stashed in a bin near the Dive Shop parking lot so Nick was poaching as you thought," he said. "I also finished up with the tire tracks. He had more than a couple of visitors that day."

"Garbage or service trucks maybe?"

"Only in the summer. I checked with the power company and every other agency I could think of who might send out an emergency truck. Nobody had sent anybody but there were at least three different sets of tracks, not counting yours. It had rained in the afternoon so one set was indistinct. After that two other vehicles were through the lot the evening Nick died."

"He must have been selling poached stuff to somebody, so maybe one of the vehicles belonged to the buyer. Was there anything near the bin where he stashed the abalone?"

"That's hard to tell, but maybe. There were lots of older tracks there anyway."

"Any tire matches?"

Lee shook his head.

"As we know, Robbie's truck was at the ferry terminal where it had been left. We had it towed in and I took tire impressions from it. They matched one set at the scene, mostly near the shop and boat ramp; and there are the repeats. Robbie's tracks weren't the ones at the bin."

"I guess that would be unusual."

Lisa Wainright appeared, slid Thomas Lee's 'Steelhead Platter' onto the table. Lee blocked his tablet with one hand so she couldn't read it over his shoulder. Archie forked in a mouthful of potatoes. Lee waited until he figured Lisa was out of hearing.

"It doesn't look good for John Robbie. Anyway, Stoney checked at Moffat's in case he'd been there but nobody had seen him since before the homicide. Moffat said he figured Robbie had been working with Nick recently. He said you'd been there."

"I was. Put it all together for me the way you see how things happened with all the traffic on the day Nick died."

Lee nodded.

"First, Robbie was there with his boat. He left and then he came back. Did he kill Nick then — probably not. Somebody came to pick up the contraband abalone from the garbage bin between Robbie's first visit and the second. At least one other vehicle came and went. I figure Robbie came back, maybe drunk, and I still wouldn't discount the fact that he killed Nick for some reason."

Archie was pondering this when Patsy walked through the door. She saw Lee and Archie, navigated her way to their table through the rapidly filling restaurant, slid into a chair next to Lee and unzipped her jacket. Lee smiled at her. She gave Archie a look full of reproach.

"You shouldn't be wandering around unprotected after what happened," she said.

"I'll be fine."

He could see that she did not agree with his assessment. He cut her off before she could say anything else. He was, nevertheless, rather glad to see her.

"We have to figure out how it all works together — all these folks driving in and out at Nick's, the fact that John Robbie and his boat have disappeared but his pickup with blood inside is at the ferry terminal. Then there's the attack on me..."

"Do we assume that is related to the case?" Patsy asked.

"Right now, I haven't a clue."

"There's something else, Archie," Lee said.

"What's that?"

"Jameson's been telling everybody that'll listen that he'll be taking over your investigation."

Archie searched out the ketchup, splashed a mound of it on his potatoes.

"I don't give a damn what Jameson thinks?"

"Apparently, the mayor's putting pressure on Fricke to replace you. Jameson is the mayor's brother-in-law so Fricke might cave."

"I've got more to worry about than Jameson."

Lisa materialized with a pot of coffee, poured some into Patsy's cup, and lingered a moment, half-smiled. She ambled away when Archie made it clear that he wouldn't talk until she was gone.

"That's one nosy woman," Patsy said.

"That isn't the half of it. Anyway, let's put all our efforts into finding John Robbie — or his body."

"Does he go out with anybody?" Patsy asked. "Does he have a girlfriend?"

"Sometimes he sees Bonnie Tran at the Zuider Zee. I've talked to her but got nothing. We've got enough with the blood in John's pickup to expand our investigation to include his known associates. Let's get Bonnie in for questioning. Let's push her more. I know she saw Robbie more recently than she's letting on. You can do that, Patsy?"

"I can do that," Patsy said.

Archie then asked Lee if there were any updates on Nick's computer. "There's not much," Lee said. "They've got some email but nothing useful. The thing is that somebody went to a lot of trouble to try to make sure that we couldn't get anything off that machine, but we're still working on it."

"Did anybody find Nick's charts yet?"

"Nope. Nothing there either."

Archie noted that fact. He waited for more from the two of them but neither had anything to add. Both seemed preoccupied. Maybe they were thinking that he was in over his head or that Jameson should take over.

"We're finished here," he said. "I want both of you to continue with your assignments, which means that Thomas will follow up with Forensics and Patsy I'd like you to talk to Bonnie Tran. Wait until her off-hours. I want to meet again at 11 a.m. tomorrow — my office."

Lee nodded, unfolded his scarf and put it on, methodically buttoned up his coat buttons, held his fedora by the brim in one hand, and brushed the nap with the other. Patsy stood too, her eyes on Archie.

"Are you okay?" she asked.

She and Lee looked concerned.

"I'm absolutely fine. Why wouldn't I be?"

"No, really?"

"I'm fine I told you."

Their concern unsettled him. Lee leaned slightly forward and peered into Archie's face as if he were probing for the truth. Patsy let out an exasperated sigh.

"Are we getting anywhere?"

"Maybe. It's what detective work is all about."

"Be nice if we made some progress before my first pension cheque arrives."

"Funny."

"Is it?"

"Maybe it is. Be at my office at eleven ready for the meeting. Talk to Bonnie — she's key, I think. You never know — you might crack the case wide open."

She frowned, repeated the little mocking salute she had given him three days before and was gone before he could think of anything encouraging to say. He watched her go, watched her long enough to have it noticed. Lee shook his head, went to the register and paid his bill.

"See you at eleven," he said. "I'm assuming I'm supposed to have something new to talk about."

"I hope so."

Lee nodded, put on his hat and headed for the door. Archie thought of lingering in case Streya came in, but then thought better of it. He saw Lisa through the kitchen door window, talking on her cell, emphasizing some point to her caller with sharp motions of her hand. Her voice was too low for Archie to hear more than muffled sounds.

He wished he could leave well enough alone. He dropped bills onto the table to pay his cheque. Then he crossed the floor of the restaurant. He paused for a moment at the ornate doors, knew he was dawdling in hopes of seeing Streya. Irritated with himself, he opened the door and went out into the night.

His preoccupation was such that he had almost forgotten that somebody had tried to kill him earlier in the day. His first instinct was, in any case, to carry on as if he didn't care about anything — if he was going to get shot, he'd get shot. But it'd be embarrassing to die in the old Dodge he had drawn from the pool. So he kept, more or less, to the shadows. Before he got in, he bent down and shone his flashlight under the car to make sure nobody had taped a bomb there. Then he flipped the hood and checked the engine compartment. He looked up as a patrol car pulled into the lot. It stopped close enough so that he could see the driver. The window came down with a whine and the same young rookie grinned at him.

"I watched it the whole time you were in there."

Archie lifted his hands in mock surrender.

"Thanks."

Gillot grinned.

"By the way, are you making a move on Detective Kydd, or is she up for grabs?"

"She's your superior in every way, constable. You got high hopes."

"You never know if you don't try. By the way, Fricke's pulling me off watching you. I guess you're not worth department resources after all."

The window hummed back up and the cruiser pulled away. As Archie slid into his car, the radio squawked and he answered it. Delia John asked him how he was. He told her he was fine, fine, and she told him not to get irritated when people show their concern for him. He asked her what she wanted. She told him that the all-points bulletin he asked for earlier had produced a result. Someone thought they had seen John Robbie in Empire City. She told Archie that if he wanted to be civil she'd give him the details. He said he'd try his best to do what she asked.

He had just started the Dodge when Streya Wainright drove up in her Volkswagen. She saw him, waved, got out and walked towards him. The old feelings bubbled up inside him. He wanted to leave, knew he should — politeness demanded that he at least talk to her.

CHAPTER 14

He sat in a bar on the Rochville waterfront and waited, his back to the wall. He rubbed a big hand through his hair, and stared at the waitress who was on the verge of walking away with his ten dollars in change. He grunted, "My change."

"See this T-shirt," she said.

Her T-shirt, cheap cotton stretched thin over enhanced breasts, read SAVE ENERGY: DON'T TALK TO ME. She started to walk away, tray balanced on her left hand.

"Back here," he growled.

"Look." She turned towards him.

"Be polite. Be respectful."

She hesitated.

"Screw you."

"Later. First, give me my change."

She hesitated, said "Fuck." Then she reached into her belt pouch and took out a ten-dollar bill.

She flipped it onto the table to make him reach for it. He flicked the money off onto the floor and then pointed at it with the toe of his boot.

"Pick up my money."

She stood hipshot, her eyes fierce on him, ribcage raised, breasts high, drawing attention to the slogan on her shirt.

"Why should I?"

"Pick up my money."

"What'll you do for me?"

He said nothing, kept his eyes on hers. Finally, she said, "asshole," dropped down on one knee and picked up the bill. She let her tight skirt ride up high on her thighs, eased back a bit so that the skirt rode even higher. She picked up the bill, slapped it into his open hand.

"Satisfied?" she asked.

He smiled, laid his hand on the tabletop and displayed heavy arm muscles, corded and ridged, for her. She lifted her chin, tossed frazzled, bleached hair, turned away. But she went slowly, back straight, ass out. He watched her over the rim of his drink, making his plans.

The sun was setting over the warehouses across the estuary. Its glow through the grimy windows of the bar lit the dirty air, highlighting the beer stains on the floor. He hated the sour, sulphured-mash smell of the pulp mill, hated the grime, hated the people who lived in the town. He finished his drink, caught her eye, held his empty glass up. She sashayed over with a fresh drink.

"It's on me." She leaned in as she set the glass down. "My name's Rochelle. Sorry if I was rude."

He laughed without mirth.

"Thanks, Rochelle. You weren't rude — really."

The bar was almost empty — the afternoon shift from the mill gone home for supper, the evening drinkers not yet arrived. She lingered, smiled at him, showed the pink lipstick on her teeth. He knew her type.

"It's quiet tonight," she said.

"I see that."

"You look so serious."

She came behind him, reached around him for his empty glass; her breasts just brushed his shoulder. The tidal flats, invisible in the dark reeked, and the stink of decay rose through the floor boards and mingled with smell of stale beer and smoke.

"Smells in here tonight don't it," she said.

"Enough to make me not want to sit here all evening."

"I get off soon."

"Cool."

The barman called her. She went away, smiled at him over her shoulder. He smiled back, wrote a note for her on a coaster, left it along with a big tip, and then he went outside to wait.

The thick night reeked of hydrogen-sulphide and the sodium lights cast horrific shadows, black on sickly yellow. He saw his own, turned lean and spectral, arms and hands long like Mr. Hyde. He liked the image. He lit a cigar to cut the smell of the mill and the tide, and walked to the truck he'd stolen earlier. He would dump it later, after he wiped it down for prints. The old woman had demanded a sacrifice and he would give her one.

Rochelle came out of the side door, her T-shirt exchanged with a low-cut, tight camisole. She picked her way across the gravel, professionally high on stiletto heels and he smelled her perfume even over the rotten-egg stink of the mill and the reek of his cigar. He opened the passenger door for her and watched as she climbed in, tight denim skirt sliding up her thighs.

"You didn't tell me your name," she said.

"Call me Chad. Anybody know you're out with me?"

She pretended to think.

"Not a soul. What do you want to do, Chad?"

He put a hand on her thigh, stroked it. She leaned back and lit a cigarette, blew the smoke out the window.

"Fun and games."

"That's what I like best."

Rochelle blew smoke towards the roof of the cab and leaned into him. She put a high heel up on the dash. Her skirt slid back to non-existence, displayed the pink lace of her panties. He checked once more to make sure no one was watching. Then he started the truck, put it into gear and took her away from the lights.

CHAPTER 15

Archie wasn't a hundred percent sure why he'd accepted Streya Wainright's invitation to visit her at her apartment; maybe it was more masochism than politeness. He still had a hard time resisting her, but it was more than that too. Mostly, he just needed to find out something about himself that he couldn't otherwise.

She answered the door almost before the bell finished its ring. Excitement, his or hers, made her eyes seem very big and bright. She had dressed up for him, subtly seductive — a semi-sheer blouse with long sleeves that half covered her slender hands and pale silk trousers that looked expensive. She looked like a delicate doll with sex on her mind. She wore subtle but effective makeup and just the right amount of perfume. He breathed deeply and stepped inside.

She'd redecorated since he'd been there. He liked the changes and he told her so. It gave him

something to say to help cover up his awkward-
ness, and she seemed genuinely pleased at the
compliment. She kissed him, helped take off his
jacket, led him into the living area, and sat him
down on the sofa. She told him that she had
food to get ready, turned up the new age music
that she favoured and then excused herself to
the kitchen.

It seemed, to him, like old times and yet not
so, but then he had a 'what the hell' moment and
resigned himself to his fate. He was spending the
evening with a beautiful and sexy woman and
the risks suddenly seemed inconsequential. He
relaxed, stretched out on the sofa and closed his
eyes, letting the music carry him away. When she
returned, he had to pull himself out of reverie
and he realized that he must have dozed off. She
brought the food to him.

"You were tired," she said. "How's work
going?"

He nodded. She watched, waiting for his answer as he put crackers and smoked salmon on
his plate. He was hungry too.

"I've been busier than hell."

"I guess it's all to do with that Donaldson
murder?"

"It's my baby."

"Who did it?"

"I couldn't say just yet. It's a work in progress."

"You must have some idea?"

"Not really. Not yet."

He looked at her. He didn't want to talk about work and told her so.

"Okay, no work tonight. I want to enjoy your company."

She moved around him, sat down, put her slender body next to his and pressed against him. She asked him if he had liked what she was wearing. He said she was very sexy and that she turned him on and that she knew it. She moved her hand down to his crotch to learn how much.

"It's good to be with you again," she said. "What happened before shouldn't have happened."

He hesitated, as if he were weighing his options. He turned to her, put his hand to her hair, and brushed it back from her ear. She put her hand over his heart; his hand almost automatically moved to her left breast. She breathed deeply, tilted forward and let her forehead rest on his chest.

"I mean it Archie. It's good to have you here and I'm sorry for what happened in the past."

"Let's forget it. I wanted to see you."

"I hope so."

"Your family and friends didn't like me around before. That hasn't changed. Your sister, Lisa, hardly gives me the time of day."

"It's the way we are — clannish. We stick together, don't have much to do with people outside the group, often just socialize with people descended from the original Finnish settlers. I don't always like it but it's just how it is."

"What about the Brother Eli part?"

"Oh, that. No. That's ancient history. Some families that have always stuck together, that's all."

She got up and turned up the music, a kind of a slow rhumba. Then she pulled him to his feet, danced him away from the couch, her sensuous body swaying with the music. She circled him, dipped in a dance move so that her hair fell coquettishly over her face, and then she slid behind him and drew a long fingernail across his shoulders. He reached after her, found her hand, led her around to him, studied her as she danced. She moved into him, ran her hands down his stomach and into the front of his jeans. She grabbed his belt, guided him to the sofa and pushed him down on it.

When she had him positioned the way she wanted, she straddled him, leaned over him so that her red hair cascaded around her face and tumbled over his hands. He toyed with it, gathered it up, turned her head with it and kissed the bare nape of her neck. She tossed her head so that her hair lashed his face. Then she eased herself upright and rolled her shoulders back so that her breasts pushed against the sheer fabric of her blouse — glimpses of pink aureole for him. She purred deep in her throat. When she kissed him, her tongue probed deep, and her breath came hot from the center of her. Then she laughed, pulled away and stood up. He reached for her, but she stepped away, still laughing.

"I've got some good wine. I'll get us some. It's too early for the evening to end. If I let you go on, we'll be in bed and you'll be asleep before I know it."

"I won't fall asleep. Come back."

"The wine first."

"Diet cola for me, with lots of ice."

"Really? Are you sure? It's very good wine."

"I'm sure."

She went to the credenza and filled one of the goblets she had placed there earlier, got his Cola from the refrigerator, poured it over ice. He was half out of the trance she'd created in him. He looked around the room, told her again that he admired her paintings and sculptures; some of them he hadn't seen before. She pointed out her latest and told him she called them her "Anthropologicals." The style was familiar but he couldn't remember where he had seen it before.

She said that red was her favourite colour and that she had used the most violent reds to express her innermost feelings and her passion. That bothered him a little, which she seemed to sense because she laughed a little as if she'd been only half-serious. She sat down close to him and looked him in the face. Her expression changed suddenly.

"It must be nice having Patsy Kydd working with you?" she said.

That surprised him.

"She's part of the team."

"She's attractive, so — you must be tempted."

He saw the jealousy in her eye, the green monster she'd called it before. But she had put the image of Patsy Kydd into his mind and it wouldn't leave. The spell really was broken now. He told Streya that he thought he should go.

"You're kidding?"

"I've got a lot to do. Lots of work."

She looked hurt, contrite.

"I was out of line. I'm just a bit jealous that's all. Is that so bad?"

She cuddled in closer, the warmth and softness of her body began to arouse him again. He put his arm around her and she stroked his cheek with her fingertips. He made to kiss her but she spoke before he could.

"First, tell me about your case, about what you've learned. It's obviously on your mind."

"I can't talk about it, Streya."

"I won't say anything."

"I'd rather not think about my work right now."

She moved her head on his shoulder and he could feel her sweet, hot breath on his neck. She persisted.

"I'd really like to know."

"I don't want to talk about it."

"You must have found something interesting?"

"Like what?"

"Whatever Nick was up to that got him killed. What evidence have you found?"

"We didn't find anything you need know about."

"It's just a girlfriend's curiosity, Archie."

"I still can't discuss it."

"Suit yourself."

He had made her angry. He couldn't think of anything to say and so he looked off out the window toward the lights of town. The change in her mood made him wonder if he'd been stupid to visit her, to let her get inside his defences.

He decided it might indeed be better if he left; he set the glass down on the coloured tiles of the coffee table, and started to get up. His move seemed to take her by surprise but she moved quickly. She brushed her wine glass with the tips of her fingers. It fell on the hardwood floor and shattered. The red wine splashed across his feet.

"Oh damn, sorry."

"Why did you do that Streya?"

"You're going to leave and I don't want you to."

He mumbled a protest but he let her push him back into his seat on the couch, forced now to wait while she ran to get a cloth. When she came back, she kneeled at his feet and peeled off his wet socks, patted the wine away.

"Forget I asked about your work okay? Let's just have a nice evening for old time's sake, please?"

She smiled at him, looked up at him from under her brows — aggressive or submissive, he couldn't tell. Lascivious, certainly. His resolve disintegrated. She ran her hands under his jeans' legs up his calves, withdrew them, placed them on his thighs and worked her way up. It seemed natural to take her hands and to draw her to him, to bring her lips to his.

She unbuttoned her blouse slowly and then lifted her arms so that he could pull it off over her head. He leaned into her warmth, into the sweet scent of her, close enough to feel her nipples tighten and stiffen under his breath. She ran her fingers through his hair.

He hesitated. She nuzzled into him and started to unbutton his shirt. He let her tug the tails of his shirt out of his pants. She unbuckled his belt and pushed herself away from him. She posed for him, drew an invisible and complex pattern on her naked breasts with the tips of her fingernails. Then she undid the tie on her silk trousers and they slipped to the floor with a soft hiss of fabric on skin.

"Stay with me?"

He couldn't say no, not anymore, not against her. Anyway, he had no will to truly resist, no desire to stop the momentum of it — too far gone for that. He lifted her easily, carried her to the bedroom, deposited her on the bed. She helped him struggle out of his clothes, and he rose up onto her, crooked her legs with his arms and entered her.

Later, lying in the angle of his arm, she ran a finger down his belly, as interrogative as a gesture could be and he knew that she still had her agenda.

"Will you tell me about your investigation?"

The unusual curiosity again, out of place, insulting. It was as if a transaction had occurred and he was supposed to pay for the sex with information. He didn't answer. She persisted.

"Why is it such a secret? Why won't you tell me?"

She couldn't seem to help herself, like she had a job to do, and couldn't rest until it was completed. He sat up slowly, eased her off him.

"Forget my work. I don't want to talk about it. How many times do I have to say it?"

That made her angry. She sat up half-draped, pulled her knees up to her chin.

"Get the fuck out then."

"There's no reason for this."

"You're such a bastard."

He had nothing to say to that — maybe he was. He pulled on his jeans, put on and buttoned his shirt. Then he went looking for his boots. She followed him, leaned against the wall, arms folded. She watched while he pulled his boots on.

"Archie?"

"What?"

"I still want you, Archie. I want us to be the way we were."

"Yeah, sure you do."

"I mean it. We had a good time tonight — mostly. Let's go somewhere, have a picnic, get out of this stupid town, even for a few hours."

"What would that do?"

"I don't know. I've made you angry. I really would like to spend some time together, like we used to. I can make the picnic — the food you like. Please?"

He thought about it.

"Where would we go?"

She seemed happier, stood on her toes and kissed him. She paused to think about it, so that it was as if the idea had just popped into her head.

"How about we go out to the islands, maybe to Cat's Cradle Island?"

"I can't go tomorrow," he said.

"Can we still do the picnic soon?"

"Sure."

"Come back to bed, please. I won't ask you any more questions and I won't be jealous."

She convinced him. When he left her place early in the morning, he still wasn't sure what was going on, just that Streya had decided not to ask any more questions. There was something to be said for not over-thinking the situation, for just going with the flow, for not seeing enemies and complications everywhere — his fallback position these days. Probably, it was like she said. She was curious, and no more than were half the people in the town. What bothered him more was that, a few times, he thought about Patsy Kydd when he was making love to Streya Wainright.

CHAPTER 16

When Archie phoned the police department in Empire City, he was routed to a detective named Doug Dolan. Dolan was the cop who thought he'd seen Robbie, twice — once two days or so before at a sandwich shop and then, more recently, at a café called the Sunburst in the center of town. Both times, Robbie had been with a middle-aged Asian woman — not bad looking, Dolan said, but not the kind of girl most guys would take home to meet mother. They'd had lunch in the sandwich shop and had not lingered. It was a different story at the Sunburst where they had stayed for quite awhile. He told Archie what he had seen.

They talked about Robbie and discussed what he might be doing in Empire City, keeping the company he was keeping. Dolan said he had theories. He suggested that Archie come down to talk to him; he thought he might be able to help, to put Archie in touch with people who might be useful. The conversation ended abruptly when Dolan had to take another call.

When Archie called back, Dolan's superior, a lieutenant named Emile Pared, said that Dolan had already gone home and that he'd be gone from the office for a couple of weeks on a preplanned holiday. Pared said he wasn't about to give Archie Dolan's home number. He said he hadn't heard anything about John Robbie from Dolan, but when Archie pressed, he said he'd do a meeting. Archie had to be satisfied with that. He knew of Pared by reputation but that didn't reassure him.

He drove into Empire City early the next morning. He wanted to check the sandwich shop first and then, most importantly, to find the Sunburst Café where Robbie and Bonnie Tran had spent time. There was a chance that he might spot Robbie there, since Dolan thought the owner and Robbie knew each other.

The sandwich shop was on a main avenue and very busy. Archie couldn't see any reason why Robbie would do anything at such a place other than eat. It was too public. The Sunburst, on the other hand, was on a side street, almost an alley, in an area that was becoming gentrified. It was almost empty of customers.

He parked, went inside, bought a coffee, tried to find out from the longhaired youngish manager if Robbie had been there. The manager, whose name was Parker — according to the embroidery over the pocket on his white restaurant jacket — shook his head. He said he didn't work evenings but that Archie could ask his partner who did. Archie said thanks, took a newspaper from the counter and went to a booth that gave him a view of the front door. Not that it mattered. Aside from the owner and, he assumed, a fry cook in the back, he was alone. Nobody came through the door while he was there. It might be that the real breakfast crowd would start arriving at nine or so, long after he had gone, but he doubted it. He'd never seen a business that looked more like a front than the Sunburst. Robbie would not feel out of place there. Archie finished reading the paper and headed out for his meeting with Pared. He could check back with the partner later — if there was such a beast.

Empire City Central office was housed in a newer three-story building that tried very hard to pretend it was anything but a cop shop. It even had commissioned art in the lobby, a sculpture that featured a strangely shaped block of stone propped up by shrouded metal figures. Neither the sculpture, nor the layout, made much sense to Archie. He checked in at the desk, took a seat on an uncomfortable designer chair in the lobby, and waited.

Emile Pared came from behind an imposing wall of frosted glass decorated with swimming salmon. He had a linebacker's build and he seemed vaguely familiar. He dressed well too. His overt friendliness belied his reputation as a hard, sadistic officer.

Pared smiled like a banker, made small talk, and then guided Archie through to the elevator that took them up to the third floor. Pared's office had a good view of the harbour but had a functional blandness to it that didn't give away much about the man. He had a small, colourful painting on one wall that reminded Archie of Streya Wainright's work. This one suggested a religious theme, but what that theme might be, Archie could not tell.

Pared motioned him to a table where he had laid out mug shots ready for viewing. Archie glanced through them, saw nobody that even half resembled John Robbie and said so. Pared said he didn't know much about Robbie — Robbie didn't usually spend time in Empire City, he thought. Dolan knew him from years back.

Pared asked what Dolan had said he'd seen. Archie said that Dolan had thought that he had spotted John Robbie at a sandwich shop in the east end of the city and at the Sunburst Cafe, with three guys who could have been Vietnamese. Dolan had thought that one of the Vietnamese looked like Bill Tran.

Pared seemed to think that was funny. He said that Bill Tran seemed to be everywhere these days, according to Dolan. Archie said that he had heard that Tran was affiliated with the Four Winds Triad that was trying to establish a presence on the coast; that might mean that Tran was doing some consolidation but Pared dismissed that idea as well.

Archie, now wondering if Pared had his own agenda, said that Dolan had sounded certain, that he came across as a good, very observant cop. Pared acknowledged that Dolan was observant but figured that he had gangs on the brain. That coloured his thinking. On his own, he had decided that Robbie was up to triad stuff, speculating about arranging a robbery or even a hit with Tran. Big things. Pared said it was nonsense.

"I doubt that scenario myself," Archie said. He decided to play his cards close. "John's too old. If he was meeting Tran it would more likely have something to do with a little dope smuggling."

Pared caught his jaw between his fingers. He ran squared fingers over the stubble shadow on his cheeks, the rasp of it clearly audible. He seemed to be considering his next move.

"In that case, we'd better follow up," he said.

Pared then said that he would have patrols check the east side for anyone resembling Robbie. He knew that Tran had had his muscle there, a couple of ex-bikers named Scorpion and Jumbo.

"Scorpion and Jumbo?"

"Walter Bertram King and Daniel Yip."

Pared reached for a file, a sheet on Walter Bertram King. Archie noted the conviction for murder and others for assault and armed robbery, the pitifully short incarceration in juvenile detention. Jumbo's sheet told a similar story: a local boy, from a good home, then gang membership, then some nasty stuff with weapons, drugs, extortion and home invasion — two arrests and no convictions. Pared interpreted Archie's look as a political comment.

"Products of our criminal justice system. Great, isn't it?"

Archie didn't reply. He was thinking about Robbie, what he might be doing talking to guys like Scorpion and Jumbo.

"Robbie had some biker connections in the past. There must be more to it. Where are these guys now?"

Pared shrugged, scratched his forehead. His smile was warm and collegial.

"Dolan didn't arrest anyone so there wasn't any follow-up."

"I'd like to know if these two guys turn up again."

Pared said he would keep Archie informed. He seemed to going out of his way to be helpful and accommodating; it made for a nice change, compared to what Archie was used to in Harsley.

Pared also gave Archie a complete tour of Central Office, of the large and spotless labs, the warren of offices, even the firing range, trying his best either to make Archie feel welcome, or to make the point that Archie was from a hick police station — likely the latter. Archie decided that the purpose of the whole exercise was to let him know that there was nothing more he should do, or that he need do, in Empire City; Pared had everything under control.

"I'd like to go talk to Dolan," Archie said. "I'll need his phone number."

Pared seemed surprised, irritated even.

"I'm not even sure he's in town. He won't be able to tell you anything anyway."

"I'd still like to get Dolan's number."

Pared leaned against his file cabinets, rubbed his forehead with the tip of his second finger. When it was obvious that Archie was not going away, he relented and wrote the number on a page of his desk pad. He tore off the page and slapped it down on the desktop.

"You're wasting your time," he said.

Archie picked up the phone number.

"Likely, but it's mine to waste. Appreciate your giving me the tour. It's nice to see how things are done here."

Pared almost glared at him.

"Think you can find your way out?" he said.

"I think so."

"Good. I got work to do."

Archie gave him a nod. He turned away and headed down the hall for the elevators and the exit. He heard Pared move in his office and was certain that the man was watching him, but he didn't look back. He had made the call before he got to the ground floor. Surprisingly, Dolan seemed to want to talk. Archie paused to jot down the directions to Dolan's house, walked through the spotless lobby to the doors and then out into a thickening drizzle that hadn't been in the forecast.

CHAPTER 17

Dolan's house was in a pocket of undeveloped forest, at the edge of a new and upscale subdivision. The tidy wartime bungalow was of the type that a developer would buy to tear down to make way for something larger. The new *For Sale* sign on the trimmed front lawn spoke volumes. Archie parked in the driveway behind a big three-quarter ton attached to a trailer carrying a newer cabin cruiser. He walked up the carefully-edged path to the front door, which Dolan opened before Archie had a chance to knock. Archie, not knowing what to expect after meeting Pared, stretched out a hand and introduced himself.

Dolan brushed the remains of his lunch off the front of a freshly pressed shirt and shook Archie's hand. Archie thanked him for agreeing to meet.

"No problem at all," Dolan said. "I'm heading out on holidays in the morning but I've got time right now."

He ushered Archie into his house. As expected, the interior was as neat and tidy as the outside, although Dolan had the face of a hard drinker. Archie stopped and pulled off his cowboy boots, set them on the small Persian rug that protected the hardwood. Dolan waited and watched until Archie clued in and lined his boots up military-style and then led the way into the kitchen. He seemed to have anticipated Archie's unstated question.

"If you're interested in buying a house for a coupla hundred grand over what it's worth, you can have this one," he said.

"I'll think on it."

"I bought out here about twenty years ago and development caught up with me. Now I'm holding out until I get my price. These aren't my kind of folks here now. But just because the place is going to be knocked down, I'm not living in no pigsty."

Archie didn't know how to respond to that. Do you compliment the guy on his housekeeping, or on his foresight in buying the place? In the end, he said nothing. Dolan motioned Archie to a chair at a 50's vintage table and took a seat himself. Archie eased onto the yellow vinyl, rested a hand on the chrome-edged melamine tabletop. Dolan settled in across from him. "You want to know about John Robbie."

"And Tran if you have anything you think might help."

"I know Tran. I know Robbie from being up your way. I'm sure that it was him that came to a meet they had on the west side. He's a tough little fucker. Then I seen him again downtown at the Sunburst. He had that Vietnamese chick with him that he used to hang with. She's tough too — still good-looking though. I think she was connected with Bill Tran in some way."

"She's his sister."

"Right — I remember now. But Tran's not part of what you're doing is he? Robbie's the prime in a murder case you got up in Harsley?"

"He's definitely a person of interest. I'd bring him in if I could find him. There was the thought he might have been hit but you saw him..."

"He's alive. I'm sure of it. You couldn't kill that little prick."

"Your guy Pared seemed to think I was wasting my time."

"He would. He doesn't like cops from out of town working his beat."

"He's not on Tran's payroll, is he?"

The expression on Dolan's face didn't change.

"Not that I know of."

Archie figured that Dolan was close enough to retirement that he wouldn't want to do anything that might interfere with his pension. Dolan seemed to read his thoughts.

"Pared's clean as far as I know. Anyway, I'm pretty sure it was your man at the Lin's restaurant the other night, and it was definitely Bill Tran he was talking to. Tran had some of his guys there too and like I said, the Vietnamese woman was there too."

"Did you hear any of what they were saying?"

"I could guess but that wouldn't be much help to you. Your man looked nervous to me. Tran looked pretty serious."

"What's your guess?"

"I'd say he was looking for something from Bill. The woman seemed to be doing a lot of the talking. She looked upset."

"I guess Robbie figured that since she's Bill's sister, Bill might do something for her. Did it look like she was asking for money?"

"She was scared, is what I'd say, or very nervous."

"You think they needed to patch things up with Bill perhaps?"

"Like maybe they got messed up in some Triad gang stuff accidently, you mean? That I couldn't say. I only saw them for a minute or two."

"Then what happened?"

"They left."

Archie wondered about the wisdom of apprehending Bill Tran and questioning him. He mentioned that to Dolan who shrugged. He thought that Archie would be wasting his time, that Tran wouldn't say anything, and that his word that he had seen Tran wasn't worth much to the powers that be.

"Myself, I've hauled him in more times than I've got fingers. Now Pared and some of the others think I got a fixation."

"You say you thought Robbie looked scared."

"Scared is the wrong word. He was nervous, edgy, I'd say. The woman was too."

Archie had more questions but Dolan said he had to get his stuff ready to go on holidays and it was obvious he wanted to terminate the interview. Archie thanked him and went to put on his boots. Dolan was seeing him out the door when Archie's phone rang. Somebody had found another dead body.

CHAPTER 18

As Thomas Lee and Patsy Kydd watched the body being placed on a gurney, two divers stood nearby, dripping water on the asphalt. One looked pale, like he was going to throw up — understandable under the circumstances since the woman's body was missing its head. Archie, who had just returned following his visit to Empire City, had watched the retrieval from his car.

He shut off the engine and got out, legged over the parking lot fence, and walked to where Lee was standing making notes.

"Not a pretty sight." Lee said. He indicated the dripping corpse being wheeled up the ramp. "Not the worst thing I've seen in this business but it's right up there. Worse for the guy who found the body. He's sitting over there if you want to talk to him."

Archie looked towards a pile of driftwood logs where a middle-aged man sat, chin in wind-reddened hands, staring fixedly out to sea. A little dog sat near him, looking in the same direction but with one eye cocked to check up on the condition of his master.

"I've talked to him," Lee said. "He doesn't know anything. Apparently the dog ran under the wharf after a stick. When the dog didn't come out, he went under himself — saw the body floating there. He's kind of shaken up. Like I told you, the head was missing from the body."

"Not what you want to find when you're out for a stroll," Archie said.

He felt suddenly, and embarrassingly, light-headed. He could see Lee was watching him like a hawk.

"You look pale."

"I'm okay."

Patsy came by. Her step was light and her demeanour seemed almost jaunty. She stopped, looked at Archie and frowned.

"What's up?"

He was relieved that the light-headedness had started to pass.

"I get taken by surprise sometimes."

"Dead bodies don't really bother me."

"Well they bother me — a lot." He turned from her to Lee. "Any idea who the victim is?"

"Her name was Rochelle Arnesto. She worked in a bar in Rochville."

"How can you tell without a head and without clothes?"

"I'm going by age and size. She has a mermaid tattoo on her upper thigh. You can see it on the body. That tattoo, and the woman wearing it, went missing a few days back. The missing persons report was called in by her place of employment, the bar in Rochville. The barman working with her that night remembers her talking about meeting up with a customer who'd been there earlier on the evening she disappeared. Problem is, nobody can remember him or his vehicle."

"And now she's dead — brutalized," Patsy said.

Archie nodded. He looked at the body as the gurney passed. The coloured mermaid tattoo was clearly visible on the unearthly white of the skin. He had no idea what this murder meant in the scheme of things or why the killer had beheaded the victim. He had a hunch that it was related to the Donaldson murder but he couldn't figure out how. He tried to muscle his thoughts — demanding more of his brain but getting less.

He had some notions about gangs and triads, but nothing conclusive, nothing that would even begin to say, yes, this is what happened. And without a hypothesis to test, he didn't have a clear path to follow.

Jim Stone drove up, got out and went over to look at the body. He walked over to talk to Archie.

"Ray says that what happened here has to be retaliation for something," he said. "He says if you want he'll try to find out if the victim had any ties to gang activity."

"Thanks, Stoney. Tell Ray we're okay for now."

"If you say so."

Archie saw that his rebuff had confused Stoney.

"It does look like the stuff from those Mexican gangs in Juarez you hear about," Stoney continued.

"I'm not ruling it out. I'm just letting you — and Ray — know what the deal is. If I want help, I'll ask for it."

Stoney shrugged, rolled his eyes. He walked away, went to talk to the divers who were out of their wetsuits and getting dressed. After a few minutes, he got back into his squad car and drove away.

"Wonder what's up with Stoney?" Patsy said.

Archie shrugged.

"Who knows? Let's think about this for a bit. Anything suggest itself?"

"If anything it reminds me of those John Does from years back," Lee said. "The skeletons the biologists found on Parcelle Island."

Archie shot him a questioning look. He had never heard of any headless John Does and said so.

"You were barely out of high school back when it happened," Lee said. "This is maybe fifteen years ago. I think Ray Jameson handled the case. Nobody claimed them so Ray decided that they were squatters and that they'd starved to death."

"And they didn't have their heads?"

"They were in a bad state. Ray said animals probably dragged the heads away. We put out a nationwide — missing street people and the like. You know how those things are. We didn't get anything definite. It's the only other time I've seen the results of a decapitation."

"How long before Ray closed the file?"

"Not long."

Patsy spoke up.

"It's not reasonable that animals would take the skulls and not disturb the other bones. Porcupines chew bones up; rats scatter them. I can't think of any animal that just takes skulls and hides them."

"Except for human animals?"

"Mind if I take another look at the body?" Patsy asked.

Archie looked at her in surprise.

"It's what I'm trained for."

"Then be my guest."

She walked over to the back of the ambulance, spoke to the attendants and then unzipped the body bag. If she had any qualms about examining a gruesome corpse, she didn't show them. She took out her loupe and studied the horrifying edges of the wound. Archie stood at her side. She pointed to the neck of the corpse with the pen she had taken from her pocket.

"See this line here?"

Archie tried to quieten his squeamish mind, He looked where she was pointing, swallowed hard and nodded.

"The blade the killer used was not straight. It was curved or wavy and very sharp. The killer knew exactly what she or he was doing. She was cut from behind. The cut between the cervical vertebrae is clean. It's how a butcher would do it."

Lee leaned over the gurney and grunted. Archie swung his gaze out towards the sea, away from the body before he looked at the wound again. He glanced at Patsy.

"Good — I hadn't considered the edge of the weapon yet," he said. "I'd like you to see if you can determine if the blade used on Nick Donaldson was similar to the one used on our victim here. I also want to take a look at those skeletons from Parcelle."

The detective in charge of the forensic unit came by and Archie consulted with her. Then he went to his car, glad to have a good reason to leave the body. He left further instructions before he drove away.

Back in his commandeered command room, he studied the pictures on the bulletin boards. He'd put up a full spread, showing the murder scene with close-ups of Nick's body and his wounds. He thought about how he'd reorganize around the photos of the latest homicide. While he was pondering, Delia John interrupted him with a message from Fricke. She handed him the pink memo; he tossed it on his desk without reading it.

"The Chief wants to see you right away. He's over at Mayor Estes' office."

"Pretend you didn't see me."

"Didn't see who? I hear voices but there's no one there."

She grinned, lifted her chin, shook her long, black hair. Then she turned her back to him and walked away, swinging her hips. He glanced after her. He returned to the board and his mental organizing. After a few minutes, he left his office and walked down the hall in the direction of the lab.

CHAPTER 19

Patsy was waiting for him at the lab. She had retrieved two folders from the Cold Case files, turned the one she'd just been looking at to face Archie. Decapitations weren't all that common and he wondered about a link between the murdered woman and the bodies found fifteen years earlier. He knew that an expert could identify the marks of different cutting edges on bone. He hoped that Patsy would be able to do that. He picked up a photograph of a skeleton — complete except for the skull. She handed him a second photo showing the other skeleton, which was also without its skull.

"These are slightly out-of-focus. Photography seems sloppy or hurried. In general, the crime site recording is lousy."

"That's not good. These are no help at all."

Patsy looked relaxed, more confident than usual — bone work was more in her field of expertise. Lee brought in two large cardboard boxes on a trolley, set them on the stainless steel tabletop. Patsy lifted the bones out of one and expertly arranged a skeleton on the table. Then she turned to the second box and a second skull-less skeleton materialized on the table adjacent to the first. She took bones from the one and switched them to the other; made a 'tsch' sound, tongue on teeth.

Lee looked at her over his reading glasses. Archie could see that he was impressed.

"Like I said — two John Does," Lee said. "The one in the second box looks like it has been around much longer, judging by the stains on these bones. A biologist found these skeletons on Parcelle Island. He was there to study bats."

Patsy picked up a long bone from the first skeleton, looked at it, and switched it with one from the first.

"Not two John Does," she said finally. "A Jane Doe and a John Doe."

She held up the pelvis for them to see. Archie tried hard to see the difference.

"This is a female," she said.

"Not what I expected," Archie said.

She put it down, took a little tape measure out of her pocket, measured the long bones. Then she used her loupe to examine the pelvis.

"Obviously a woman, epiphyses fused, pelvic striations show children — two of them. She was between twenty and twenty-five — a small woman, slender, not more than five foot four. She did some hard work, but the bones show no signs of significant disease. She was healthy."

Lee beamed. Archie looked at him and shook his head.

"I guess this is the one they thought was put there first. I don't think so. The stains are water stains. They probably say more about where the bones were in the cave than anything else. If anything, the woman's skeleton was out there much, much longer. There's more deterioration, more weathering of the bone. I'd have to get a better sense of the microclimate within the cave to do that; I ought to go to that island and have a look."

Archie grunted and pointed to the bones from the first box.

"What can you tell us about him?"

She ran her long fingers through short curls.

"He was a big guy. He had his leg broken and set. The right femur had a healed fracture. It healed up fine except he might have had a little limp. He was muscular. You can see the size of the attachments. He had a slightly twisted back and a touch of arthritis. He had Chicken Pox when he was a kid. I'd say he was in his fifties when he died."

She measured a long bone with her tape and did a quick calculation.

"He was a little over six feet tall."

"What about these marks here on the cervical vertebrae? Could they be made by the same kind of blade used on Rochelle?"

Archie pointed to a number of striations on the bone, each about half an inch long.

"Cut marks, Archie. I saw them — maybe."

"What about with the woman?"

Patsy didn't have to look.

"She's has them too — again maybe."

"Two more murders," Lee said. "How could Ray have missed this?"

"Maybe he didn't," Patsy said.

Archie scratched his head. He didn't want to get side-tracked.

"Is there anything else you see that might help identify them?"

"Nope."

"What about the coroner's report and the examining doctor's notes?" Archie asked.

"Nothing," Lee said. "I couldn't find them. I think they were the same individual at that time. It could have been Doctor Wainright, Streya's father, but I just don't know for sure."

"Keep all this to yourselves for now," Archie said.

He would have liked to have had more time — and more data too — but both seemed in short supply at that moment.

"You're going to revisit what we know about the wound on Donaldson's corpse, Patsy. We can't spend too long on this; it might not be our case soon anyway. But headless bodies and almost headless bodies —that's too much of a coincidence not to check out. I need a link, soon. Thomas, I want you to look for any links between Rochelle and Donaldson."

Lee nodded, shrugged on his Burberry, grabbed his tablet, turned away and left the room. Patsy informed Archie that she was going to examine the skeletons further before she returned them to storage. Archie wondered how much more information could be got out of the old bones. He had lots to think about once he had got through his meeting with Fricke.

CHAPTER 20

Fricke took his time getting started — unusual enough to put Archie on edge, that and the act of offering Archie a mint from the bowl he kept on his desk. He was wondering about the wait until Ray Jameson joined them. Jameson walked past Archie and took a handful of mints from the bowl and popped one into his mouth. Then he picked some files up off a chair resting against the sidewall of the office, dropped them on the floor and took a seat. Archie would have to turn his head to look at him. Fricke harrumphed and cascaded into his big chair.

"Shit, Ray, I had those files organized," he said.

"There're fine, Cal," Jameson said. "Can we get on with this?"

Fricke harrumphed again and then he looked past Archie toward the still-open door.

"You been doing a good job, Archie, right?" he said.

He had picked up a thick-barrelled fountain pen from his desktop. Archie watched him take the cap off, replace it and then repeat the operation.

"I've got to meet Lee, so if this is going to take awhile, I'd like to do whatever it is later."

"Thomas is part of what I'm going to say. He's been up at the archives wasting time. You got Patsy Kydd doing God knows what. You got a pickup belonging to a suspect spattered with blood, you got no suspect in custody or even close, right? You been down to Empire City and stirred the pot. You also got no idea about where you're headed with this thing and that's putting it mildly."

Archie leaned back in his chair and glanced over his shoulder at Jameson. Jameson grinned and shrugged his shoulders.

"I'm not worried," Archie said. "If Robbie's not dead, I think he's not that far away. Ray thinks he can do better. You obviously think so too. Why don't you get to the point?"

"Alright. Here's the deal. You got until next Friday. After that, Ray takes over and you might or might not be part of the team, depending on what he thinks is best. I got the mayor and the media to worry about. If you would have nailed

Robbie, things would be different. Anyway, it happens all the time that guys get reassigned."

"Is that a fact?"

"That's a fact." This came from Jameson. "You got no experience, Stevens. You only got the job because it looked good — Indian cop gets big case and that kind of shit. It takes more than ambition and good intentions to do this job. You got to know what you're doing from day one."

Archie kept his eyes on Fricke. He rose from his chair.

"I've still got a few days," he said. "I don't see much point hanging around here."

He stalked out of Fricke's office, leaving the two of them to amuse themselves — by going over his failings most likely. He still had time, a little less than a week. He should call Lee and update him but decided instead that his priority was to find Lars Norgard. For some reason, he sensed that figuring out Norgard was key.

Norgard lived on his fish boat, the Thetis Island, but it wasn't in its berth. Archie went down the list of hangouts — the Satsuma Café, Avril's Donut Shop, Wilkie's Garage and checked them all out. Finally, he cut back to Moffat's where Laci Laitenen seemed to have anticipated his visit; she seemed to be waiting for him, in fact. She was trying her damnedest to be friendly. When he asked about Norgard, she almost tripped over her tongue to tell him her story.

"He came back after you left, bought more beer, said he was going fishing. I think he went out in his boat. You won't see him now for weeks."

It was a line, rehearsed and he could see that she was pleased with herself for getting it right. He wondered how far he could push her before she used up the script she'd memorized.

"Funny — he didn't say anything about going fishing when I was here."

"Just decided to go, I guess."

He looked around, didn't see any of the regulars.

"How come you don't have any customers?"

She puffed air out through silicone lips.

"Slow day."

He could see her struggling to stay friendly, not easy for Laci Laitenen. She seemed to be unnaturally nervous too, evidenced by her folding and refolding a bar coaster.

"I'll need to talk to Moffat."

"He's not available."

Archie's phone buzzed. He checked the call display, saw that it was Lee and walked away from the bar to answer it. Out of the corner of his eye, he saw Laci edging closer in order to listen. The bar phone rang and he saw her go behind the bar to get it. He was almost out the door when she called him back. He told Lee to hold.

"That was Lars. He says that he'll meet you at the gravel pit on Sunny Valley Road if you're interested. He says he'll wait a half an hour and if you're not there, too bad."

"Let me talk to him."

He started back towards her. She hooked the receiver back into its cradle.

"Too late, he already hung up."

He shook his head at that, put his phone to his ear and acknowledged Lee.

"I've got some important information," Lee said. "We'll need to meet right away."

"Can't you tell me what it is over the phone?"

"I'd rather not. I went to check something out in our archives and found a mystery I think we ought to discuss."

Archie looked over his shoulder, aware of Laci who was pretending to clean a table.

"I'll go outside so we can talk without being heard."

"That won't do. This needs to be a face to face."

"I've got something I have to do. I'll meet you as soon as I can, maybe by noon. Where will you be?"

"I don't know right now. I'm on the highway heading towards Harsley. I'll have to get back to you."

"As soon as I finish up this way, I'll meet you."

There was silence on the line and then Lee came back on.

"Sooner the better, Arch," he said.

"I'll do the best I can."

He ended the call; he saw Laci watching him. He couldn't read the look in her eyes. He pointed at her as he made his way towards the door.

"I'll need to talk to you some more, Laci. I'll send somebody over."

"Whatever you say."

She leaned her hip into the bar, arms crossed over her chest, unmoving.

"I don't want you leaving Harsley right now. No quick ferry trips — no anywhere. Understand?"

"Like I said — whatever you say."

The harsh light from the window touched her face and bleached out her skin. He saw that her mascara had run and she'd fixed it. She'd been crying. He wondered who or what the tears were for. She had such hard eyes it was difficult to imagine her crying for anyone, and he wondered what that meant. On the way to his vehicle, Delia called him and told him that Forensics had identified the blood in Robbie's pickup. It was Nick Donaldson's, which meant that Archie could have an arrest warrant issued. The blood didn't change much in his mind. Robbie had not killed Nick. Not the way Archie had it figured. Not without a motive.

CHAPTER 21

Happy Valley Road was northwest of town and a long drive from Moffat's. Archie had plenty of time to ponder his next moves. Ideally, Norgard would know where Robbie was holing up, the arrest could be made and, maybe, he might get the answers he wanted. That was the ideal anyway. He pushed a button on the player, selected the Tedeschi Trucks band, turned up the volume, and drove.

The trip took an hour but Norgard had waited for him at the gravel pit. Archie passed an old Pontiac and saw a white Dodge panel van parked near a broken down D-9 Cat. Norgard was sitting on a rock drinking a beer. Archie parked, got out and walked towards him. He was aware that the van was now behind him. The situation made him even more wary and reminded him too much of the ambush on Chinese Cemetery Road. Stupid really. There were procedures a person was supposed to follow so that situations like this one didn't put a cop's life more at risk than it already was. And now he had no choice. He brushed his hand against the lump that was the SIG in its holster under his jacket, and carried on.

Norgard watched him, crushed the can he'd just emptied and tossed it aside. Then, still seated, he reached into the case in front of him, pulled out another can and popped the tab. Archie, ready now to draw and shoot at the slightest provocation, relaxed slightly.

"You said you'd pay for information on Robbie," Norgard said.

Archie had stopped about ten feet from Norgard.

"Sure. What's up, Lars?"

"You have to give your word that you won't arrest me if I do you a favour and tell you where Robbie is."

"You got my word."

"And I'll need five hundred bucks."

"I can get that for you."

Norgard crushed the second can, reached into the cardboard case. When his hand came up, it had a black automatic in it. Archie raised his hands slightly. He heard the panel door of the van slide open behind him. Norgard motioned with his pistol, motioned him to turn around.

John Robbie stood by the open door of the van, holding a pump-action Remington in one hand. He pointed it at Archie.

"Hi, Arch," he said.

"You look like hell, John," Archie said.

Robbie snorted.

"I didn't kill Nick so there's no need for you looking for me."

"Don't work like that, John, and you know it."

"I could kill you here. Lars won't say nothing."

Archie had changed positions so that he could see Lars out of the corner of his eye. There was a better than average chance that a man would miss with a snap shot from a pistol. The same was not true for a shotgun.

"I guess I'd be wondering what the point of that would be. Everybody's looking for you, John. At least with me, you got a cop who doesn't think you planned to murder your partner."

"You got that right. I didn't plan it nor did I do it. Might have even been able to save his life but I just got back a bit too late."

"What's Lars got to do with all this?"

"It's up to Lars to tell you that."

Archie stood waiting for something to happen, for Robbie to get to the point, for an explanation. For long seconds, nothing happened.

The air was still and he could hear ravens talking off in the bush somewhere.

"This is way too mysterious for me, John. Are you going to tell me why you and I are here, so I can get on with my day?"

"I don't even know for sure — not sure what's in it for me. Maybe you can get me someplace where I can be safe but I doubt it. Maybe you'll cut me some slack, give me a few days. You could give me half of that five-hundred now too."

"I can't do that."

"You used to be a straight up guy, Arch."

"We've got Nick's blood in your pickup to complicate things."

Robbie laughed half-heartedly and shook his head.

"That's nothing to do with me and that's a fact."

He sat back down in the open doorway of the van, the shotgun loose across his lap. He looked very tired, all the cockiness gone. Sitting down, he looked even smaller than he was. He moved like he was going to bring the Remington up to point but instead he turned, laid it on the floor and slid it into the van. Then he stood, turned, and climbed in after it. The door slid shut and a couple of seconds later the van started. Archie made to move but Norgard told him to stay put. He watched Robbie ease the van around the D-9 and then he gunned out of the gravel pit, spraying stones.

"Give him five minutes," Norgard said. He reached into the case with his left hand, pulled out another beer, popped the tab, and took a swallow.

"This ain't a real gun," he said.

"I know it isn't," Archie said. He walked across the gravel to where Norgard was sitting. Norgard handed him the air gun. Archie pointed it at one of the discarded cans and pulled the trigger. The can spun away across the stones. He shot it again and again before he tossed the empty weapon to Norgard.

"Don't forget my five c-notes," Norgard said.

"I won't — I'll put in a chit."

Then he turned away and walked back to his car, leaving Norgard on his rock drinking beer.

On the highway, he tried a half dozen times to reach Lee but he was either out of range or away from his phone. John Robbie was the priority now anyway. Archie called the dispatcher. He had her put out a bulletin on the panel van and its license number and then he did a U-turn and headed off in the direction of the Zuider Zee. There was still an outside chance that Robbie would hook up again with Bonnie Tran.

Arnie Bulkwetter was at the restaurant when Archie arrived, half reading a newspaper, half watching Bonnie Tran write the day's menu on a white board that was set almost too high for her. Bulkwetter shot Archie a conspiratorial grin — Bonnie looked good from the back, hands high over her head, shirt lifted a hand space to reveal a tattoo on bare skin and a pleasantly trim dorsal curve.

Archie shrugged, sat down. He tossed his keys on the counter to catch her attention. She didn't look back until she'd finished — Special #3: BLT $7.99 includes fries. When she turned to face him, she had a look in her eyes that he couldn't read, like she wanted to tell him something. She slid him a menu, watched Bulkwetter who drained his cup, got up and left. When he was out of hearing, Archie focussed on Bonnie.

"I saw John earlier today, Bonnie," he said. "So I know he's nearby. I got a warrant for your brother too."

"Good luck with that."

"Luck doesn't have anything to do with it. We'll have him in custody by this afternoon."

"And then what will you do?"

Her expression was a schoolgirl smirk that took Archie by surprise. It took years off her and erased the hard edges somehow. It made him smile.

"Scare the pants off him, I reckon."

"If you can do that then breakfast is on the house," she said.

She poured coffee for him and brought him the apple pie he asked for — even added a free scoop of ice cream. He had known Bonnie Tran for a long time, had even been on friendly terms with her during the wild years. He remembered how Bill Tran had been, how Bonnie had tried her damnedest to keep her brother out of her life — not that it had worked.

CHAPTER 22

The forensics team from Rochville had taken advantage of a generous law and order grant and now had one of the best labs Archie had ever seen. Nice facilities and a real budget gave detectives like Rick Grift, who ran the place, a comfortable arrogance that seemed natural even to Archie. Hard not to be smug when you really do have it all. Besides, Grift was a decent enough guy. Archie had driven up to Rochville to get results from the forensics sweep of the Donaldson place. Grift greeted him like a monarch welcoming a foreign dignitary.

"Hope you had a good trip," he said.

It was a remark that didn't warrant a reply since Rochville was only forty miles from Harsley, but Archie, without cracking a smile, insisted that he had indeed had a pleasant journey. Grift nodded gravely and then led him through a maze of labs and offices into a larger space where several lab-coated technicians were busy at their stations. Grift continued through to his own glassed-in office. Archie had asked Grift to have his team give the dive shop a second look.

"I did like you asked for old times' sake," Grift said. "Your department's budget for this doesn't cover much of the cost of the tests."

Archie shrugged his shoulders.

"You've got the elected representative in your district," he said. "We've got the opposition. Result is that you get the goodies."

"Could be we're just more deserving," Grift said. "But it wouldn't hurt to vote the other way next time."

"I'll think about it. Did you find anything?"

"Don't know how we missed it the first time. It's not what we're used to here, missing things. How'd you know?"

"I didn't. I just thought that it was a possibility. I had a hunch."

"Good hunch."

"I thought it was worth testing Nick's locker area and the safe for chemicals."

"Well we did and we found traces of cocaine in the safe," Grift said. "There was just enough to get a sample we could use."

"I figured it had to be more than abalone poaching," Archie said. "There aren't enough of those around. I checked with Sky Johnnie at

Fisheries. Robbie and Nick spent a lot of time on the water so they had to be doing something out there. We're close enough to the border. I thought there might be some indication that drugs had been kept on the premises. I'm still looking for motive and I don't see one in mollusc poaching."

"But you see it in drugs?"

"I don't know, maybe. It just has to be eliminated is all."

Grift nodded.

"And the samples from the pickup? Did you get anything there?"

"Blood isn't John Robbie's but you know that," Grift said. "As I said earlier, it's from your victim — Donaldson. We checked the truck for the usual stuff, found semen smears and the like. I'll send them off for DNA analysis if you like but that'll take time. Plus that *will* cost you."

"I don't know if I need them but hang on to them anyway."

"And the other thing you wanted to know about?"

"The wetsuit was drenched in blood. They found blood all over the cab of that truck. But he bled out in his shop. He must have been wearing the wetsuit when they cut his throat."

"Okay — what does it all mean?" Grift said.

"I don't know," Archie said. "I'll have to figure that out."

He left Grift and started back to the station. He speed-dialled Lee. This time Lee picked up. He wasn't happy

"Isn't it enough that we have a complicated case without you going all mysterious on us?" he said.

"What are you talking about, Thomas?"

"I'm talking about meetings in gravel pits, lone-wolfing it, jeopardizing yourself and the investigation. Teams coordinate — or had you forgotten that?"

Archie almost said something he would have regretted. But he stopped himself. He knew why Lee was angry. He knew that he should have been open with his team; he was too ready to operate on his own. On the other hand, he was the boss. Lee might not be too pleased — that was obvious — but Archie expected that Lee would get over it.

"What did you want to talk to me about earlier? Archie asked. "You said that there was a mystery we ought to discuss. What as it?"

"It's important but I still think we need to talk face to face."

"Alright — I should be back by ten tonight. We can talk then if you're still around."

"Where are you going?"

"Later."

He ended the call and tossed the phone on the passenger seat. Archie planned to drive to Empire City — he knew Fricke's views on that, which was one of the reasons he kept his plans to himself. But Archie wanted to check on Pared; something about what Pared had said, or done, or how their conversation had gone, had bothered him. He was also hoping that he might see someone or something that would confirm some fragments of his theory.

The road was empty, most people being home for dinner at that time of day. The rain came; gusts of wind made driving miserable. It would take him at least a couple of hours to get to Empire City and soon he was wishing he'd called it a day and gone home.

He passed the entrance to the side road, which ran past the lot where John Robbie lived. He had sent Lee there but Lee had said that he'd found nothing of significance in his quick search. Trusting to the other detective's thoroughness was well and good but Archie had to see for himself. At the very least, he needed to try to get more of a sense of Robbie and his lifestyle. Without a search warrant and without a key to the trailer home, he would need to break in but he was prepared to do that. He slowed down and made a U-turn.

The road was narrow and rutted, it being more of a Forestry supply road than anything else. It had obviously not been maintained beyond the occasional grading — no reason it should be since the logging there had long ceased. The only things at the end of the road now were the devastated slopes of the mountain and Robbie's old house trailer.

He came to the clearing, stopped the car and scanned the property. The scene was one of desolation. The trailer was an ancient twenty-seven foot with faded paint and enough moss to give it a greenish glow, slowly decaying into the landscape. The mountainside, now barely visible in the failing evening light, was a wasteland of stumps, new birch and alder. Thankfully, the rain had eased.

He parked the Dodge on the pad where Robbie had usually parked his boat and trailer, turned off the ignition, got out and walked to the front door, now blocked with an 'X' of yellow police caution tape. He ripped it down and went to work on the lock. Getting inside took him no time at all.

He turned on the lights. If Robbie had left in a hurry, his living space didn't show it. The kitchen was messy, bachelor messy, but it wasn't *getting the hell out of Dodge* messy. The other rooms were in the same condition. The bed was neither made nor unmade. A few items of clothing hung on a chair in the living room. Empty beer cans and full ashtrays occupied the coffee and end tables. He knew immediately that someone other than a cop had been in the trailer and had searched the place, although whoever had done so had been very good at his job. If anyone had asked how Archie knew that Robbie's space had been searched, he wasn't sure he could have said. Nothing obvious. Subtle things like the TV remote control being an awkward reach from the right hand corner of the couch where it was clear that Robbie sat to watch TV had been moved a little, or the tobacco can too close to the sink — that sort of thing. Nothing by itself told the story. Together — well, that was a different.

Archie hoped the intruder had been unsuccessful. He began his search certain that there was something important still to find. He could be very methodical when he needed to be plus he had good instincts. He took his time, found nothing inside. The object had to be outside then. He walked the area of the trailer pad, head down like an archaeologist, and then, with his light in hand, he crawled under the structure. He rolled onto his back and shoulder-bladed his way along the length of the structure. He ran his fingers along the floor joists. Near the line for the propane tank, his probing fingers found the thing.

A cellphone was tucked into a holder fixed to an extraneous 2x4 attached to the foundation of the trailer. He crawled out and tried to turn it on, but the battery was dead. He took it to the Dodge, plugged in his car charger and connected the device. Then he returned to the trailer, turned out all the lights, closed and locked the door. He attached and arranged the caution tape before he got back into his car. Then he drove back down the logging road to the highway.

He was tired but his mind was racing. The smart phone was still charging but the unit lit up when he pressed a key. He scrolled down through the messages. Within moments he knew why Robbie had hidden the device so well. Now there was little point in going home to sleep — he would be far too preoccupied. He turned south for Empire City as he had originally planned. His meeting with Thomas would have to wait. Two hours down, two back, maybe an hour looking around. He'd be home by two and then he'd sleep. The last text message on the smart phone mentioned the Sunburst. There were other folders on the smart phone but they were locked and he couldn't open them without a password. He would get the techies to look into that.

CHAPTER 23

Just north of Empire City, Archie found a cut-off that took him past the Sunburst Cafe. There was little traffic at that time of night — he was glad of that. He turned onto the avenue close to the cafe. He was not surprised to see lights on inside, although it was very late. He drove on past the building, turned right onto a side street and then circled the block. He parked where he was certain the car wouldn't be conspicuous, on a street kitty corner from the café. Then he cut the ignition and settled down for a wait.

He watched until his eyes grew heavy, contemplated ending his vigil but finally the lights of the café went out. He checked his watch — one in the morning. Five minutes later, a dark red Volvo sedan pulled up in front of the café. Two people came out the front door of the Sunburst. They got into the back seat of the sedan, which pulled away immediately. Archie slid lower in his seat, out of sight he hoped, and watched it pass. He had recognized one of the two passengers as Parker, the manager of the Sunburst; the other had stayed in the dark and was in the sedan before Archie could get a make on him.

When the car was gone, Archie got out of the Dodge. He took his Maglite and crossed the street to the alley alongside the building. There he paused, checked his back trail and then hurried to the side door of the café. He checked the lock — a dead bolt setup too good for him to pick quickly. Then he looked for a window he could use; he found one he thought would suit. Moments later and, he hoped, with a minimum of noise he was inside. He rubbed his eyes to help them focus. He knew he was really pushing his luck. If he'd been smart, he would have gone home and slept like a normal human being. Then, in the morning, he could have taken John Robbie's smart phone to the station and waited until the password situation was resolved. But he hadn't gone home, and he was in the middle of an unauthorized Break and Enter, so such thoughts were a waste of time.

He eased his way through shelves stacked with tinned food and other supplies. His night eyes were good and he refrained from switching on the Maglite until such time as he really needed it. The last thing he needed was to get busted by Empire City cops and have to call on Pared to get him out of jail.

He found nothing unusual on the first floor so he followed a hunch and went down the stairs into the basement. Four large upright freezers occupied one wall. He knew what they contained even before he opened them. He switched on the Maglite and then checked all four, one at a time. Two were filled with frozen abalone, certainly bought from poachers; the others were filled with freezer bags packed, so far as he could see, with bear paws and other contraband that would be destined for China.

He guessed that there was an illegal fortune in the freezers. He was so engrossed in mental calculations that he didn't hear what was going on behind him. A baseball bat swung hard caught him square across the shoulders and drove him forward. The shock of the blow shot through his body.

He recovered enough to turn away, tried to dodge the next swing — too late. The heavy wood whistled into his ribs and knocked the wind out of him. He fell gasping for breath to the floor. The internal lights in the freezers had taken away his night vision and he felt helpless. He saw only the dark mass that was his attacker. He raised his arm to deflect the next blow, which glanced off across his forearm rather than hitting him in the head. He grunted against the pain and stood up, angry. Somebody said, "Enough."

The lights came on. The big man, Jumbo, whose picture Archie had seen with Pared, pushed Archie forward with the head of the bat. Scorpion stood off to one side holding a Glock. This he pointed at Archie's face. He waved it indicating that Archie should turn around and face the other direction. Archie saw that Scorpion grimaced as he moved and guessed why. With no option, he turned to face the man who had ordered the attack.

Bill Tran sat on one of the bottom stairs, a bottle of Steam Anchor beer in his right hand. Tran was a small man, almost delicate, but the right side of his face had been scarred in a knife fight early in his career. The effect of the wound had been to sever nerves in the cheek causing his smile to be lopsided. People often couldn't decide if he was serious or having them on, but most knew it was safest to assume that Bill was deadly serious, even if he appeared to be joking.

If Bill was surprised to see Archie in the basement of the Sunburst, his face didn't show it. He raised the beer as if he were making a toast. His smile lifted only the left side of his mouth.

"Didn't expect that you'd figure this out, Archie, but I guess you did."

"You've branched out, Bill," Archie said. His forearm throbbed and his ribs pained like they had been broken. "I didn't figure you for this sort of thing. Should have, I guess, but didn't."

"You shouldn't be sticking your nose in this, Arch. It's dangerous. You could get yourself killed."

"Don't threaten me, Bill. I don't like it."

"Then stay the fuck out. This isn't even your town, you got no jurisdiction here."

"You're still a two-bit bullshitter, Bill. Like you always were."

Archie knew what was coming but didn't react in time. Jumbo swung the bat into the back of his legs, knocking him off-balance. He caught himself, turned to face the big man who had just swung the bat.

"Damn you," Archie said. "I'll remember this."

Jumbo grinned, hefted the bat. His eyes flicked to his partner, Scorpion, for an instant. Archie hit hard and fast. He drove a straight left into Jumbo's nose, which exploded in blood.

Jumbo swore, took a step back and put a hand up to his nose. Archie heard Scorpio laughing behind him. That seemed to enrage Jumbo who advanced on Archie, one hand trying to staunch the blood flow, the other brandishing the bat.

"Settle down, Jumbo," Tran said. "You've had a bloody nose before."

"I'm going to cripple this fucker."

As Jumbo hefted the bat, Archie caught him with another jab with his left, his right still numb and tingling.

"Fuck you!" Jumbo said. "I'll kill you."

"I said stop!"

Tran was angry now, angry that his order wasn't being followed. It was always bad news to cross Bill Tran. Everybody knew that. Scorpion quickly moved in and eased Jumbo back a step.

"Do what he wants, stupid," he said. "Settle down. Be a professional."

Jumbo shook his head, retreated half a step and then he lowered the bat.

"That's good, Jumbo," Archie said. "Do as you're told."

"Don't make this worse, Archie," Tran said. "It's going to get rough enough as it is."

"What's holding you up?"

"I want to know what you know."

"Jesus, Bill. I'm here. You know what I know. If I was a local cop, I'd arrest you."

"That's funny."

"Not so funny, Bill. You should have been put away years ago."

Tran shook his head, ruefully like he had failed to make some dimwitted person understand something very simple.

"For old times' sake, I'm not going to hurt you too bad, Archie. But you have to know that if you don't keep your nose out of my business, you won't have a nose."

He nodded to Scorpio who aimed the Glock at Archie's head. Tran stood, turned and walked away up the stairs.

"Now what?" Archie asked.

He almost thought he heard the whistle of the bat and then everything went dark.

Cold damp and harsh morning light brought him back to consciousness. A landscape of stained brown appeared before his eyes. He felt a hard rib of vinyl under a bruised cheekbone and realized that he was curled up in the back seat of the Dodge. He pulled himself upright, grimaced against the sharp pain in his back. Lots of things hurt. He had a dim recollection of Bill Tran telling him not to come back if he wanted to stay alive.

He hauled himself out of the back seat, found his keys in his pocket. He checked for the smart phone that he'd found at Robbie's but it was not on him nor was it in the car. Curious, he checked his face in the mirror. Aside from a red welt on one cheekbone, he looked not too bad. It was his back, ribs, and chest that really hurt — they had worked him over like the professionals they were. He was angry, but he was also very hungry. He needed a good breakfast. Gingerly, he turned the ignition, peddled the old engine back to life, turned the Dodge around and headed back to the Sunburst Café.

The hippie owner looked surprised when Archie limped through the door. His hand was on its way to the cellphone near the cash but Archie pointed at him and waved a dismissive hand. Parker nodded and spread his hands in the interrogative.

"A menu," Archie said. "I want breakfast."

He sat down in a booth that gave him views of both the front door and the length of the narrow seating area all the way to the back. He didn't expect trouble but he sure as hell wasn't going to limp out of town with his tail between his legs.

"You got guts, buddy," Parker said. "I hear that you're lucky to be alive."

"Three eggs scrambled, bacon, hash-browns, white toast, coffee," Archie said. "Try not to poison me. It's been a rough night."

"Breakfast is good here. You'll like it. Just so you know — what goes on here with Bill doesn't have anything to do with me. I just run breakfast and lunch."

It hurt to laugh but Archie managed it anyhow.

"If you say so, Parker. Just bring me my breakfast okay?"

"Right on."

He keyed the order into the register and then went to get Archie cutlery, which he set on the table. Other customers arrived and found their tables. Most seemed to be regulars and Parker repeated their usual orders back to them. Archie was beginning to believe that Parker really was an innocent dupe, would like to have believed that. In any case, he had other things, other people on his mind.

Breakfast was as good as promised. Archie finished up, lingered as long as his aching ribs would let and then, between spasms, lifted himself out of the seat. Parker came over with the bill. Archie took it from him, balled it up and tossed it into the booth he'd just vacated.

"Tran can pay this for me," he said. "He owes me breakfast at least."

"I guess I'll just make this one on the house."

"Suit yourself, Parker."

"I will, I will."

Feeling somewhat revived, Archie walked out into a cutting wind that brought on a painful shiver. He'd had enough time with Tran to make sense of part of the puzzle. He put in a call to Pared about the lockers filled with contraband, mostly to see where that would lead. Pared seemed surprised, said he'd look into the matter when he had time, which meant either that he would do nothing or that the contents of the freezers be moved before he got there. Likely, the freezers were empty already. Archie nodded agreement to himself. Then he turned the ugly nose of the Dodge towards home.

CHAPTER 24

"What the hell happened to you?"

Patsy gawked at Archie like he was the victim of a train wreck. He had forgotten that he was wearing some of the results of last night's adventure on his face, although he had imagined that Jumbo and Scorpion had taken care not to do too much in that department. He had tried to get through the building to his office without being seen, to avoid questions from the Chief as much as anything. He was relieved when he didn't encounter Fricke, but Patsy was at his door waiting for him. She looked him over, concern on her face. She'd be seeing things Archie thought were minor, like the bruising on his right cheek and the dried blood around his ear. She touched one of the tender areas on his jaw and he wished that he had gone home first and cleaned up.

"I took a fall," he said. "I'm clumsy, always have been."

"Ha, ha."

He tried a smile. She shook her head.

"You look like hell, Archie. Bruised up and dragged out — that's you."

"Thanks. When I need a compliment I'll come to you."

"You should go home."

He shook his head.

"Too much to do. Call up Lee. We'll meet in my office in twenty minutes."

"Archie — Jesus!"

"No — just the three of us."

She grinned and tossed her head. It was the first time he had made a joke.

She turned on her heel and walked away down the corridor. He watched her go, his eyes lingering too long. He caught himself at it. Something about the package — her figure, her walk, her carriage, the set of her shoulders — was alarmingly fascinating. He mentally chastised himself and headed for the washroom to try to clean up as best he could. Inside, he looked at his face in the mirror; saw fine wrinkles around the tired-looking and reddened eyes. He filled the bowl with water and went to work. He was drying off when Chad Reddin walked in, glanced at him and went to a urinal.

"You look like shit, Stevens," he said.

"So I've been told."

"Fricke talk to you yet?"

"What about?"

"What I heard is that you were sticking your nose into Empire City business and Empire City don't like it."

Archie tilted his head.

"You know what Fricke can do."

Reddin finished up, washed his hands and passed Archie on his way out. At the door, he turned and grinned.

"He'll be glad to hear you tell him, I'll bet. Empire City don't like much what we do but this is the first time I ever heard of a Harsley cop working their beat. You must be nuts or stupid."

"Go away, Reddin."

Reddin said something Archie didn't hear, pulled back the door and left the room grinning. Archie took a plastic container of Aspirin from a cabinet near the door, popped three in his mouth, then bent down and took a gulp of water from the faucet. Jumbo and Scorpion had been good — the pain kept increasing as the day went on. He made a mental note to pay that debt back as soon as he could.

Fricke did look angrier than usual. Archie had gone to his office to get things over with. Fricke waited for Archie to get inside his office, and then instructed him to close the "fucking door," after which he expressed his strong view that Archie should let him know when he was trespassing in other jurisdictions. Archie was getting used to being on the carpet. He waited until Fricke had finished and then told him what he had in mind and what he had discovered. At first Fricke seemed unimpressed with Archie's plan but, gradually, the thought that he could stick it to the Empire City department seemed to intrigue him.

"So you met Pared. What did you think?" he asked.

"I'm not sure what to make of him. He seems okay but I don't think he liked me around much. He tried to put me off talking to Dolan. I doubt very much he did anything about the contraband. He blew me off when I told him about it."

"He's highly territorial," Fricke said. "Plus he thinks we're strictly bush league. He doesn't like to share intelligence or resources. I hate the prick."

"You know Dolan?"

"I know him."

"He seemed like a good cop, like he knew his job."

"He gives that impression alright. I worked with him years ago. You have to be careful with him."

"How so?"

"He's always got something going on that you don't know about. That's what I remember. Of course, he could have changed."

"Do people change?"

Fricke shook his head.

"Not in my experience."

He was obviously turning something over in his mind. He picked up a sheet of paper, looked at it, looked at Archie, handed it to him.

"Read that, Detective, and tell me if you can see a way out of it."

Archie read the letter, which was on official mayor's office stationary. In it, the mayor expressed concern about Archie's rapid promotion, his inexperience in homicide cases, and his supposed lack of focus. The upshot was that Mayor Estes wanted Archie demoted and replaced; he strongly suggested Ray Jameson or, even better, Chad Reddin as an alternative. Estes thought Reddin would have approached the Donaldson murder directly and would already have a suspect in custody. Fricke was told to move on the matter immediately. Archie looked at Fricke, tossed the letter back on the chief's desk.

"I'll resign before I'll accept a demotion."

"I know that. I told Estes to go do something nasty to himself — not because of you but because I don't like to be threatened, especially by a politician like Estes."

"Where does that leave me?"

"It leaves you with responsibility for the Donaldson case and for whatever you've got going on but you got a strict, strict time limit. You either find something, like now, or you *will* be writing parking tickets — or I'll give you something that'll make the man in you so mad, you'll quit. It might even happen to me — a demotion, I mean. I might find another job but you won't. Estes will see to that. That brings me to what you found in Empire City."

"The contraband in the freezers?"

"That and the fact that you got beat up by Bill Tran. I don't like people beating up my detectives. Sends the wrong message. You're going to have to do something about it."

"Like I said, I told Pared about the freezers."

"I heard — they were empty. That's not what I meant anyway."

"I know. You don't have to worry on that score."

Fricke rubbed a big hand over the sweaty expanse of his forehead.

"You got to give me something, Archie, You got a good head on your shoulders but even I can't figure out exactly what you're up to."

"I've got to do things my way."

"Maybe you do but you could make it easier for me by keeping me properly informed at least."

"If you'd rather, I'll turn the case over to another detective. If you don't like Jameson, you've got others to choose from. Your choice, Cal. Either you leave me be or you get somebody else."

"You're a prick, Stevens. You know that? I can't give in to Estes on Jameson, as you well know. Even if I wanted him, it'd look like I was caving in and that I'm not going to do. So, get your ass in gear and arrest somebody PDQ. You got that?"

Archie grinned, nodded. Fricke shook his head like an old walrus and waved him out of his space. Archie walked through the main office area oblivious to the curious looks he got as he passed. Patsy and Lee were already in his room when he got there. Patsy peered at him as if she were looking for bugs. Apparently satisfied with what she saw, or didn't see, she settled back in the old leather side chair and slouched, her hands linked across her chest, legs out. Lee, standing near her, rubbed his eyes and looked into space.

"Something on your mind, Thomas?" Archie asked.

He thought Lee might tell them what he had found in the archives but Lee didn't do that.

"Since you ask — yes, there is."

"And?"

"Things are getting sloppy. The whole idea of you going to Empire City, doing your own investigation, working without the team, or even team input bothers me. I like to do things professionally. I believe in jurisdiction, in procedure. I believe in the team. Otherwise, the whole thing turns into a gong show. I don't like it."

"So, you figure I'm not professional, not a team player — is that right?"

Lee looked up, met Archie's eyes, obviously peeved.

"That's right, I do."

Archie crossed his arms, sat on the edge of his desk. He admired Lee's policing skills, his organization and his thoroughness. He wanted to keep him on his team but he damn well wasn't going to let Lee dictate the terms. In the old days, he might have lost his temper; he didn't have that luxury now. Besides, Lee was right. He should have included them. He thought for a moment about the correct response, the right way to handle the matter. Patsy was looking at him from under her brows.

"You agree with him?"

"I do."

"You have to do what you think is right, both of you. I'm not going to change my approach, or explain why I do things. You don't agree with my decisions — I can accept that. You can say whatever the hell you like and it won't matter to me. What does matter is what you intend to do. If you want to work with me, great but if you don't, well, I'm sorry to lose you."

He repressed the urge to try to mollify them.

Lee stood up, shook his head.

"I'll have to think about this," he said. Then he turned and went out the door. Archie shrugged. He looked at Patsy, who was now very glum.

"What about you?"

"I'm staying for now. I think you know what you're doing. I'll talk to Thomas. You hurt his feelings by going lone wolf on this."

"That wasn't my intent but I'm not begging him."

She sat up and looked past his shoulder.

"You called a meeting," she said. "What is it about?"

Archie rapped his fingers on the edge of his desk. Maybe it was normal to have dissension in the ranks, maybe it was the same in every team, but he wasn't quite sure what to do about it. He dropped back into his chair and told Patsy what he thought about Nick's involvement in the Tran smuggling racket. She nodded as he outlined his strategy — so far as it went. He didn't tell her about the part of the case that really bothered him, about thoughts he'd been having about the Children. He wasn't sure what to do in that regard and was reluctant to confide in her, or ask her for her thoughts.

She sensed this fact and showed her irritation by tapping her foot and shifting in her chair.

"You take the cake," she said. "You want to piece it out a little at a time. It's called being proprietary. How do you expect anyone to have any confidence in you as a team leader? How can Thomas trust you? How can I?"

She had a point. He told her so, told her that he wasn't keeping things back because he was, as she said, proprietary, but rather that his suspicions put him into such strange territory that he felt like a Sasquatch hunter, or something like it. Even entertaining his ideas on what was really happening in Harsley, what Nick had really got killed for, seemed too far out to be true. She seemed satisfied with that. He beckoned her to follow, led her out through the office, out the back door, through the parking lot and to his car. They both got in. He looked straight ahead and gave her his thoughts on the Children.

She waited until he had finished saying what he had to say, her scepticism obvious on her face. He knew what she was thinking. He would think the same if someone had advanced the theory to him, anybody would. But he could not get past what now seemed obvious to him. She had been watching him and now she looked away.

"This is incredible," she said. "I don't know what to say about it."

"Not much to say. I'm not even sure how to do what I need to do given the time Fricke's given me."

"There's still talk that Jameson is going to replace you."

"In a way, I wish he would. Nick's murder is only one part of this — almost a distraction. In the meantime, there are things that have to be done. Part of what I need you to do is to run interference for me. Are you willing to do that?"

She put her hand on the door, ready to get out, turned to look at him.

"I believe in you," she said. "What you say makes sense to me and I think you have to pursue it. I'm part of your team and you're still the boss, at least for now. I'll do what you want. By the way, the wound edge on Donaldson's neck suggests a wavy blade. You asked me to check."

"I thought it might," Archie said.

She got out of the car.

"Patsy."

She held the door open and looked back in.

"This could get very dangerous."

"I know. Did Thomas tell you what he'd found in the archives?"

"No, he didn't — why?

"Just wondering," he said.

She shrugged and walked away — a small figure, not very cop-like. He started the car, wondering if he really was as incompetent as others were starting to think. He decided he didn't have time for such doubts. He had to find out if Pete Wilson could get him a ride to Cat's Cradle Island right away. Once he'd arranged that, he would get his dive gear. Sooner or later, if he wanted to confirm what he was thinking, he was going to have to get wet.

CHAPTER 25

Cherish's diesel rattled to life and she eased back from the wharf, leaving Archie behind on the weathered float. He had decided to postpone his dive. Instead, he had asked Pete Wilson to drop him off on Cat's Cradle Island near where Walter had said he had seen Nick Donaldson a day or so before Nick had died. Pete waved through the pilothouse window and Archie watched until the boat was out of sight and around the point.

He saw no sign of the recent activity he had expected so he searched out the old road that led through a long-deserted and overgrown orchard. Then he followed it into a dense clump of dark spruces until he reached a dead end created by windfall. He wasn't sure what he was looking for, some sign of activity, maybe a marijuana plantation or processing area — something criminal anyway — but that might be harder to find than he had imagined. He did a circuit through the bush but found and heard nothing.

Back at the windfall, he saw another path that seemed to go south and he crossed thigh-deep fireweed to get to it. It was the lesser of the two trails that Pete had marked on the map, the one that should take him to the south side of the island but also the one Pete was less sure about. With the main trail blocked and overgrown it was his only choice. He sidestepped a massive rock and followed the path under the trees and into the forest gloom. Somewhere in the deeper parts of the island a raven croaked, hollow and lonesome and another answered it from far off.

The trail narrowed as he walked and soon he wasn't sure he was still on it. The bush and trees were very wet; he pulled his collar up against a stream of icy-cold water that spilled from the bough of a cedar. He checked his GPS but he couldn't pick up a signal and so had to depend on his instinct. Gradually his route became more difficult. Often the path led him away from the seashore, up behind rocky outcrops and down gullies clogged with nettle and devil's club. When he caught a glimpse of a pale, cloud-shrouded sun, he realized that he was heading towards New Jerusalem. Finally, he came to a well-used footpath marked with many boot tracks and the walking became easier.

He was soon out in the open again, skirting the forest edge, happy to be close to the water but cautious too. He checked his SIG, made sure that there was a round in the chamber and continued, listening for sounds of activity as he walked. The sun came out for an instant and lifted his spirits. The going was much easier and he began to make up the lost time.

He cut across a smaller side trail and stopped. Caught up in a low tangle of Mahonia was a single long bud of marijuana. He picked it up and sniffed it, knew from the scent that it was high-quality weed. He dropped it back where he found it and proceeded cautiously up the path.

The plantation was hidden within a stand of vine maple, the plants long harvested. He checked the area and found nothing, not even a tool. He made a note of the location and then went back to the main trail and continued on his way. The ravens called to each other again and the thought that somebody might be signalling crossed his mind but he dismissed it. The pot gardening season was long over for the year and there was no reason for anyone to be guarding harvested fields. He checked for more paths and fields and found evidence of more harvests.

There was every chance that Nick had somehow been involved with the grow-ops on the island but Archie still had to find the reason he was murdered. He needed to hurry now. He was getting hungry, and he was cold. He checked his watch; he had to cover a lot of ground if he was to meet Pete at the prearranged time. He crossed yet another path that seemed to cut diagonally through the forest in the direction of the rendezvous, turned onto it, and picked up his pace.

The trail soon changed direction and, now committed, Archie realized that he was heading in the wrong direction. Instead of cutting across the island, he was now trending south. This took him back into the forest, which was now darker and gloomier than ever. The arrival of a soaking drizzle added to his discomfort.

He had no choice but to hurry — he had no desire to spend a cold, wet night on the island. As he walked, he heard movement in the bush nearby and a branch snapped. Something was paralleling him. But when he stopped and turned towards the sound, it ceased. A deer on the move, he thought, and carried on.

Deeper into the forest, he was no longer sure exactly where he was. The light level was soon so low that he thought he might have to dig out his flashlight. Nearby, he heard the raven call again, a single, long, wavering croak, like a death rattle, and then a lonely answering cry.

He grew apprehensive. He scolded himself for being taken in by the atmosphere and upped his pace to a ground-consuming stride. At last, he was free of the bush and out in the open. He looked around, only half-surprised at the scene that lay before him. The extensive meadows of the once cultivated fields of the Children of Eli stretched up into mist on the slopes of the mountain; the ruined buildings of New Jerusalem were visible through the rain.

He cursed to himself. His wanderings had taken him almost a mile out of his way. He had a long walk ahead of him before he could get to where Pete would be waiting, and he was already soaked through.

Exasperated, he searched for the remains of another road that Pete had marked on the map, one that should lead back to the landing. The map showed the circular layout of the deserted community and the locations of the four cairns that marked each of the cardinal directions, like a compass.

The houses were mostly tumbled down, roofs caved in, walls tilted — except for one. The temple and lodge where Brother Eli had once lived, his Presbytery was still intact and looked solid. Archie thought he smelled smoke. Indeed, a faint blue haze drifted down across the slate roof from the Presbytery chimney.

He strode up the path towards the building. The door was ajar. He called out and, when no one answered, he took a quick look inside. Empty beer cans and sandwich wrappers littered a long table, and a garbage can was full of junk. Somebody's bedding was spread across an old couch. He felt the stove, which was still warm. Likely, he had disturbed a squatter; someone taking advantage of free accommodation but there was always a chance that a sentry for the grow-op was staying here. He drew the SIG and then put it and the hand holding it into his jacket pocket. He was now certain he had been watched earlier and likely was still under surveillance.

He went out a side door and eased along the wall, his senses on high alert. But he saw and heard no one. According to Pete's map, the front door of the Presbytery faced the old road leading south. He walked quickly out into the open, found the road immediately, and picked up his pace. He was wary now, half expecting an attack from behind.

Within a half an hour, he was at the rendezvous. At the other end of the beach, Pete nosed an inflatable dinghy up onto the shingle, a sandwich clenched between his teeth. Archie walked up the beach to meet him, feet crunching through loose, wet cobbles.

"How you doing there, amigo?" Pete said. "Things go well?"

Archie tossed his pack into the inflatable.

"I found some interesting stuff but I got turned around up there and had to retrace my steps. That's what took me so long. I'm ready to go home."

The wind had picked up noticeably, and shifted until it was blowing in from the southeast. Pete nodded. He held the bow while Archie climbed in and then he shoved off.

"I'm just waiting for you, buddy boy," Pete said. "There's a hockey game on TV tonight that I don't want to miss."

"What kind of sandwiches have you got there?"

"You *must* be hungry."

Pete laughed, started the motor, and turned the bow of the inflatable towards Cherish anchored in deeper water. Within minutes they were aboard.

Archie got a sandwich from the cooler and was relieved when the filling turned out to be cheese — you never knew with Pete. He might have bitten into tuna and peanut butter. The diesel kicked in and Archie went on deck and scanned the shoreline as he munched the sandwich. They were almost out into the channel when two figures, tiny in the distance, came out of the forest and stood watching as darkness descended.

CHAPTER 26

A rchie didn't like diving alone, especially late in the day when it was dark and rainy; he wouldn't have done so except that his curiosity about what Donaldson had found on the bottom was overwhelming. His visit the day before to Cat's Cradle Island had convinced him that drugs were part of the story. The other part had to do with Brother Eli gold coins and whatever else Nick had found on the bottom of the sea. He'd anchored the police zodiac over the place where Walter had said he'd seen Nick diving, and now he was fifty feet below the surface, feeling the piercing cold, trying to get his bearings.

He checked his compass, tried to remember his underwater navigation. He'd made three passes back and forth paralleling the reef, without success. He was on his fourth pass when the wreck appeared from out of a green blizzard of sea snow. The sight of it pulled him around, finning hard to stay in place against the current, trying not to overshoot the timbers, the debris field, the scattered artefacts — no doubt now that he had found the wreck he expected. He was about to descend for a closer look when he heard the throbbing slash of propellers above him; a shadow obliterated most of the remaining light.

He looked up. The bubble-defined, silvered hull of a large vessel, its engines throbbing, lay beside the tiny shape of his zodiac. He waited, wondering if he should surface immediately, or take some samples from the wreck first, something to prove his theory to Fricke. He decided on the latter, dropped to the bottom, picked up a small dish and a piece of metal, secured them in a pocket on his vest. He kept one eye on the hull right above him.

He almost didn't see the divers passing like shadows not twenty feet away, three black figures armed with spear guns. They turned towards him. Archie rose from the bottom. The lead diver pointed his weapon and fired. Archie reacted immediately, finned backwards as the spear bubbled past. He kicked up sand with his fins, erasing visibility, and swam hard for the kelp forest. He heard the swish of propellers above him, knew that surfacing now would be a mistake. He checked his direction on his compass, and then headed in the direction of the shore.

When he reckoned he had gone far enough — and when he was almost out of air — he surfaced, rising up slowly into a raft of kelp fifty meters or so from the shore. He saw a dozen or so dozing harbour seals on a large rock and looked to the vessel pursuing him, a modified fishing trawler or maybe a Harbercraft. He tried reading the name on the stern but it swung away from him. An outboard whined to life near him — his zodiac — and he knew that they were using it to look for him.

The kelp provided some cover and he hoped that the slick, black neoprene of his hood would look like the bladders of the plant if he stayed still. The fact that the seals had scarcely looked in his direction was a good sign. He lowered his head slowly, face rubbing into the kelp stems, mouth barely out of the water, pulled off his mask lest a flash off the glass faceplate gave him away, grimaced against the salt water burning his eyes. His tank was now only an encumbrance. He made a decision, unclipped the straps on his vest and eased out of his rig.

The zodiac came closer — he felt the vibration of its outboard through the water; came closer to where he lay concealed. He scarcely breathed at all, fought the urge to turn and look, expecting that, at any moment, a metal spear would pierce his skull and kill him. And then he heard the throb of a diesel, the sound of another boat arriving. A walkie-talkie squawked and he heard a woman request instructions. Archie eased around to look.

A pleasure boat, seeing activity that looked much like a search, had come to investigate. As the boat closed with the trawler, the zodiac peeled out to intercept it. Its wake washed over Archie's head and filled his mouth with salt water. From the kelp mat, he could see a trim woman in a wetsuit and hood standing in the bow of the zodiac as it ran up to meet the gill-netter; she had her feet braced, one hand on the painter like a circus rider. Her two companions sat on either pontoon of the boat, heads down, spear guns out of sight. The skipper came out of the pilothouse door to greet them. He wore dark glasses and a ball cap low over his forehead.

The zodiac came to a halt. The bow rider made a sweeping motion with her arm, indicating that they were searching for something in the Bay. The skipper said something in reply; the bow rider shook her head in polite refusal. The skipper nodded and went back into his pilothouse. Archie guessed that that he had been told that the group was diving, that they didn't need any help but thanks anyway. Before Archie could do anything, the yacht had cruised out of the bay. At least, they hadn't killed the man. Archie breathed a sigh of relief.

Archie knew that he only had a few minutes before they picked up the search again. He eased out of the kelp and let the current swing him past the rock. The seals watched with sorrowful, liquid eyes, half propped on their sides; some went back to sleep. Then the zodiac's ignition whined. They had seen him! The outboard coughed and started with a roar. The seals woke, panicked, and splashed into the water. Archie gave up on stealth. Adrenalin flooded his body; he broke the surface, arms pumping in a free-style sprint, scarcely heard the roar of the zodiac as it spun round, slammed into its own wake and came after him.

He swam as fast he could, long strokes reaching ever for shore. In the shallows, he tore off his fins and let them go. At last, his feet touched bottom. He clambered up the slippery, wrack-covered rocks and onto the beach, ran pell-mell towards the bluffs that ringed the bay. A metal spear zinged past him and clattered off the shingle. He heard the rattling crunch behind him as the zodiac beached, heard the woman shout out orders. He dove into a thick line of alders, got to his feet, veered, climbed up the steep slope, traversing higher and higher, wishing he'd kept his training up.

The slope was overgrown with nettle, wild rose, and broom but he muscled through scraping thorns and heavy brush. At the top, he glanced over his shoulder; saw two of them paralleling him, running along the beach fifty feet below. He wished he knew the island better. He slid across a ridge of sandstone and then, suddenly, he was on an old deer trail and making speed. He got his second wind and felt better. His wetsuit helped protect him from thorns and branches that slid off the slick neoprene as he pushed on.

He slowed, allowed himself a pause to catch his breath. He heard a noise on the trail ahead and looked up to see — he had been headed off. One of them was waiting ahead of him, spear gun ready. As he swung it up to point at Archie's chest, Archie charged, pushed the spear gun aside, and knocked the man off his feet. Something sang past his cheek — he felt the wind of its passage; knew that the others were close behind him. He sprinted for a thicket of Ocean Spray, and dove through it.

His momentum brought him to the edge of a steep ravine, off balance, unable to stop himself. He clawed for a handhold, missed, picked up speed, tumbled out of control down the slope, slammed hard into the corrugated trunk of a huge Douglas Fir and stopped. An aluminum spear spanged off the thick bark near his head. Painfully, he got to his feet, sidestepped a bush and dropped into nothing.

It was almost dark when he came to, learned by feel that he was caught in the crook of a heavy tree limb, held against the trunk, saw enough in the low light to know that he was twenty feet off the ground. He listened for the sounds of his pursuers but heard nothing. He hurt. He felt for broken bones, decided that, beyond a concussion and some scrapes plus the lingering ache of his Empire City injuries, he was all right.

Getting out of the tree seemed to take forever but he managed it. Then he made his way down the hill to the bottom of the gully. He was exhausted, cold and hungry. He picked his way along the old streambed but couldn't find enough water to wash the salt out of his mouth. When he could go no farther, he climbed up the bank as far as he could manage, found a comfortable hollow amongst the roots of a giant cedar, snuggled deep into a pile of dead leaves and rested.

In the middle of the night, the rain began to fall. He leaned his head back and opened his mouth wide and drank the sweet water. He had seen withered salmonberries when he had gone to ground and found them now by touch. He ate handfuls; the normally gritty, tasteless fruit now seemed delicious. The moon came out. It made him more visible if he moved but he felt better nonetheless and some of his strength returned. Soon his teeth stopped chattering and he began to feel warm.

He thought about his options. He wasn't quite sure how he could get home, but he would — hail a passing fish boat maybe. He knew one thing, which was that he wanted to find out who had attacked him and get the bastards. His eyes grew heavy. He watched an enormous banana slug begin its slow way across a patch of fungus. Before that creature had finished its transit, he had fallen into a deep and dreamless sleep.

CHAPTER 27

The combination of spent adrenaline, fear and sleeping rough had left Archie drained. At first light, he stumbled down through heavy brush until he reached the shore. There he got lucky. A passing fish boat answered his hail and sent in a dinghy to pick him up. By the time the captain dropped him off on a wharf close to home, Archie, wearing borrowed clothes and boots, had been fortified with two bowls of oatmeal, half a quart of orange juice, and lots of coffee. He felt better, went home to change and then headed to the station. He debated about reporting what had happened but he owed Fricke. He found him in the coffee room. Fricke looked at Archie over the rim of the stained coffee mug he held in his beefy fingers.

"You look like death warmed over, Archie. Did you put in an all-nighter?"

"In a way. I spent last night on Cat's Cradle Island."

"What the blazes were you doing there?"

"I was diving — I'm entitled to time off — and then I got stranded."

"You didn't have a partner — and a boat?"

"I don't believe in the buddy system. I had the department zodiac but lost it in the tide change. Just bad luck."

Fricke looked sceptical but after a deep gulp from his mug, he shrugged.

"The zodiac's tied up to the wharf. I saw it this morning. You were unlucky all right— or lucky. And don't badmouth the buddy system."

"Story of my life. Glad it's back though. Wouldn't want the cost to come out of my wages."

Fricke held Archie's eyes but Archie was determined not to give Fricke too much. Finally, Fricke turned away. He looked back over his shoulder.

"Remember what I said about results, Archie."

"Sure."

Archie had a lot to sort out, beginning with who had attacked him and why. The zodiac returned to the dock was a further mystery. He had had a better look at the big man with the spear gun than with the others but that didn't help much. He had only had glimpses of the others; all had had worn neoprene scuba hoods making identification almost impossible. He ran a computer search through several databases, clicked through a dozen or so mug shots and got nothing. Then he called the dive shops he knew. His inquiries about missing zodiacs, divers, spear guns, and recent equipment rentals got him nowhere.

The attack had done one thing — it convinced him that many people had an interest in Nick's activity. What had seemed to be a number of lines of inquiry that had little to do with each other on the surface were indeed connected — and Cat's Cradle Island was, in some way, their nexus.

He had lost the wreckage artefacts but he was certain that they were from a luxury yacht and just as certain whose yacht it had been. Now he needed to find out more about the woman whose decapitated body was still in the morgue. If he could get an ID on the victims in the cave also, he might get closer to confirming his theory before Fricke got fed up and booted him off the case.

He went to his office, still deep in thought. Moments later, Patsy showed up at his door. When he looked up, hoping to look irritated enough that she'd leave him alone with his thoughts, she shook her head, came in and closed the door behind her. She walked up to his desk, shoved some paperwork out of her way and sat down on it, half-facing him.

"How are things in the House of Secrets?" she asked.

"Haven't you got things to do, like getting me some DNA results, for example?"

"Those don't happen overnight and you know it, Archie."

"Alright."

"The zodiac you used when you went diving turned up. Thought you might like to know that."

"I heard."

"Okay."

She looked him over, searched his face with her eyes. Self-consciously, he leaned back in his desk, picked up a pencil and rapped it on the desk. He glanced at her, looked unexpectedly into her eyes, brown shot with green. Then, suddenly, he was describing what had happened to him. He had surprised himself. She seemed taken aback, concerned.

"Jeez! Did you tell Fricke?"

"No, I didn't," he said. "It'd complicate things for him but things are becoming slightly clearer for me."

"What do you mean?"

"Remember the coin and the reference to Brother Eli?"

She nodded.

"Thomas told me. Eli ran his little cult like a dictator. The Children, or Divine Spirits whatever they're called, gave him everything they possessed. Some of them were very wealthy people so he got rich fast. The cult was secretive and used intimidation and murder to maintain control," she said.

"That's right. He also owned most of Cat's Cradle Island — made it his base of operations. One of the odd things he did was to buy gold, maybe even have it stolen for him, and then melt it down and have it cast into coins with a dedication to him on it."

"Like the coin Nick found."

"I imagine that's one of them."

"But you're not suggesting that the Children of Eli tried to kill you — surely."

"The originals are all long gone so far as I know — or they'd be very old. I think there's something still happening with that island but I just don't know what it is. Maybe it's just that somebody's using their old networks, something like that."

"Are you going back there, back to that island?"

"When I can, yes."

"Will you take me with you?"

"Why would I want to do that?"

"You need backup at least."

"I'll think about it."

"Can you do me a favour?"

"Like what?"

"Give me a ride home. My car's being serviced."

"I can do that. I need to go get something to eat anyway. Give me fifteen minutes."

She signalled agreement by pointing her index finger at him emphatically, and then she was gone, leaving him wondering just what, in God's name, he was up to with her.

In the car, she suggested that they have dinner together at her place and he searched for an objection. There were, indeed, many good professional reasons not to go but he couldn't seem to think of any that would save him from himself. He was old enough and experienced enough to understand what was happening. Either she was falling for him, or the other way round. As they drove, the rain, which had been intermittent all day, committed itself. Outside the steamed windows, wind-whipped spume drummed against the vehicle as it splashed through the sheeting water covering the highway. The scanner mumbled and when he reached for it their hands touched. For a moment, neither moved until he said, "Turn that down, would you," and put his hand back on the wheel.

The rain hammered down with renewed intensity and the car now boated down the flooded street. The heater seemed to be working overtime to steam up the windows and the windshield wipers barely helped; Archie's ability to see anything beyond fifty feet or so was nil. The effect was isolating but he found it discomfortingly pleasant to be with her, alone, almost as if they were suspended in time. It was mesmerizing. He resolved to break the spell that he seemed to be weaving for himself with conversation.

"How are you liking the department?" he asked.

She leaned back against the door so that she could look at him. He sensed that she was amused by his tactic.

"I don't know. I'm still making up my mind," she said.

He hunkered over the wheel, peering through the windshield into the rain.

"I guess I haven't made it easier."

"You haven't been real welcoming but I expected to have to learn my way around. I feel better about everything now."

"What made you decide to become a cop?" he asked. "I looked into your employment file. You should be at a university — as a professor."

He heard her shuffle around in the seat. He glanced at her. She lifted her shoulders, indicating she wasn't sure.

"I wanted more action, I guess. Plus there were a couple of big headline cases involving women that made me think I could be of use."

That took him by surprise. He started to retreat into his thoughts and caught himself before he got in too deep.

"How about you?" she asked. "According to Delia and Thomas, you used to be Hell on wheels when you were young. You used to be friends with half the criminals in town."

"You've been asking about me?"

"You were checking up on me."

"That's different. You were supposed to be working for me."

"Anyway. Why did you change from bad apple to cop?" she asked.

He didn't like being questioned and he told her so.

"No more questions then," she said.

They drove on in silence for five minutes or so.

"Was it because of your mother like Delia says?"

"Delia doesn't know anything."

"It was because of your mother then."

"Maybe."

"She was one of the street women murdered by Foster, wasn't she?"

"None of your damn business."

"You don't need to get upset."

"I'm not upset. I'm private. I don't like people asking about me, or discussing me, or trying to figure out my motives, okay?"

"Okay. Sorry I said anything. I just thought it might be something we could both relate to."

He laughed bitterly.

"Both relate to — are you kidding? You're a professor's daughter with a hobby — catching serial killers. I don't know what I am."

"I'm sorry, Archie."

He stared into the night, his hands loose on the wheel.

"She was my mother. My kid brother died and she thought it was her fault — or my old man's — I never could figure that out. She started drinking; they split up; she took up with a loser and ended up on the streets. When I was thirteen, I went looking for her. I found her and she promised to come home. And then Foster got her. If the cops on the mainland had done their work properly, he would have been caught years before. Maybe she would have come home. I like to think so. First I hated all cops, hated everybody. Then I decided that I could do something; that I could be the better cop and maybe save lives. Now I know better. I've grown up since then. Satisfied?"

She said, "Yes," and put her hand on his arm, letting it linger there for a second. Then she turned forward, looked out into the darkness and the rain. Suddenly, the scanner squawked and she turned up the volume.

"A homicide at a restaurant called the Zuider Zee," she said. "That's the place John Robbie's girlfriend runs."

Archie swore. He flicked on the emergency lights, reversed direction and spun the car through a river of water. The Zuider Zee was on the other side of town and they could get there faster if he used an access road that ran like a by-pass around the town. He accelerated down the highway, trying not to hydroplane and then made a sharp left into the road access. Someone on a dirt bike almost cut him off as he made the turn, forcing him to cut the wheel hard to avoid a collision. He slammed on the brakes, hand on the door ready to exit.

The bike skidded to a stop and the rider righted his machine. For a moment the two vehicles stopped side by side, the rain dancing through the bright arcs of their headlights. Archie looked across at the sodden figure crouched over the handlebars, unrecognizable because of his helmet but familiar nonetheless.

Then the bike accelerated away and was gone down the road into the rain before Archie could react. For a moment, he thought about going after it, but decided against it.

"No license plate," Patsy said.

"Forget about it. We're not going to catch the bastard in this weather and on this road. Call it in though. Maybe there's a cruiser close enough to intercept."

She called in, confirmed what Archie already suspected — that no cruisers were in the area.

Archie swore, looked off into the rain in the direction the bike had gone. Then he put his emergency lights on and accelerated towards the Zuider Zee.

Emergency vehicles had taken over the parking lot when he got there. Ray Jameson's Ford was there too. Archie slammed the dash with the heel of his hand.

"Shit!"

Patsy looked at him.

"Relax," she said. "No reason he shouldn't be here."

Archie said nothing, got out of the car, slammed the door behind him, regretted doing so. He heard her door close, the normalcy of the sound a reprimand to him. She paralleled him as they walked towards the brightly lit restaurant; she ducked under the caution tape he stepped over. They climbed the three steps to the porch together. She followed him through the door and into the dining room. Jameson's sidekick, Reddin, was sitting at a table drinking coffee, a baseball cap in an evidence bag on the table in front of him. Reddin saw Archie, raised his cup in salute, grinning he said, "You fucked up here, buddy." He leered at Patsy who ignored him.

They continued on through the kitchen, towards the bungalow and the sounds of activity there. Jameson, a cold cigar clenched in his teeth, scowled when he saw Archie. Archie looked beyond him to Bonnie Tran's body on the bed; a dark bruise on her neck and a red cord that had been used to strangle her lying on the floor near her outstretched arm.

"You should have brought him in, chief," Jameson said. "Robbie got to her. He was here not a half hour ago — took off on a dirt bike."

Archie could think of nothing to say. Was it true that he had almost collided with the man he'd been trying to arrest and who had, apparently, killed again? Jameson pushed the point home.

"I don't get it."

"I guess he got fed up with her or maybe she threatened to rat him out. He probably thought he had a good reason."

"This doesn't make any sense."

"You got above yourself, chief. Too much too fast," Jameson said.

"You're sure Robbie was here?" Archie asked.

"He was here. He went out the back door while we were still out front. Guess he wanted to shut her up."

"Why didn't you arrest him?"

Jameson's eyes narrowed.

"Chad saw him first, almost got a shot at him before he took off out into the rain."

"And then what?"

"He took off on a dirt bike down the dirt road at the back. We got his cap though."

Archie shook his head.

"You got his cap."

"So fucking what? You're not involved here," Reddin said.

"Did anyone go after him?" Patsy asked.

"No, sweetheart, nobody went after the guy that soon to be ex-Detective Stevens should have nailed a week ago. Not yet anyway."

"I'd like to look around. You have a problem with that, Ray?'

"Like I said, you got no business here now." Jameson punched in a number on his cellphone, lit a cigar. "I think it's time you got your ass out of here."

"When I'm ready, Ray."

Jameson tried and failed to stare Archie down. Then he came forward, trying to intimidate, trying to make Archie move out of his way. They stood nose-to-nose, eyeball-to-eyeball. At last, Jameson looked away for the briefest of moments, and eased back.

"Amuse yourself then," he said.

"How come you happened to be here, Ray?"

"Like I'd account to you."

There was so much contempt in his voice that, for a moment, Archie suddenly felt like dropping him, felt like driving the man's nose into his face. Instead he walked away and got on with what he had to do.

He took his time. Patsy seemed unsure of her role but she stayed close to him. He saw an empty Black Cat can on Bonnie's dresser and knew from experience that only money or dope would have been stored in it. He glanced at Bonnie's body and suddenly had the overpowering feeling that he had been in some way responsible for her death. That shook him.

When he'd been there as long as he could stand it, he went out of the room, past Reddin, past cops stringing out the caution tape and into the parking lot. Patsy followed; he saw the look of concern plain on her face. He felt sick to his stomach. At the car, he stood in the rain, his hand on the door handle, waiting until the waves of nausea subsided. Patsy got into the car, looked out the window into the rain. He didn't know what she was thinking and, at that moment, he didn't care. Through the window, he heard Fricke's voice on the radio — a demand that Archie come in immediately.

CHAPTER 28

The drive back to headquarters with Patsy involved an uncomfortable silence. When she had tried to talk to him, Archie grew sullen and withdrawn so she gave up trying. Parting at the station door, they adjourned to their separate offices without words. He was losing control of events and he knew she knew it.

He was barely inside when Fricke called him on the interoffice line and ordered him to his office. Archie was not in the mood for a dressing-down from Fricke. He wanted to ignore the summons but that really was out of the question. He kept his jacket on and stalked down the hall. Fricke was busy signing papers, watched over by Chad Reddin, who had returned from the crime scene. Reddin was leaning against a filing cabinet, a phony look of sympathy pasted onto his face.

Archie took a position near the wall opposite Reddin; his black mood deepened. He waited, watching Fricke work over the thick barrel of his fountain pen. Fricke was taking his time, putting off whatever he thought he had to say.

"Doesn't make any sense at all," Fricke said. "All these killings and then John Robbie tooling around like he hasn't got a care in the world don't make sense."

He paused, maybe to let Archie agree with him, or maybe to get some conversation going. Archie kept his thoughts to himself.

"We needed John Robbie in custody, Archie," Fricke said.

"We're still looking."

"Bonnie's death means that you screwed up. You should have had Robbie — not taken off in working hours to go diving. You got an explanation for that?"

"Not right now."

"The thing is, Archie...," Fricke said.

Reddin pushed himself away from the filing cabinet like he was a bouncer about to eject a troublesome guest from a nightclub. Archie had heard that he had been a bouncer before he became a cop. He had the look anyway.

"What he's trying to say, Stevens, is that you can't do the job. You got no sense of what your priorities ought to be and that's an obvious fact."

Archie looked at Fricke.

"What's he doing here anyway?"

Fricke started to say something but Reddin interrupted.

"It's no fucking wonder," he said. "A guy comes right off the fucking reservation and figures he knows everything. You do a few courses and then you get promoted over what you should. There's no fucking way that's right."

"Shut up, Chad," Fricke said. "I'll handle this."

"I'm just saying the truth, Cal. It's what everybody's saying."

Fricke, on the verge of rising, sat back in his chair. Archie wondered if he agreed with Reddin. Reddin wasn't finished.

"You're too much like your old man — a fucking loser. Ray says so."

Archie caught his breath, told himself to walk away. He even turned to go but halfway to the door, the wild thing got loose. He pivoted on the balls of his feet as he grabbed Reddin's shirt and slammed him into the cabinets, upsetting the bowling trophies Fricke had displayed there. Reddin swore and shoved back. Fricke bulked in between the two men.

"Archie, I'm reassigning you."

"Go to Hell."

"I'm not saying that was your fault — but it doesn't look good for the department. You're too new and too inexperienced. You know Mayor Estes questioned the fact that you got the Donaldson case in the first place."

Archie had a hard time making the words.

"So you take away my case. What do you figure I'll do around here?"

"I don't know yet. Ray will handle these new killings. You can do something with the Bill Tran gang stuff — maybe. The poaching and all could keep you busy."

"This stinks."

"Ray's got seniority, and he's got support at city hall. The press is all over this fucking thing."

"You still got a job at least," Reddin said.

Fricke cut him off.

"Shut up, Chad. You cause way too much trouble."

Reddin shrugged, massaged his jaw and then stepped back.

"Look, Arch, Patsy Kydd can work with you, no problem," Fricke said. "Ray doesn't think she has anything to contribute to his investigation anyway."

"She'll help you on clam patrol."

"I told you to shut up, Chad," Fricke said.

"Can't help it, Cal. Stevens rankles me no matter what."

He focussed on Archie.

"I heard what your old man looked like when he died? Him dying there, and begging for help, all ripped up."

Archie wasn't sure what happened, just that suddenly Reddin's face exploded in blood under his fist. All his self-discipline, the holding in, was for nothing. Reddin was bent over. He held his hand to his face, the blood leaking out onto the tiles.

Archie cocked his fist again but Fricke and some other cops from the squad room were all over him, pulling him back. Nothing much he could do about what had happened now. He was well and truly screwed. He just wished that he'd done more than just tag Reddin. He knew that he'd better start thinking about looking for another job. Fricke reinforced that.

"You're suspended, Archie, until further notice."

Archie shook off the arms holding him. The other cops backed off. He took another look at Reddin, who was now standing, holding his nose, mad as hell and cursing. Archie made a dismissive hand motion and then stalked off towards the exit.

Archie was invisible now; other cops passed him in the halls like he had the plague, which left him feeling more isolated than ever. The pain of his humiliation was almost physical and the thought that Reddin had outmanoeuvred him was unbearable. He wanted to pretend that it didn't matter, that it was just one case that hadn't worked out, but he knew better.

His mind was all over the place, like a moth at a lamp, and that didn't help. He knew that he ought to retreat into professionalism. He ought to go to his office and work, or go back and apologize to Fricke. He did neither. He left the building, got into his car and drove off, heading for the town limits.

CHAPTER 29

Shivering, Archie climbed out of the pool, dried himself off, and stood on a flat rock, waited as his uncle Tony cleansed him with sweet grass smoke and eagle feathers. Tony, haloed by the early morning sun and smoke, asked him if he felt better after the Sweat.

"Less confused, for sure," Archie said. "Yes, better. Was there an animal, like a mink in there with us last night?"

"I told you that you had a gift," Tony said.

"What was it?"

"Better to say who. I can't talk about what you saw without risking offense to him."

"I don't actually believe I saw anything," Archie said. "I'm not really thinking straight this morning."

"You saw what most people couldn't. Leave it at that for the time being. Did you learn what you wanted in there?"

Tony nodded in the direction of the still-smoking sweat lodge.

"I don't know," Archie said. "I'm tired and scalded. Now I'm frozen. But I feel stronger and I'm thinking clearer. I wasn't asking for solutions and didn't get any."

"That's the way it is sometimes. You get what you need not what you think you need."

Archie nodded in agreement. Then he got slowly to his feet.

"I have to get going, Tony. I'm still employed as far as I know — or maybe I'm not. Thanks for helping me out. You didn't smell something like coyote last night did you? Just for a second, just before dawn."

"Nope, but I know the coyote is not your friend. If you smell coyote, head for the hills. For you, bear smell is good; coyote smell means danger."

"Sure, if you say so. You've helped me lots over the years, Tony. I'm just starting to realize how much."

"I'm your uncle, which for our people means I'm more like your father. I'm happy when you come to me."

"Usually I can handle things but lately it's like I'm climbing a mountain with a sack of rocks on my back."

Tony laughed as he buttoned up his shirt.

"We all think we can handle things on our own. That's our big-headedness always getting the better of us — but I know what you mean."

Back in the Dodge and still shivering, Archie checked his messages. Thomas Lee had sent him a text, reminding him about the archives information — like it had been Archie's fault that Lee hadn't delivered it. Archie made a resolution to try to be more careful with peoples' feelings, and not only because it was the right thing to do. In the meantime, he was famished. He saw the sign for Avril's Donut Shop and made the turn.

Half an hour later, with a Trucker Breakfast under his belt, he was back on the road, fighting the old Dodge's tendency to drift to the right. He had texted Lee but he still hadn't had a reply — that worried him a little. He tried Patsy but got the message that she had the day off and was unavailable.

He thought about recent events, more clearly now after the sweat. He thought it unlikely that Robbie had killed Bonnie Tran. It didn't jive with anything he knew about the man. Tran would be looking for Bonnie's killer, certainly. If he decided it was Robbie then Robbie was toast. He ran through the three murders, Donaldson, the decapitated woman, Rochelle, and now Bonnie. The odd one out was Bonnie but what did that mean?

He reviewed as he drove. He had a good idea what had happened at Nick's on the night he died. Drugs were involved, likely cocaine. Abalone poaching too, but that was incidental. Robbie had been at Donaldson's Dive Adventures that night. That was certain. He had found something there that changed everything for him, something more than the body of his partner. And he hadn't killed Donaldson.

He tried Lee again but still couldn't connect. He began to think that maybe Lee was still irked after all. He put that thought aside, avoiding getting into a mood about it. Bonnie Tran's funeral was the next day. Bill would certainly attend. Archie wanted to talk to him before that. He put in a call to an informant he knew and learned where Tran spent most of his time. As a gangster with a moderately high profile, his location, for many reasons, was the subject of curiosity — and was monitored by many.

Because Tran likely knew the Dodge he was driving, Archie left it in the parking lot of a mall at the edge of Empire City. Then he took a cab to Magic Nails, an acrylic fingernail outlet in a strip mall — Tran ran his businesses out of the back of the shop.

Archie found a vantage point in the window of a coffee shop across the highway and watched. Tran came out of the place just after noon. His man, Jumbo, led the way, then Tran, then Scorpion. The three lingered for five minutes or so, smoking and talking. Finally Tran said something to Scorpion and he and Jumbo walked to a black Land Rover, got in and drove out of the parking lot. Tran lit another cigarette, smoked it leisurely, tossed the butt away and went back into Magic Nails. Archie paid for his third coffee, walked out, crossed the road to the front door of Magic Nails and went inside.

The shop was busy — four or five women were having their nails done. The manager, a tiny Vietnamese woman, looked up from a computer screen and asked Archie if she could help him. Archie shook his head. He walked past her and through the door at the rear. The manager, angry now, followed, a loud and persistent tail.

At the noise, Bill Tran appeared from out of a side door. He had changed into a white tracksuit, the blue stripes incongruously sporty. He saw Archie, waved the manager back, and motioned Archie to follow him through the scuffed hollow-panel door and into a small office furnished with a small metal desk, an easy chair, a T.V. and little else. Tran turned to face Archie. He half sat on the edge of the desk and folded his arms across his chest.

"I thought you got the message," he said.

"I don't get messages," Archie said. "It's a failing of mine."

Tran traced the outline of his right orbit with his finger and then examined the tip for whatever he hoped to find there.

"I've been waiting for you," Tran said. "I knew somebody would come from Harsley but I figured the visit would look a lot more official than a suspended detective."

Archie wondered how Tran knew about his suspension.

"I wanted to see you in private," Archie said. "Before Bonnie's funeral happened."

"If you came to tell me to keep my cool, you might as well go home."

He bowed his head for the briefest of moments. Archie found it surprising. He thought for that instant that Bill really was touched with grief, but the look in the man's eyes when he looked up dispelled that illusion. Tran shook his head.

"They had Emile Pared call to tell me. Can you imagine that? I hate that fucker and everybody knows it."

This came as a surprise. Normally, his own department would have sent Ray Jameson, the lead detective now on Bonnie's case. He had to assume that somebody had passed the duty onto Pared. In any case, it went against procedure and whoever did it would have known that it would only antagonize Tran further.

"I'm sorry about Bonnie," Archie said. "I truly am. I'm still looking for John Robbie and I wanted to find out from you where he is."

Tran laughed.

"You have to be joking."

"I'd rather you didn't kill him."

"Would you now? What if I told you that I wouldn't touch a hair on his little weasel head?"

"Then I'd consider that a promise."

"Let's wait and see. I saw you waiting so I sent my boys out for cigarettes. They'll be back any minute.'

"I don't give a shit about those two."

"You still got the marks from last time."

"Yeah, I owe you for that. Lay off Robbie and we'll call it even. Otherwise I'll forget I'm a cop. Right now I got little to lose anyway."

They stood there; neither one looking away. The hum of women's voices, of the spray guns and air pumps seemed far away. But the stink of nail lacquer and other chemicals from the front area permeated the air, making it difficult to breathe. Finally, Tran scratched his temple with his fingertips.

"I'll think about it Archie, for old times' sake. I didn't like laying a beating on you but that's the way things happen sometime. Now, do you mind leaving me with my grief?"

Archie nodded and turned to go.

"What I can't figure out, Bill, is what exactly you're up to."

"Early days. Maybe one day you will. Who knows?"

"I guess."

Archie left it at that. He walked out through the nail shop; conversations and nail work stopping as he passed. He was glad to be out of there. He had no confidence at all that Bill would do what he said. He tried, once again, to contact Thomas Lee but without success. He was about to start the Dodge when Fricke called him to tell him Thomas Lee was lying unconscious in a ward at Harsley General. He had been ambushed and shot.

CHAPTER 30

Archie stopped an IC doctor who was on his way to the ward, got an update on Lee's condition, which was that he was in an induced coma but there was hope. Lee had been hooked up to drips and monitors and was not yet breathing on his own. Archie continued through the wards until he got to Lee's room. He nodded in the direction of the constable sitting down the hall, apparently on guard duty, and got a brief wave in return.

Lee's partner, Philip, was at his bedside, had been since Lee had been brought in. Someone had made up a cot for him, which meant that he planned on staying. They talked about Thomas awhile before Philip excused himself, saying that he wanted to get a cup of tea. Archie, worried that whoever had tried to kill Lee might try again, figured he could trust Philip at least — he wasn't as sure he could rely on the department to provide protection. When his nurse came, Archie asked her about the things Lee had on him when he was admitted.

"They're in his night table, locked up."

"I'd like to see them."

She hesitated, took a ring of keys from the pocket of her smock, knelt and opened the night table door, retrieved the basket containing Lee's things and passed it to Archie. She lingered as he checked through them.

"Did he have anything else on him?"

"Just what you see except his cellphone and gun. A cop named Reddin took those."

"There was nothing else?"

She put her hand to her cheek, rolled her eyes towards the ceiling, trying to remember.

"Yes — there was a notebook, spiral bound. The policeman took that away too."

He handed back the basket containing Lee's things. When she had gone, he lingered at Lee's side, waited until Philip returned. Archie asked him if he was going to stay with Lee. Philip nodded.

"Where else would I go?"

Archie wasn't used to giving comfort. He knew he should say something to help. Instead, he said, "I've got to go." He turned away.

"He'll make it," Philip said. "Thom and I belong to the Harsley Operatic Society. Some of the other members are going to spell me."

"That's good. Better he's not alone.

"He won't be."

Archie's mind returned to the undelivered message.

"I don't see his computer tablet. You don't have it, do you?"

"Not me — I wondered about that myself. Maybe he left it at his apartment, charging or something."

"You don't have a key to his place, do you?"

Philip nodded. He scanned Archie's face as if trying to make up his mind if he ought to trust Archie or not. Finally, he dug into his pocket and hauled out his key ring. He wrestled with the key and the ring for a moment or two, separated it from the others and handed it to Archie.

"He has a security system. The panel is just inside the door. You have 15 seconds to enter the code — 45784."

Archie repeated the code and then pocketed the key.

"Call Detective Kydd or Chief Fricke if anything goes haywire. Don't trust anybody else," he said.

Philip looked concerned but nodded. Archie wasn't sure what else he could do at the hospital

— it wasn't a place where he felt comfortable anyway. He made his exit as gracefully as possible. He had no time to waste. The tablet that Thomas was never without should have been amongst his things.

He went first to Lee's office, made a surreptitious search but didn't find the tablet there either. Nor was it at Lee's spartan apartment. He searched the condo thoroughly, feeling slightly awkward about invading Lee's personal space, but drew a blank. Finally, he drove back to the police compound — empty at that time of day. He found Lee's car, got his Slim Jim, had the door open in ten seconds and easily disarmed the alarm. He reflected briefly on the irony that his misspent youth made things he was doing as a cop much easier.

The tablet wasn't anywhere obvious. He was starting to think that Lee's attackers might already have it but he had a strong, inexplicable feeling that the device was hidden in the car — that Lee had been smart and concealed it well before the ambush. He tried to think what Lee would do if he knew he was being followed and might be caught, and where he might have concealed something so important if he had enough time to do it. Lee was careful to a fault. Archie didn't doubt that he would have pre-picked places to hide things in his vehicle.

He contemplated the interior for a few moments. Then pushed back the seats and felt around under them. The device was tucked into a pocket sewn into the under-fabric. Archie eased it out of its hiding place, put the seats back the way they had been, relocked the door and left.

Later, at a corner table at Avril's Donut Shop, he figured out the word "Philip" was the password — so much for Lee's security. Archie unlocked the device and began to read. What he learned worried him. He shut down the tablet and put it away.

He sat for a moment, considering his options. He tried and failed to contact Patsy Kydd. That worried him. Then he called dispatch to ask about her.

Delia John took the call. She said she'd overheard Patsy talking to Stone about going to Parcelle Island to look at where some skeletons had been found. Other than that she wasn't sure. She told Archie that she wasn't supposed to be giving information to a detective suspended from a case he seemed unwilling to let go. She laughed. Then she asked about Thomas and ended the call. Archie wondered how that had come about — that Patsy had taken it on herself to go alone to Parcelle Island. She was on days off — that's what he thought. He drove to her house, but her car was gone and the lights were out when he passed. He left another message on her phone and carried on.

CHAPTER 31

It was too late in the day to go to Parcelle Island, but Archie had no desire to go home. He still ached a little from the beating he'd had from Tran's boys, and from his experiences on Cat's Cradle; his eyes were scratchy with fatigue. He thought about calling Streya, thought about paying her a visit, but changed his mind. As he drove, he wracked his brain, trying to reconcile all parts of the puzzle. Dealing with the overlapping pieces tested him; trying to solve them one at a time only seemed to confuse matters. He knew, almost instinctively, that John Robbie was important but he still couldn't quite understand how the man fit into the whole. It didn't help that he didn't have any idea where Robbie was. Bill Tran might know but he wasn't saying.

Archie stopped for a bite at the Satsuma — it being on his way. He saw nobody there he knew but, as he watched out the window, he saw Arnie Bulkwetter across the lot.

Bulkwetter was at the top of his stairs, his hand on his office door, talking with Mayor Tom Estes. He seemed to be trying to convince Estes of something but Estes seemed angry and resistant. Finally, Estes made a dismissive motion and hurried down the steps. At the bottom, he turned and yelled something at Bulkwetter. Then he got into his car and drove away. Bulkwetter gave the car a mock salute. Then he made his way down the stairs and across the lot to the Satsuma. He seemed surprised to see Archie and not happy about it either, but he put on a grin and lumbered to Archie's booth.

"You look like hell, Detective," he said.

Archie shrugged. He could smell the liquor on the man's breath and Bulkwetter was sweating. As Archie studied his face, Bulkwetter's eyes darted to the kitchen.

"Lisa doesn't seem to be here, Arnie, if that's who you're looking for."

"I had some business with her but I got errands to do."

"Why don't you sit for a minute? We can talk."

Bulkwetter shifted his feet. He seemed nervous and Archie's curiosity naturally increased.

"You look like you've got something on your mind, Arnie? I'll buy you a coffee. We can talk."

"I'd like to linger, Archie, I really would. I'd like to chitchat but I got to get going. I'll have to take a rain check."

"Whatever's best for you, Arn. You haven't seen Lars Norgard recently have you? I'd like to talk to him."

"He hasn't been around. Look, Arch, I've really got to go. I'll see you."

For a large man, Bulkwetter could move quickly when he wanted to. He was out the door before Archie could say more.

Natalie Lindeman brought him a menu. She smiled at him like she was genuinely glad to see him. Archie ordered a sandwich and coffee, picked up the morning paper and scanned through it. He saw an editorial on derelict boats in the Coffin Bay anchorage, a rant against dumping unusable, junk craft and about the district's need to clean up the waters. It was a fortuitous read. It reminded him that a few years back, Lars Norgard had lived on a boat in Coffin Bay.

His order arrived and he started to eat, pulling up maps on his smartphone as he did so. Coffin Bay was a busy fishing harbour in summer but off-season, it was virtually deserted. A man who didn't want to be found could do worse than to take up residence on one of the twenty or so boats mouldering away at anchor there. He zoomed in on a cluster of three of the larger boats; saw that one had a small tender tied to the aft rail, suspected that that might be the right vessel. He'd have to hurry. It was already dark; if Norgard was coming ashore, he'd be doing so when he couldn't be seen. Archie called for the bill, left a generous tip, and headed for the Dodge.

At Coffin Bay, Archie parked his car up behind the service bar, which was closed for the season. Then he walked down to the wharf, stopped above the adjoining beach, and scanned the scene. He planned to wait — all night if necessary, hoping that Norgard would show. Norgard would likely leave his cramped quarters as often as he could. Archie wasn't looking forward to the wait; the damp cold was bone penetrating. He shivered and stuck his hands deep in his pockets. At least, he'd eaten and had enough Satsuma coffee in him to keep him awake. In the darkness, widgeon whistled to each other on the black water below him.

He looked for a place to conceal himself, found a spot behind storm-deposited and interlocked driftwood and made himself as comfortable as possible in the hollow behind a huge cedar stump. He was out of sight, he hoped, of anyone coming ashore from the moored boats, about fifty feet from the shoreline. He could make out the dim waterline and the beach through the screen of twisted roots. He had waited for about an hour when the onshore breeze carried the sound of creaking oars and moving water to him. He rose, stiffly, from his hiding place with the SIG already cocked. He was waiting at the beach when the dinghy came ashore; its occupant shipped oars and stepped out onto the shingle. Archie flashed the Maglite beam and John Robbie turned to meet it. The light showed a haggard face lined with worry and strain.

"Hello, John," Archie said. "I wasn't expecting you."

"Hello, Archie." The tone was halfway between exasperation and resignation. "I didn't expect you either. How'd you find me?"

He tossed the painter end into the boat and waved Archie's light away from his face. Archie thought Robbie looked a century older than when he had last seen him. He uncocked his pistol, put the safety on, slid the gun into his jacket pocket. Robbie hauled out a pack of Winstons, tapped one out, lit it.

"I was looking for Lars actually. You're an added bonus."

"You won't find Lars. He's long gone."

"Gone?"

"He left on my money. I never did trust that prick and he proved me right. Can I tie up my dinghy?"

"No need for that — I'm going to use it. Come on up and don't do anything stupid."

Robbie laughed, shook his head.

"It's too late for that. My whole life has been doing stupid."

He climbed the bank, head down. When he got to where Archie was standing, he stuck out his wrists ready for the cuffs. Archie clapped one on the right wrist and then turned Robbie around and secured the other so that Robbie's hands were behind his back.

"John Alan Robbie I'm arresting you on suspicion of murder. You have the right to a lawyer..."

"Spare me the rest," Robbie said. "I know it off by heart."

Archie laughed and finished what he had to say. Then he marched Robbie up to the Dodge and put him in the back seat.

"The longer I'm down there searching that boat you've been living in, the colder you're going to get sitting in the back of this cruiser, John."

"You won't be searching long," Robbie said. "I got sloppy, not careful enough. Beyond that, I got nothing to say."

"That's up to you, John. It must be tough being in the middle like you are. Anyway, I'll be back for you when I've checked out your lodgings."

He closed the door. Robbie, hands cuffed behind his back, stared straight ahead. Archie made a quick circuit of the area but, so far as he could see, there was no one else around. After checking his messages, of which there were none, Archie started down towards the beach and the dinghy. As he suspected, Robbie had a weapon, a sawn-off shotgun, lying on the forward bench. Archie unloaded it and wedged it firmly into a narrow space between the hull and the seat bracket.

It wasn't easy finding Robbie's boat in the dark but after bumping up against two other derelicts and checking them out, Archie found the right one; identified it by the high rail he'd seen on the zoom. He tied off the dinghy, checked the SIG in its holster and then climbed aboard. He crossed the deck silently, keeping low, listening for sounds that might indicate that anyone else was aboard. Finally, he opened the door and went inside.

The boat was a derelict on the outside but inside, Norgard, or Robbie, had created a comfortable living space, complete with a leather recliner, a small TV, and an oriental carpet. There was also a laptop. Now that he was closer, perhaps, to an arrest, he resisted the temptation to check through its files without a warrant. Even doing what he was doing was close to an illegal search and could get any case he built against Robbie thrown out of court. As it was, he could claim that he was looking for Lars Norgard who he assumed might be present — anyway there was a warrant out for Robbie. So long as he didn't cross that invisible line between legal and illegal, Archie was probably okay. He started to search and found the coins right away.

CHAPTER 32

The two Brother Eli coins lay on the galley table, along with some other items that looked vaguely religious, including a rusted wavy-bladed dagger. The purple velvet pouch in which Robbie had kept the coins lay nearby.

Archie photographed everything with his phone camera but left the things where they were. He examined the rest of the boat, found Robbie's phone, and checked it for recent calls. Bill Tran had called and, to Archie's surprise, so had Jim Stone — three times. Nick Donaldson had also called the day he died. Archie slipped the phone in his pocket.

He turned out the light, waited until his night vision returned and went on deck. Back in the car, Robbie would be shivering by now. Archie climbed down into the dinghy, unhitched it and rowed to shore. After he'd beached the boat, he retrieved the empty shotgun and walked up to where he'd left the Dodge. He stopped and stared. The Dodge was gone and John Robbie with it. Archie cursed and rapped the gravel with the butt of the shotgun. After a minute or so, he called Pete Wilson.

Pete arrived a half hour later. He didn't ask Archie why he was afoot although the question would certainly have occurred to him. Pete was used to waiting for people to tell him things in their own good time. If they didn't feel the need to explain, that was okay with Pete too. Archie's visit to the reservation seemed to have been enough to patch up their friendship. He had always known he would have to make the first move. He guessed he'd made it. As far as Pete was concerned, picking up a buddy in the middle of the night was just something a friend did without asking the reason why.

Archie climbed into the cab of the pickup and dropped the sawn-off shotgun on the floor. He grunted thanks to Pete and then asked him to take him to the police station.

"You're wondering what I'm doing out here afoot, aren't you?"

He was angry at himself and he imagined the tone of his voice likely reflected it but Pete seemed amused. He put the pickup into gear.

"It's your business. I imagine it's either cop-related or else you got a girl out here. I'm only curious to a point, especially about your fabled love life."

Archie shook his head. Losing a prisoner, handcuffed in the back of his own vehicle, was embarrassing. He still couldn't figure out how it happened. He surprised himself by blurting it out, by telling Pete what had happened. Pete roared with laughter.

"Jeez, Archie! You mean your prisoner un-handcuffed himself and then stole your car?"

Archie was not in the mood to be kidded.

"Shut up, Pete. It's not that funny."

"It's funny. You'll see the humour in it one day."

"I know you're right but today isn't the day."

Pete snorted through his nose trying unsuc-cessfully to stifle his laughter.

Archie looked out the side window. Robbie's escape meant that he had help, that the place wasn't as deserted as Archie had thought. He'd have to report the Dodge stolen; he wasn't sure he had the balls to go to the station and endure the scorn that Jameson, Reddin, Humber, and the rest would lay on him. It made sense if Bill Tran was Robbie's help. He had rescued his man and that told Archie a great deal. The loss of the Dodge could be a small, if embarrassing, price to pay. He resigned himself to the inevitable and called in and reported the theft of his car. He heard Delia repeat his words and then loud laughter from somebody in the office before he clicked off.

Pete, hungry, insisted they stop by Avril's Donut Shop for something to eat. They parked and walked to the front door; saw Walter George through the window; the place was otherwise deserted except for Avril, the owner. Walter, a regular at Avril's, spotted them and waved them over as they walked through the door. Pete pointed to the Canuck cup in Walter's hand.

"Now he's taking it out on dates. Can you believe it?"

"Can't let down my guard," Walter said. "What are you two up to?"

"I'm just giving Archie a lift — seems he lost his police car."

They called over to Avril for coffee and donuts. The lights were harsh and the bright melamine table tops an affront to Archie's tired eyes. They sat down; Archie slouched in his seat, almost too tired to be hungry.

He listened as Pete told Walter about the car. Walter laughed so hard he almost choked on a mouthful of coffee. When he had recovered, he looked over the rim of his dirty-blue cup at Archie, said, "I remember when we were kids.

Archie borrowed a cruiser one night to get us home and now he's lost one. What goes around comes around as they say."

"I hope not or this is only the beginning but you might have something there, Walter," Pete said.

Avril brought over their order. Walter put down his cup. He looked serious.

"I heard Thomas Lee got shot," he said. "I'm sorry to hear it. Thomas is a good guy, always fair."

Archie nodded, took a swallow of scalding coffee.

"Thanks. He's a good cop too. They got him in an induced coma right now. They're hopeful."

"Are you making any progress on the Nick Donaldson killing?"

"I'm more or less suspended right now. Maybe I'm halfway out the door for all I know. Otherwise Thomas Lee's in IC in the hospital and Patsy Kydd took the weekend off. I'm working by myself in a kind of unauthorized lone wolf fashion."

Walter said, "You were interested in Cat's Cradle Island, right?"

"I sure am."

"I saw Jim Stone yesterday. He was coming from the direction of Cat's Cradle in that little

boat you cops use. You guys got something official going on over there."

Archie shook his head. He was very focussed now.

"He had Patsy Kydd with him on the way
out," Walter said.

"And on the way back?" Archie said.

"No — he was alone when I saw him later."

"You do mean yesterday afternoon?"

"Yeah, it was yesterday afternoon."

"If he had her with him, they would have
gone to Parcelle Island, not Cat's Cradle. There
were some bones found there and maybe she
went to check the area out. Stoney has a boat so
he'd be the natural guy to take her."

Walter set his cup down, screwed up his
face. He looked at Archie with one eye cocked.

"Arch, when I see a babe like Patsy Kydd, I
know it. And Stoney was coming from Cat's
Cradle Island, not from Parcelle, though that's in
the same direction. He didn't have her with him
later. My best guess is that he'd been to Monkey
Beach because that would be the heading he was
coming back on."

"That doesn't make any sense," Archie said.

"Just telling you what I saw. You want that
donut or can I have it?"

Archie was already on his feet.

"It's all yours, Walt. I've got to go. I need to borrow your pickup, Pete. You mind?"

Pete rolled his eyes. Then he tossed his keys to Archie.

CHAPTER 33

Archie stopped at Patsy Kydd's to check to see if she was home but there were no lights on in the house. There were signs that she had been there recently though, like yesterday's newspaper in the blue recycling box. He went looking for her car and found it almost out of sight behind a cube van at the end of the next block. That was unusual. He returned to her house and knocked on her front door. When he didn't get an answer, he went around the back and broke in. He felt awkward doing that and had to remind himself of his purpose, which was to confirm to himself that she hadn't returned from Parcelle Island — or Cat's Cradle Island for that matter. He wasn't sure what he'd do if she actually came home and found him inside her home.

She had an old-fashioned answering machine for her landline and he forced himself to check her messages. One of the messages was from Jim Stone, asking Patsy to meet him at the wharf. That would have been yesterday.

Archie left the house. In his vehicle, he called Pete Wilson and was able to talk him into taking his boat, Cherish to Parcelle Island, which should have been Patsy's destination and therefore the best place to start. When Archie arrived at the dock, Pete and his boat were waiting, lights on. Pete pushed the starter as Archie jumped aboard and backed her out into the harbour.

When they were underway, Archie and Pete discussed strategy. It was possible that Walter was wrong about Cat's Cradle Island being Stone's destination, but Pete doubted that Walter would make such a mistake. Archie grunted agreement and nodded at the glowing green screen of the radar, which showed the outline of Cat's Cradle off to starboard and the smaller Parcelle dead ahead.

"Lots of steep drops on that island. Best wait for daylight," Pete said.

"Sounds about right."

It was barely light when they arrived at the landing on Parcelle Island. Pete, yawning, eased the boat in on the current. Archie knew that the landing was one of the few safe places to go ashore. He looked up at the sheer cliffs that climbed up into the heavy overcast, which were shorn off by the cloud layer a few hundred feet above his head. The island was a sanctuary for seabirds. It was uninhabited and only rarely visited. On sunny days, the cliffs rising out of the deep green water made for spectacular scenery; on misty, wet days, like today, Parcelle Island was forbidding.

Pete accelerated up the current past the dock and then throttled down. He let the boat drift back to the float and held it there expertly. Archie jumped out onto the surprisingly sound dock and hitched the bowline to a cleat and waited while Pete cut the motor and jumped down off the boat and secured the stern. Almost immediately, Archie's communicator squawked and he heard Stone's voice, incomplete because of the static. The call ended abruptly. Pete made an interrogative gesture with his right hand but Archie shrugged and put the device in his pocket.

"The cliffs screw up the signal — just as well. I don't want to talk to him just yet. He knows way more than I do right now."

"Shouldn't you ask him about Patsy?"

"No phone connection anyway. When I ask him, it will be in person."

The fact that Stone had tried to call was significant. Archie wondered what he was up to. He searched the area near where they landed, found woman-sized footprints in a patch of mud close to the trail and big boot prints near them. Other prints confused the track. Beyond the landing area, rocky ground frustrated him. He gave up trying to interpret the tracks in the mud and rocks. When Pete looked at him, he shrugged.

"Might become clearer higher up," Archie said.

He consulted the map of the island he'd brought, folded it over so that the two side by side red X's he'd marked on it from memory were visible, saw the contour lines bunching tight together, marking the bowl where the cave was supposed to be. That was high above them, on a ledge under the cliffs. He indicated the path with a nod of his head.

"We'd better do this. Before the fog gets any thicker."

Pete said, "Right."

Archie led the way up the trail. Pete shouldered the pack he had brought and followed. When they got high enough, he pointed to a knife-edge of pale sandstone, hundreds of feet high, on Cat's Cradle Island across the channel.

"That's Cormer's Surprise, that straight drop over there."

"Why do they call it Cormer's Surprise?"

"A guy named Cormer, connected to the Brother Eli group, walked straight off about fifty years ago — three hundred feet straight down."

"First time I heard about that," Archie said.

"Lots of stories are buried around here."

They continued upwards. The trail was well marked but overgrown, partially blocked by trees blown down in autumn storms. They were able to get around most the fallen trunks and branches but had to climb over some and scramble under others. Archie pointed to a side trail.

"We go that way. You getting tired?"

"Before you get tired — never. But I can think of better ways than this of spending my time."

"You're growing that belly — just wondered."

"Don't worry about me, Archie."

They had to struggle through more deadfall. The trail went up and then plunged into a steep-sided depression lined with tangled alder and Vine Maple. Cormer's Surprise rose high on the opposite shore. Fog had started to fill up the channel and was following them up the trail.

They made their way higher and then suddenly the trail was clear and easy to follow. They found the cave without difficulty, its entrance a low, horizontal notch at the foot of a spur of harder siltstone. Pete sat down on a rock to catch his breath after the steep climb. Archie, hiding his worry, scanned for signs that Patsy had been there.

He walked over to the cave mouth and crawled inside, used his flashlight to check the interior, which was more spacious than he expected but empty. On one wet rock, he saw two more footprints, little more than muddy smears. One was the same size as the small ones he'd seen earlier; the other was from a large boot — the mark of a size thirteen police-issue sole. Feeling a new sense of urgency, he eased himself back out of the cave and onto the cleared, flat space, the porch in front of the cavern. Outside, Pete, seated on a rock, munched a sandwich, a thermos cup of coffee in his other hand. He raised the cup.

"Want some?"

"In a bit, maybe. I have to think."

"Tough to do two things at the same time, I should know."

"I'm going to check around a bit more. You might as well relax."

"Exactly what I plan to do."

Archie walked around the clearing. The natural bowl in which the cave was situated was almost like a miniature auditorium, or place of ceremonial, made more spectacular by Cormer's Surprise on the opposite shore, rising above the trees like the prow of a great ship. Below him, the fog roiled heavy in the channel like a river of smoke.

He left Pete with his sandwiches and coffee and climbed back down to the trail, hurrying more than he should. He put his foot on some wet moss and missed his footing, slipped part way down the rock face, caught himself, cursed, turned to look back. Then he saw them — a line of darker curiously shaped stones set every three feet or so — almost invisible amongst the broken rocks under the rim but there nonetheless. He scrambled back up, lost sight of them, and then found them again.

The stones were pentagons, each about two feet across. He squatted down, took out his notebook and sketched the line of them. Then he laid the notebook down, reached for the nearest rock and tried to move it. When the stone refused to budge, he sat, chin in hand, and contemplated it.

One of his techniques was to slow down the process of looking by turning it into close observation. He did this now with the stones, listing in detail everything he observed — stones angled at thirty degrees, facing Cormer's Surprise; slightly darker than the surrounding stone; edges chamfered, thinner at the lower left and upper right; corners slightly grooved as if for hand-holds.

That gave him an idea. He moved to the closest stone, grasped the opposing left and right corners and tried a clockwise turn. When that didn't work, he tried counter-clockwise. The block moved in his hands, rasping and squealing, and then he was able to turn it. It came away abruptly to reveal a dark, squared cavity. He realized that he had been holding his breath and reminded himself to breathe. Then he got down on all fours and peered inside. Through dead eyes, a woman stared back; coils of blond hair wrapped her temples.

He steadied himself. He had started when he saw the head and he shook his head at his reaction. He looked again. The head sat on a decorated pedestal, neck down. The skin was stark white and the lips were tight and thin across the maxilla. Symbols covered the walls of the niche, and a small bag of desiccant lay open at the base of the pedestal, presumably to speed mummification. It was all quite remarkable.

He got to his feet, followed the line of stones, chose another, tried to turn the slab. When it refused to budge, he reset his hands and pushed harder until the stone turned in its grooves and he was able to lift it out. The niche also contained a head, older, its blond owner long dead, about the age of the female skeleton he had seen in the police lab. He snapped some pictures with his phone camera and made brief notes. He stopped when he heard a noise on the trail above. He turned to see Pete standing there, a stunned look on his face.

"So, it's all true about the Divine Spirits." Pete's voice was barely audible. "I heard you fall so I came to take a look."

He looked past Archie.

"What's that over there?" he asked.

He pointed to a small patch of navy blue under a bush. Archie slid down and retrieved it. It was a police ball cap. He turned it over and saw Patsy's name in black where she had written it. He held it up for Pete to see.

"We got to go," he said. "Right away."

They went down to the boat and went aboard. An hour and a half later, and after a car ride, Archie dropped Pete off at Avril's. He refused to tell Pete what he intended to do. Back on the island, before he found the heads, Archie had decided it was time to visit Stone.

Stone lived in an apartment above an auto parts shop away from all other buildings in the north end of town. The auto shop was long closed when Archie arrived but lights shone from second floor windows. He parked out of sight behind the building and got out. He checked the loads in his pistol, opened the side door and went up the stairs. On the landing, he listened at Stone's door. He stood to one side of it and knocked. The strong supernatural stink of coyote almost nauseated him.

Stoney yelled out something Archie couldn't quite make out. Archie called out his name, declaring that he was passing by and wanted to talk. There were a few moments of silence and then Stoney shouted that he should come in. Archie opened the door with his left hand, his right on the butt of the SIG Sauer in his jacket pocket. Stone was sitting in a recliner, pulled upright; the chair was skewed half away from the door so that his right hand was hidden behind the arm of the chair. He did not smile.

"What can I do for you, Archie?"

"I think you know what I'm here for, Jim."

"I do."

He saw the movement just in time and threw himself to one side. Stone fired three deafening shots from a Colt .45 Government. Then he struggled out of his recliner, flailing the big automatic as he fought for his balance. Archie fired, half-heard, half-sensed the SIG Sauer's nine-millimeter slugs tear into Stone's gut. Stoney stumbled and fell, the Colt sliding away from his hand. Archie, shaken, walked over, kicked it away. His ears rang from the shots. Stone held his bleeding midsection, "You're a better shot than me, huh, Archie? Fuck you."

Archie, feeling strangely detached, sat down on the edge of the couch, the SIG Sauer held loosely in his hand. He looked across at Stone, felt the adrenalin pumping through his body. He waited for Stone to settle. Stone tried to move towards his pistol, failed, swore through clenched teeth, and lay back down. Then Archie watched, as if it were a scene in a movie, as Stone pulled himself up so that his back rested against the arm of the recliner. The front of his blue shirt was soaked dark with blood.

"You got to get me some help, Arch." The voice was soft, pleading, no defiance now. "Gut shot is not good."

Archie leaned forward, slid his SIG Sauer into his jacket pocket, no need for it now. He sat on the edge of the sofa.

"I have to find out what you did with Patsy, Stoney?"

Stoney tried to laugh.

"Oh — her — I figured you'd come for her. You got a thing for her. I could tell. Streya could too."

"You want me to call an ambulance, Jim?"

Stoney groaned, squirmed against the pain.

"Arch — she wanted to go to Parcelle and that's the truth. I dropped her off. They wouldn't have done anything to her yet... Shit — I need help right away, man."

"I reckon you do — you'll be dead in an hour otherwise. What do you mean — they wouldn't have done anything?"

He saw the fear in Stoney's eyes.

"What's going on, Stoney?"

"Things got fucked up. Somebody fucked up."

He almost spat out the words.

"And Patsy?"

"They have her — for the ritual...two birds with one stone."

"What ritual? And who fucked things up?"

"Everybody, everything, Archie — Jesus, this hurts."

"Tell me quickly, Jim. Give me names. Then I'll call for an ambulance."

Stoney nodded and then started to talk, words in torrents. He said he'd taken Patsy to Monkey Beach. He spoke about meetings on Monkey Beach, about the sacrifices, about using human heads to focus cosmic energy. When he thought Stone had said all he was capable of saying, the old cop picked up the pace again, sometimes cursing, sometimes pleading. He told Archie about Brother Eli's children — the sons and daughters of the prophet. He passed out before he could tell Archie their names. Archie walked over, felt for a pulse but Stone was dead.

For a few minutes, he sat on a chair and studied Stoney's inert form, a thousand thoughts rushing through his mind. Then he got up, and made a quick search of the apartment. In Stoney's small office he found a photograph of three young men and a boy, brothers maybe. He recognized Stoney right away — Arnie Bulkwetter and Tom Estes too. The boy looked familiar but he couldn't quite place the face. At last, he was starting to understand. With his gloves on, he took the photo out of its frame. Then he dumped the frame into the wastepaper basket near the desk.

He had lingered long enough. Hurriedly, he wiped his prints off everything he might have touched and then, disguising his voice, he called for an ambulance from Stone's phone. He went out using the fire escape. When he found the opportunity, he would need to lose the SIG in the deepest water he could find. Otherwise he'd likely have to fight a murder charge. He was amazed at how complicated his life had become. With Thomas Lee in hospital and himself a pariah at the station, he would have to go find Patsy alone. He had to get to Cat's Cradle Island as soon as possible if he hoped to save her. He didn't want to expose Pete to the risk. Archie would have to get a boat himself.

What had happened at Stoney's had shaken him. He drove awhile, pulled off the highway as soon as he thought it safe to do so. His hands shook. His state of mind worried him. He felt disconnected from events and he hated the sensation.

He was thinking about his options when Streya Wainright called him. He knew that she had a runabout that would get him to the island; she might also know something about the Children of Eli that would help him find Patsy. Stone had said as much. Without thinking too much about the possible complications, he asked her. He was obscure about his true mission. She said she would come with him, that she would meet him at the dock at first light. He ended the call. A faint coyote smell lingered in the air.

CHAPTER 34

He had parked close to the wharf and was standing beside Pete's pickup when Streya drove into the lot. She smiled when she saw him. She seemed cheery, unnaturally so. Her mood bothered him; he knew that it could change in an instant.

Fatigue plus what had happened at Stone's had him in a strange otherworldly mental state anyway — moments of fitful sleep had been a theater for disturbing and confused dream fragments. He almost told Streya more but decided against it. Her good mood wasn't likely to last considering how he planned to use her. He made some small talk; he was aware that she was searching his face and watching his eyes. He turned away, motioned towards her boat, a battered, 12-foot Zodiac. He had borrowed a machete from Pete's truck and he placed it near the bow and then climbed aboard.

"I'm ready," he said.

She took her seat at the outboard and he cast off.

"I appreciate that you're giving me a lift. You didn't have to come. A loan of the boat would have been enough."

She smiled.

"I wanted to come. I hardly see you anymore."

It took time to get to Cat's Cradle Island and when they had arrived a heavy mist smothered the light of early morning, deadening all sound except for the soft burr of the zodiac's ten-horse motor. Streya steered for the beach. Archie turned to look at her. She was bundled up in her jacket against the cold and damp, as silent as the fog. He was still not sure how much he should tell her, but he had no real reason to doubt her — just a strong feeling that to do otherwise would be a mistake.

When the bow sighed up onto the sand, she followed him out and together they hauled the craft above the high tide line. He grabbed the machete to help with brushing. For a few moments, they stood together, isolated from the silent world by damp air. Suddenly, she leaned in and hugged him and whispered that she loved him.

"I have to level with you," he said.

She put her fingertips on his lips to silence him.

"I'm glad you came to me. I know this island. Where do you want to go?"

"I want to get up near New Jerusalem using the back way," he said. "I thought you might know the trail."

Her face darkened and she looked sad.

"I do but I want you to tell me why we are really here."

He had no choice now. He had a hard time telling lies. He did his best. He told Streya about Patsy's disappearance, said that he felt responsible for his detective and why he thought that she might be on Cat's Cradle Island because of him. He said he thought she might be following up leads he'd told her about and that he had aroused her curiosity about New Jerusalem. If her boat had run into trouble, than the old settlement is where she'd head. He also told Streya that Patsy was defying department orders. Some of his explanation was true. Streya looked at him long and hard. Then she shrugged, repeated that she was glad to help, that he should forget that she had ever been jealous of Patsy.

He nodded.

"I didn't know how much you knew about this place."

"Maybe you should trust me more?"

She turned away and started up a faint trail. He followed her. She said she recognized the shape of the rocks, and the strange forms in the sandstone that had been carved by wind and wave. She said she knew where he wanted to go and set a good pace. She walked quickly, singing softly to herself as she went. The song was strange to him and he guessed it must be in Finnish. She anticipated him.

"It's a folksong — kind of like a love song but tragic."

"It's nice. Has a religious sound, like a benediction or something."

"Yes." She laughed. "There isn't any blessing in it."

"It's still pretty."

"Lots of sad things are."

She stopped him with a hand on his arm.

"Promise me you'll always be careful," she said.

He felt powerfully attracted to her at that moment. He was losing whatever distance he had cultivated. She turned into him, raised her face, lips parted, her white teeth perfect — her hot breath from deep inside. She pushed into him, crushing her down jacket, bent her head up to his and kissed him. After a minute or more, she pulled away.

"I liked that," she said.

He looked into her eyes but saw something unpleasant within them. That seemed to break the spell. What the hell was he doing here with her? What craziness, or power, had brought him to this place in this way?

She laughed softly, saw the confusion in his face, he guessed. Then she eased past him, turned away from him and walked on. She seemed so sure of herself, sure of her directions, that he almost stopped her to ask her what was up but he kept the question to himself. He followed her like a stunned sheep.

The trail was clear enough but other trails led off of it, each of which was deep and well used. Streya glanced back and seemed to anticipate his question. She told him that she knew where she was going because she collected art materials on the island and aside from that she had a good head for directions. As for himself, he was deeply affected by the place, but whether from some ancestral memory, or because of the tone in his grandmother's voice when she had warned him about the island, at Kokishilah, he couldn't be sure.

"Be nice if the mist lifted," he said. "It bothers me."

Streya laughed.

"I thought you'd like it — makes everything more secret."

He wondered what she meant by that.

"I don't want to be seen, that's true."

She stopped suddenly and he almost ran into her.

"What if the Children of Eli get you, Archie?"

Her comment surprised him and he was on his guard immediately.

"You *do* know about this, don't you?" she said.

"I don't know anything. I know the Children used to be a force here, that's all."

She laughed. He hesitated, not sure now what he should say to her now. He decided to play innocent.

"I'll worry about them on Halloween when the goblins come out."

"You're so transparent, Archie. I think you should be very careful — really."

"Why do you say that?"

"Because I love you."

He didn't know what to say about that.

"I'll be careful," he said. "Let's keep going."

He should have told her he loved her — maybe he did. Another man would have. She turned towards him and gave him a look that he couldn't interpret, sadness or madness — something. The trail had become less distinct. She stood aside, pointed towards a screen of cedars and to the path faint beneath them

"Can you hold the branches for me while I go through? I'll follow you."

He hesitated. Then he nodded, pushed aside some branches and started through. A branch whipped back on him and slashed him across his cheek. He wiped moisture from his eye, said, "Damn."

She followed him in. She laughed, hard-edged, cruel. The suddenness of her mood change chilled him.

"Poor Archie," she said.

She peered up at him, false concern in her eyes. He blinked hard, tried to focus, waved her off. She dipped her head in mock reverence and almost ran off through the thicket, disappearing almost immediately. He could hear her singing the Finn song as she travelled. The sound grew fainter and then all was silence. He called out after her, but if she heard him, she didn't reply.

He tried to decide what to do; he hadn't anticipated that he'd be searching for two women on the island. Streya couldn't have gone far and she knew more about the island than he did. She might just be in one of her moods. He followed her trail deeper into the forest, listening for sounds of her.

She came up on him from behind, silently, and startled him. He turned, glared at her. She laughed, brushed back strands of red hair that had pulled loose out of her braid. Her blue eyes were very bright — beautiful and strange, her voice soft and seductive. She talked as though nothing had happened.

"I like it here, Archie — just you and me all alone in the fog. I like the fog. It cuts us off from the world and everybody else."

But he was angry.

"I haven't got time for tricks. A fellow officer is in danger."

Streya's face darkened.

"A fellow officer — ha, ha, ha. Patsy Kydd, your new love."

The husky softness had gone from her voice. She looked into the forest as if she expected to see someone. He looked where she was looking but saw nothing but the darkness of the trees. She looked back at him and smiled, a nice smile, not crazy like the last.

"Don't be silly. I'm getting soaked from this damned fog," she said.

"I'm sorry."

"Sure you are."

She looked away.

"Rose Mountain is over there," she said. "Do you know about that? We can't see it because of the cloud but it's there right up behind New Jerusalem. There are caves under Rose Mountain. They say the Children used them for their rituals. Very spooky."

"So, I've heard."

He drew the machete he'd brought out of its sheath, sized up the bush ahead, but she took the big blade from him before he could think. He tried to read the look in her eyes, tried to figure out what was on her mind, failed in that. She grinned.

"I need the workout. You can take over when I get tired."

She took a tight grip on the machete, hacked the dense Ocean Spray down, legged over a fallen log and then disappeared once again into the fog. He took off his cap, scratched his head and then followed the noise of slashing until, suddenly, the sounds stopped. He called to her. When she didn't answer, he picked up his pace, following the trail she'd put him on.

Emile Pared was waiting for him in a small clearing backed by a wall of rocks. Archie stopped. Wes Means was there too. Means laughed, said,

"This has been too easy."

Archie, sliding his hand back to his belt for his SIG Sauer, inclined his head in Pared's direction. Pared grinned.

"We're everywhere, Stevens, you poor, dumb bustard."

Archie stretched for the SIG, and didn't find it. He was wondering if he'd dropped it on the trail and was silently cursing his bad luck, but then Streya appeared with the machete in one hand and his SIG Sauer in the other. The crazy look was back in her eyes. Pared walked to her and stood beside her. For the first time, Archie saw the resemblance, knew that they were brother and sister. That was a surprise.

CHAPTER 35

Archie watched as the robed figures lifted their goblets and drank from them. He recognized that the cups were made from the calva of human skulls and knew now that the stories he had heard were true. The Children of Eli went about their ceremonies in their Pavilion of Stars in a purposeful and practiced way. At times, they stopped and seemed to meditate or to go into a trance. At last, after a long series of prayers, they seemed to relax and began to talk amongst themselves as if they were at an ordinary meeting. Archie had recognized those from Harsley, including Chad Reddin and Mayor Tom Estes; the others must have come from elsewhere.

It was all so fantastic. Archie tried to think of an escape plan but the numbers against him seemed overwhelming and escape was not likely. He had been under guard since Streya and her

brother had brought him to the Presbytery in
New Jerusalem where they had turned him over
to Arnie Bulkwetter, Chad Reddin and Lisa
Wainright. They had refused to answer his questions. They had hustled him downstairs. Reddin
had insulted him; Estes and Lisa had actually
criticized him for not leaving well enough alone.
Then they locked him in a cellar room, turned out
the lights and left him alone.

Archie remained in the dark holding cell for a
long time. At one point, he even fell asleep.
When, at last, they came to get him, he felt more
rested than he had for a long time. The Children,
now hooded and robed, had taken him out of his
cell. Then they had hustled him upstairs, outside
and into a dark night. Archie was surprised;
many hours had passed since his capture.

At first, he tried to talk to them but they
seemed intent on their purpose and did not respond even when he mocked them. They bound
his hands behind his back and then led him up a
trail to the base of Rose Mountain and to what appeared to be the entrance to a disused mine. That
had led into a network of tunnels. Now he was in
a large, natural cavern, its ceiling decorated with
hanging, silver stars. He sat in an elaborately
carved oak chair, upholstered in faded red velvet.
They had lashed his wrists securely to the arms of
the chair so that he could not move. Seated, robed

figures surrounded him and he knew that he was the centerpiece of some ritual. There were several women there; he couldn't tell which one was Streya though one of them certainly was. He was also sure that she had led the men who had tried to kill him during and after his dive in the waters off Monkey Beach.

The Children's costumes and chants were supposed to impress and terrify, but Archie saw shabbiness mostly, as if the costumes had been bought at a thrift sale. The participants remind-ed him of amateur actors playing parts. A wom-an bent and arthritic seemed to be the leader of the fifteen or so devotees. She wore a purple robe and had concealed her face with a mask that modeled the face of a beautiful young god-dess. The old woman called for silence. Her old voice was high-pitched and grating, not, Archie realized, unlike Arnie Bulkwetter's.

"I speak for all the Worlds and all the Mes-sengers. We will begin. Bring in the other."

A hidden door opened in the wall of the cavern and several more robed figures entered dragging Patsy Kydd between them. One side of her face was bruised and blood had dried on the corner of her mouth. She looked surprised when she saw Archie and even tried to grin. They brought out another carved chair, dragged it over so that it stood beside his and forced her into it. When they had secured her, they stepped back and away from their captives.

Archie was immensely relieved that Patsy was still alive. She shot Archie a wry look.

"Don't trust Stoney Stone," she said. "That bastard is one of them."

"He was one of them," Archie said. "He's dead now."

"That's the best news I've had all day. How did that happen?"

He kept his voice low, told her. She looked at him intently, eyes searching. She was obviously surprised and relieved. Then she nodded at the Children — the so-called Divine Spirits — assembled at the far end of the cavern.

"Can you believe this?" she said.

He didn't know what to say and shook his head. Then he said, "It'll be alright," as if maybe it would.

But that was a vain hope and they both knew it. She grinned at him as if to let him know that he needn't worry about her, that she was a professional too.

"You came looking for me," she said. "That means a lot."

She looked around and rolled her eyes.

"Can you believe this Halloween crap?" she said. "I wonder if they give out candies."

That made him laugh, which earned him a cuff from the Divine Spirit who had suddenly appeared behind him. Archie cursed the man.

The chanting started up again and just as abruptly ceased. The Ultima stood and, in a wavering voice, sang a song in the Finnish dialect, much like the one Streya had sung to Archie earlier. The Children formed a crescent before her, bowed to her in their turn; they seemed to be ranked according to the colour of their robes and they sung repeats of parts of the Ultima's song. The Ultima then made elaborate and theatrical gestures with her hands. Arms were raised. A mask slipped and Archie recognized Laci Laitenen. She repositioned her mask and, with the other acolytes, made a parade around the chamber. Finally, they returned to their carved chairs and drank from their skull cups. Patsy used the diversion to ask Archie how he happened to be there.

"I came to the Island with Streya Wainright, which was stupid really. She led me into a trap. They blindfolded me and brought me here."

"Do you think Streya is one of those masked idiots?"

"I guess she is but I can't tell which one. She was there when they grabbed me of course but I don't know where she is now. Chad Reddin and a Rochville cop named Pared were there and must be in the crowd. Estes is here too."

"Estes?"

"He's one of four brothers. Stone was one; Estes and Bulkwetter are the others. I think Pared might be the fourth. There are probably others, given the fact that Eli had multiple wives. His group's been running drugs, and the town, for decades. "

"Damn. Can a person trust anybody in Harsley?"

"I'm not sure — Cal Fricke probably and a few others."

Patsy shook her head.

"We've got to get out of here," she whispered.

"You got that right. These folks cut peoples' heads off."

The Children finished their ritual and then formed into line. Yet another chant started. A yellow-robed Spirit walked to one of the bare rock walls of the chamber and passed a hand over a sensor. A rock-faced door opened electrically to reveal a dark passageway into the rock. Two burly Children freed Archie's wrists and hauled him to his feet; others took Patsy away in the opposite direction. He called after her, told her he'd come for her but a hard fist to the kidneys cut short that hopeful reassurance. He grunted and stumbled, swore at the man who had rebound his hands behind him.

Pushed into line, he had no choice but to follow the Children into a tunnel that seemed part natural cavern, part mineshaft. It was lit by softly glowing lights set at intervals into the living rock. But it all looked cheap, like a down-on-its-heels horror house, the kind Archie had visited at the Harsley Fall Fair when he was a kid. Even the bulbs at his feet were recycled Christmas tree strings. Mostly, though, he thought about getting his hands free and smashing somebody in the face.

The procession stopped at a heavy wooden door covered with symbols. The yellow-robed figure lit tall red candles that stood on either side. The chanting dropped to a whisper. The Ultima made a sign, spoke words. Yellow Robe bowed, inserted a large and ornate key into the lock, spoke more words, and opened the door. The Ultima entered the chamber. His minders pushed Archie forward and he followed the Children into the cavern, this one very large. Its high vault disappeared into darkness over his head.

Slowly and haltingly, the Ultima crossed the room and seated herself on a low chair at the foot of a tall throne. A figure, wrapped in heavy brocades, sat there, eyes apparently focussed on something at its feet. The hair rose on Archie's head. The eyes were sightless and long-dimmed, and the body dried and horrible.

Brother Eli had never left the island. He still watched over its pots of the gold coins that bore his name. Bales of marijuana and kilo blocks of cocaine stood stacked and ready for shipment nearby. Before Archie could get his bearings, two of the Children dragged him to a brass disc set into the floor and forced him to his knees facing the mummy. Archie was calm and clear-headed in spite of it all.

"Now what?" he asked.

"Shut up, Stevens."

Emile Pared was the wearer of the yellow robe.

"And the hell with you too, Emile."

The Ultima shouted for silence. Pared said, "Yes, mother," and moved away. Someone hit Archie hard on the back of the head and he fell forward, stunned. And then something sharp nicked his bare flesh. He felt his own hot blood on his neck and then the cold metal rim of one of the calva cups against his skin before he was pulled up to his feet.

Pared raised the calva goblet he had used to gather Archie's blood, saluted the mummy on its throne with it. He said something in Finnish and then carried the cup to his mother, who sipped from it. Then, the Ultima pronounced Eli's will. Archie, the sacrificial victim, would be released unarmed on the slopes of Rose Mountain; Chad Reddin would hunt him down and bring back his head. Pared and the others would make sure Archie didn't leave the island if Reddin failed. Pared leaned close to Archie and whispered, "That was Sister Streya's idea. She says she loves you, dickhead, and wants you to have a chance. This suits me just fine so I don't care. Don't get your hopes up. You won't come down off that mountain."

CHAPTER 36

John Robbie waited as Bill Tran, Lars Norgard, Jumbo, and Scorpion checked their weapons and adjusted their gear — all wore black jumpsuits. Norgard looked out of place; Robbie knew that he did too. He thought back to the deal he'd made with the gang leader. Tran had seemed pleased to hear from him, said he had a way to get at Brother Eli's treasure but that he needed another gun. Robbie had no choice but to agree to be that extra gun. He wondered if Bill cared more about the gold than he did about squaring things with his sister's killers. As for himself, he wouldn't rest until he'd made them pay for what they did to her.

He thought about the little he'd learned about the Divine Spirits from his mother, who had escaped from them, and more recently, from Lars Norgard. Now Norgard was part of the deal and had worked something out with

Tran. Norgard would lead the way. He was a guy who liked to brag after a few drinks. One long night, he'd told Robbie about the Children of Eli, about Rose Mountain and Monkey Beach, and about the happenings in a place called the Pavilion of Stars. Scary stuff, he said; best not to trifle with the Children. Robbie let him talk but remembered. Later he told Nick Donaldson about it, which likely led to Nick getting himself killed.

Norgard had tried to scare him too, telling how he'd killed a woman because Wes Means had ordered it and how they'd cut her head off and used it in ceremonies. He had brought out a weird knife with a strange blade and waved it around. Robbie had only half-believed that but now with Norgard just ahead of him, heading towards the slopes of Rose Mountain, his story had a lot more traction. Plus it jived with what his mother had hinted at all those years ago.

Tran had picked the early evening for the assault. When they were ready, Norgard led them up through abandoned fields until they reached a towering rock face on the eastern side of the mountain. They stopped at a patch of stunted cedar. Tran studied it for a moment; he seemed to have foreknowledge that they were looking at an artificial screen used by the Divine Spirits to hide a back door into the mountain. He called

Norgard up to the front, said something Robbie couldn't hear. Norgard moved to his right, unlatched the screen and swung it back. Tran asked Norgard if he had the combination to the security system. Norgard said he didn't.

Tran nodded, waved Norgard back. Scorpion moved up quickly, put the silenced muzzle of his pistol to Norgard's temple and pulled the trigger. Norgard dropped instantly. Robbie, taken by surprise, said, "Fuck!" Jumbo slapped him on the side of the head and told him to keep his mouth shut. Robbie nodded.

Tran looked at Norgard's body lying in the rocks and then at Robbie.

"You going to cooperate, Johnny, or do we kill you right here?"

"I'll cooperate," Robbie said. "You took me by surprise is all."

"He would have betrayed us once we were inside. It had to be done."

He turned, brushed dust off the keypad. Then he consulted a paper he pulled from his pocket, punched in a set of numbers and stood back as the low rock-faced door swung open. He saw Robbie's confusion, grinned, told him that a smart guy had to get the inside track on things to be successful. He said that his original plan had problems but a new one had presented itself. He seemed pleased with himself. When he had finished bragging, he checked the interior with his light. Then he motioned Scorpion, Jumbo and Robbie into the tunnel, telling them to be quiet.

Robbie looked at the weapon he carried. Tran had given him a Chinese pistol; the brand was not one he'd ever seen before. It held ten parabellum rounds, which should be enough to do the job, which was to shoot the hell out of Ray Jameson and Wes Means, if they were there and if the gun would shoot, which he doubted. Tran might not kill him, because of his relationship with Bonnie, but he doubted that meant much to Bill. Besides, he had just seen what happened to someone that Tran didn't trust or need.

They went quickly and quietly. Two hundred feet into the tunnel, a web of slender infrared beams crisscrossed the tunnel. Tran said that it was the Divine Spirits' security system. Robbie wondered how he knew so much. Tran took a calibrated blocking device out of his shoulder bag and turned it on, watched as the beams clicked off one by one.

At last, they reached a heavy steel door that Tran said was locked from the inside. He had brought small, measured charges of *plastique*. These he placed at intervals around the jamb and carefully inserted the wireless detonators. They backed off.

When they had gone far enough, Tran tapped in a number on the wireless unit and the door disintegrated. Jumbo and Scorpion followed him through the dust and chaos and into the Pavilion of Stars. Robbie stayed put and watched from the shattered doorway.

Eli's Children, taken by surprise, tried to fight back. Confused and disorganized, most tried to escape; some were shot down as they scrambled for the door. Tom Estes tore off the god-imaged mask that barely covered his large round face, grabbed an assault rifle from a rack. It jammed on him and he cried out in frustration. Scorpion, laughing, taunted him and then shot him dead with the big pistol he carried.

Tran shot down the Ultima, who crawled to the feet of Brother Eli's mummy and died. The remaining Spirits gave up, threw down their weapons, raised their hands and begged for their lives. Jumbo grinned; he killed them, one after the other, with bursts from his assault rifle.

Robbie watched, stunned and uncomprehending. At the same time, he was thinking too that it had all been too easy. He didn't see Emile Pared or Wes Means in the cavern and that made him wary. For a dozen reasons, he lingered in the shadows near the door, expecting something and not sure what that would be.

He watched Tran step his way through the carnage, cross to the rows of coin-filled jars that the Spirits had set out in ranks before the mummy's throne. Tran reached down and grabbed a handful of gold coins and waved Jumbo and Scorpion over. They came. Tran up-ended a jar and let the coins tumble through his fingers. The other two grabbed for the gold and played with it like children.

Preoccupied, they didn't notice Wes Means, Lisa Wainright and Emile Pared entering the chamber from a side tunnel. All carried auto-matic weapons. Before Robbie could call out, the siblings opened fire.

Tran took a bullet through back of the head and must have died immediately. Jumbo, turn-ing, was shot in the jaw and the shoulder. He swore, spitting blood, grabbed for the automatic weapon he had dropped on the floor. Means walked to him and shot him twice through the head. Scorpion, screaming with fear, dropped his pistol, threw up his hands and tried to sur-render. Grim-faced Lisa Wainright shot him through the throat. And suddenly it was over.

The siblings moved around the cavern checking bodies. A woman groaned and stirred. Robbie saw that it was Laci Laitenen. She said something. Lisa smiled, bent down as if to listen. Then she put the muzzle below Laci's right eye and pulled the trigger.

Then Pared called the others to him. Robbie heard something about things working out as planned, about getting the gold out and setting the charges. But Robbie didn't linger to hear more. He slipped farther back into the darkness and went back the way he had come. He still had work to do.

CHAPTER 37

Archie saw Chad Reddin on the other side of the ravine, saw him unlimber his weapon; he even saw the muzzle flash from a burst before it chopped up the alders beside him. He dove into cover before Reddin had a chance to fire again and soon he was running hard, going ever higher up the mountain. He was tired and sore and he wished he knew where he was going.

Reddin didn't seem at all confused. He was bigger than Archie, but much slower. He made up for that disadvantage with knowledge of where his quarry must go. He read Archie's dodges and diversions perfectly. When Archie tried to go lower, to get into dense cedar forest, Reddin had already circled to cut him off. Occasionally, he fired shots to force Archie to retreat, outflanked him and drove him higher.

Archie knew then that Reddin was driving him towards the cliffs at the west end of the island;

he was being pushed towards open ground but there was nothing he could do about it. When Reddin finally caught up to him, there was no place to go. He stopped at the edge of Cormer's Surprise, looked down hundreds of feet into the sea, turned and waited. Reddin stopped too. He cradled a short-barrelled H&K assault rifle in one arm, dug out his cigarettes, pulled one out of the pack and lit it.

Archie waited. Reddin seemed to be expecting him to show fear and maybe to beg. Archie wasn't going to give him the satisfaction.

"You not scared?" Reddin said. His voice was nasal, the result of Archie's punch in the office confrontation, a lifetime ago, it seemed. "You should be. I'm going to cut your stupid head off after I kill you. Maybe I'll drink your blood. What do you think of that?"

"If you're going to shoot, Chad — shoot. You're such a long-winded bastard."

"Don't worry, it'll happen. I was hoping you'd take a minute of your valuable time to review the hunt with me — figure out the places I outsmarted you."

Archie crossed his arms across his chest, stood hipshot, and contemplated his brother officer. Reddin took off his jacket and dropped it on the rocks.

"Warm work chasing you, Archie."

"Go to Hell," Archie said. "This is as good a place as any to die."

"You will die, my friend — for certain. I just want to get everything I can out of the moment."

A horn sounded down in the channel. Reddin looked surprised, like he was hearing a signal that had come too soon, turned away a little as if waiting for a second blast. He peered into the mist. It was all Archie needed. He darted across the six feet or so between them and slammed his shoulder into Reddin's chest. Reddin, caught reaching for his gun, lost his balance and fell hard, but he was on his feet before Archie could follow up. He yelled something, charged and caught Archie around the waist. They wrestled and slid, locked together, down the wet, slick, slanting rock towards the edge of the cliff.

Archie was taller but Reddin was broader and heavier. Archie hammered him with punches, bruising his knuckles on the knotted muscles of Reddin's massive back. But Reddin was sweating and panting hard now, using up his strength just to hold his opponent.

Finally, he released his grip and shoved hard. Archie lost his footing, stumbled, fell heavily into the salal. He got up immediately, saw in that instant that Reddin's move had put the man on the slanted rock where the footing was precarious.

The dirt beneath Archie's feet felt firm; he was off the slippery, sloping rock and was as safe as he could be under the circumstances.

Reddin was not so lucky. On the downside slope, he was slipping almost unperceptively towards the cliff edge. His gun followed him down, the metal chuffing off the sandstone. Reddin saw it and grabbed it as it slid by and retrieved it. He worked the mechanism and swung the barrel around to shoot. Archie could see the effect of Reddin's movement. Reddin was losing his footing. Reddin knew it too. He struggled in vain to keep his balance, to stop his slide towards the precipice. For a moment, he seemed to catch himself and to start back upwards but then he windmilled his arms and almost threw this gun away. Immediately, he righted himself, grinned wildly, deftly spun the barrel around and fired.

But Archie was already in motion. He threw himself backwards towards some deadfall. He was almost too late. He felt the hard blows of bullets but no pain, crashed sideways into the brush, twisted around so that he could see and fight if necessary.

But Reddin, who now had a puzzled look on his face, was still sliding. He struggled mightily to get back up the slope; he failed. The look he shot Archie was questioning, disbelieving. He said, "Shit," and toppled backwards into the void.

Archie tried to catch his breath. He hurt all over but his left side was the worst; it felt like someone had driven a spike through him front to back. He rested a moment, saw the blood under him; his fingers were so wet with blood that it dripped in great globules onto the rocks. Gingerly, he opened his jacket and checked his wounds. Two bullets had caught his left side, one above the other, and ripped thumb-width gashes through the flesh.

He puffed out his breath in short exhalations against the pain and rested for a few moments. Then he stood up, pulled off his shirt. He ripped off pieces of fabric. He found the purifying moss and mashed it into the wounds the way his granny had shown him long ago. He used strips of shirt as bandage and bound his torso. Then, with massive effort, he pulled his T-shirt back on, found Reddin's jacket and draped it over his shoulders.

He was dizzy and knew he should take time to gather his strength but he also knew that he had no choice but to try to get down the mountain, to go after Patsy and rescue her before it was too late. He fought the profoundest feeling of lethargy he had ever known, rallied his inner resources, and started back down.

CHAPTER 38

Archie had tried to learn as much as possible about the island from Walter and Pete and he thought that after his climb up and down the mountain and his two visits that he had a pretty good sense of its geography. He moved down the mountain, trying to get closer to where he had last seen Patsy. At the same time, he had to avoid Pared, Means and anyone else who might be waiting for him below. They would have heard Reddin's shots and would have no reason to assume that Archie wasn't dead as a result of them. He found a good trail that seemed to lead off to the south, towards the other side of New Jerusalem. It was a start at least. He set off cautiously, keeping as low as he could, making as little noise as possible. Means and Pared had brought him out of the caves through the back end of the old settlement. He'd try to get to Patsy by reversing the route.

The pain in his side was wicked, but he tried not to let it slow him. He felt the chill as he walked — the result of shock and blood loss as much as outside temperature. And then, to his relief, the wind died and he felt marginally warmer. Thick, wet clouds descended, submerging the Island in fog to the level of the sea. He welcomed the lack of visibility at first but soon he couldn't see more than a few feet in front of him — not great for a walk across the fissured feet of the mountain. To save Patsy, he had to get back into the caves quickly and find her but now conditions prohibited speed.

The mist eddied around him as he walked and closed in even thicker behind him. It was getting darker but Archie knew that the moon, if visible, would rise soon. The extra light, if the fog dissipated, might help or it might not, but at least he wouldn't feel so lost.

He had to make his way more by feel than by sight and he found it difficult to maintain the sense of where he was in relation to Monkey Beach. He found a branch that he could use as a staff and tapped his way onward like a blind man. Beyond his worry that he might arrive too late to save his detective, his biggest fear was that he would miss his footing, or step into an unseen crevasse. He didn't need a broken leg to add to his troubles. When he crossed bare rock, he knew enough to slow down, to tap his way forward. Pain frequently forced him to rest.

The bedrock sloped gently away under his feet too soon and in the wrong direction, so he reversed and went higher up the mountain. That brought him to a hole in the fog and then, quite suddenly, he could see again. Above the cloud, the night was clear and the moon was rising.

He was above a line of trees, in amongst convoluted and weathered sandstone ridges. He had walked a stretched fishhook pattern and he knew that New Jerusalem should be more or less dead ahead. He felt his side and discovered, with relief, that the bandages had dried somewhat.

He pulled Reddin's jacket tighter around him, picked up his pace and descended into the fog. He had not gone far before he heard voices and stopped to listen. Two men were arguing close by. He crept closer so that he could hear them better, recognized Wes Means' voice. The other was a local mechanic named Troy Selanne.

"Should have shot him when we had the chance."

"I know."

"You lost that fisherman, Troy. Emile will be pissed."

"Don't yell at me."

The voices moved away from him. Archie tried to follow but soon he lost them. He felt a hint of a breeze and smelled the strong, low tide smell of the beach. He walked more carefully, away from where he had heard the voices, easing one foot ahead of the other, testing his footing. And then he stopped and listened.

A new sound came to him on the breeze, a hollow "pop" and then "pop, pop, pop". He knew that the 'pops' were shots and that the shooters were close by. He searched for a weapon, found a broken branch he could use as a club. He weighed it in his hand and then crept towards the sound.

Twice he stopped himself at the edge of a steep drop where his next step would have been into nothing. Abruptly, he was out of the forest and into the long grass of the colony's abandoned fields. He heard another "pop," much louder this time and ducked involuntarily.

He picked up speed. His cuffs hissed through the tall, wet grass. Too fast! He caught his foot on something and pitched forward onto his face. He gasped as the pain in his side bit into him. Then he pulled himself up and looked back. He saw that he had stumbled on an old plow the Children had long ago abandoned, crouched, and stifled an involuntary groan of pain. He forced himself to rest a moment. He needed a weapon. Part of the plow dangled loosely from the frame. Archie looked at it appraisingly. Then he dropped his branch and wrenched off the oak-handled bar of metal.

The wind soughed and sighed through the long grass. Over that sound, he heard another. Something heavy was coming towards him — rhythmic, rattling choughs like a steam train approaching. He got into a crouch, hefted his new weapon, peered into the grey nothingness and waited.

The fog moved like a river around him, and flowed away towards the beach. The moon was rising higher and he could see a big shape, black against the night, coming fast towards him. He stood up, his makeshift shillelagh at the ready. Suddenly, the shape seemed to sense him; it ducked low, and charged, hit Archie on the rise and sent him sprawling.

He grunted, struggled for his footing, swung his iron whistling through the air and missed. The pain in his side flared aggravated by his wild swing. The big shadow stepped back, peered at him, and reached out a hand.

"Archie," Pete Wilson said. "I'll be damned."

He hauled Archie to his feet, smiled large. Archie could see his big grin even in the dark.

"What the hell are you doing here?"

"I came after you. Walter's here too — at the boat. Delia John told me she had overheard you planning an early morning ride with Streya

Wainright. Delia phoned me, worried about you going over to the island with, as she said 'that crazy chick'. And then I had a dream with a bear in it and had the idea I had to find you — knew you were in big trouble on Cat's Cradle Island. It was almost like I didn't have a choice. So here I am. Walter thinks I'm a nut case. Man, that Delia likes you. God only knows why."

"I'll thank her. You got anything to do with those shots?"

"Hell yes. The assholes are chasing me. Lucky this fog distorts everything. We'd better move on."

"You got that right."

They hurried up through the meadows until they arrived at the edge of the forest and then kept to the trees until they were sure they had lost their pursuers. Pete said he was going back to where Walter was waiting with the boat; he had a pump-action twelve gauge aboard.

"I'm going to get the old scatter gun," he said. "I don't like being shot at. We should go back to get it together."

Archie shook his head.

"I appreciate you coming to help out, but I've got to get my detective back."

"It'd be easier with a Remington pump."

"You're right about that but I haven't got time."

Before Pete could stop him, Archie had turned away. Soon he was loping through the mist, head low, holding his throbbing side, towards New Jerusalem.

CHAPTER 39

Archie decided that the Brother Eli's Presbytery was the best place to start his search for Patsy. If he could get in safely, he hoped he could find the doorway into the cave network that he was certain was in the basement of the building. To his surprise, none of the Children were on guard. In fact, no one was there at all. He shifted his hold on the metal bar and with it held ready in his right hand, crept in through the open Presbytery door. Once inside, he stopped and listened for sounds of activity. When he heard none, he crossed the dimly lit main room.

The door to the basement was half off its hinges and the smell of explosives and rock dust hung in the air. There had obviously been an explosion downstairs, powerful enough to shatter rock. His worry increased. Without waiting, he pushed the door aside and then picked his way down shattered stairs to the basement, saw that the explosion had not interrupted the power to the strand lights that, somewhat bizarrely, marked the way. He kept his weapon ready and hurried, hoping that Patsy was still alive.

He had got into the tunnels easily enough. Someone had tried to seal the entrances with explosives but the charges had failed to do the job. He saw tracks in the dust and knew those who had set the charges had exited through the door that he himself had entered.

He continued down the tunnel, trying not to inhale too much of the rock dust that partially obscured his vision. He realized that he had almost forgotten the pain of his wounds. He made his way mostly by feel but soon the walls were no longer pressing in. At last, he reached the Pavilion of Stars. He stopped, trying to take in what he saw. The chamber was faintly lit by fairy lights. He saw dead bodies everywhere — and an unbelievable amount of blood. Most of Eli's Children had discarded their masks. He recognized Laci Laitenen and several of the others. He hurried his search for Patsy.

He saw the throne and went to it; Brother Eli's mummy had been thrown to one side. He saw Bill Tran and Scorpion and Jumbo; the fact that they were there surprised and confused him. All three were dead, executed, he thought.

He moved on checking other bodies for life. He found Arnie Bulkwetter bleeding from several gunshot wounds, still breathing, still wearing the ridiculous robes he had donned for the ceremony. The body of the Ultima, her mask gone, old face serene in death, lay near Brother Eli's throne. Of Patsy, he found not a trace.

He saw a SIG Sauer very similar to his own next to a body. He retrieved it and checked the loads; he even found an extra clip. Armed now, he returned to Bulkwetter and knelt down beside him. Bulkwetter opened his eyes and regarded Archie balefully and then he spoke.

"You're still alive?" he said. "Who would have thought?"

His breathing was rasping and faint. A pink froth of blood appeared at the corner of his mouth.

"What happened here, Arnie? Why is Bill Tran here?"

"It's a bit of a blur. I guess Tran came for the drugs we had here. We should have killed him years ago, got rid of the competition. So much for deals with gangsters"

He paused for breath. His voice was almost a whisper but he continued.

"After that, I don't know much. Emile came back with the Siblings and opened fire. There was a huge bang and then I lost consciousness.

Are you going to help me, Archie, or kill me?
Emile and the Second Mother's children — they
betrayed us."

"Where's Patsy?"

"Help me, Archie."

"I don't know what I can do, Arn. You're seriously wounded. I have to look for my detective before I worry about you. You have to
cooperate with me or I'll do nothing for you."

Bulkwetter tried to rise but his face contorted with pain and he sank back down.

"I reckon Emile took her to the farm," he
grunted. "Now get me some help. You're a public servant — you're supposed to."

"I'll call somebody as soon as I find some
way of communicating with the outside world,
which I don't have at the moment."

"Can you get me water?"

"I don't have any."

He retrieved a fallen banner, rolled it up and
pushed it under Bulkwetter's massive head. He
thought he should look for water for the man
but Bulkwetter had lost consciousness and
looked like he would die very soon. Archie left
him. He had Patsy to worry about. He checked
the side tunnels but Patsy had gone. Bulkwetter
had been right — Pared must have taken her
away.

Out of curiosity, he went to Bill Tran's body and turned it over. Tran's eyes were open wide and his face rather innocent and untroubled. Archie saw a piece of folded paper in his vest pocket, removed it, unfolded and examined it. He noted the map and keypad numbers and began to piece together the story. Tran had come to get rid of the Children, to seize their drugs and takeover their networks; somebody on the inside had helped that happen.

Most of the Children were dead and the drugs were gone. But Tran and his men were also dead. Bill Tran — survivor, gangster, killer — had screwed up. Archie guessed that he had done a job somebody else needed done. Then those folks had ambushed and killed Tran and his men. A trap had been set and sprung, the bait too tempting to resist. The younger members of the Children, the ones Bulkwetter had said came from the Second Mother, weren't among the dead. The only explanation was that they had killed Tran and his men — and those of their half-brothers and sisters who had survived Tran's attack. Archie was looking at evidence of the equivalent of a palace coup. The remaining Children were even more dangerous and ruthless than he had imagined.

As he considered his next step, he looked at the dozens of overturned and empty glass jars that had once held the Brother Eli gold coins, just like the one Nick had found. He spotted a single coin that had been dropped, picked it up. He had to get moving. He'd try getting help for Bulkwetter when he could, although he thought Bulkwetter was likely beyond saving. There might be life in some of the others though he doubted it. Hurriedly, he checked bodies. He was also looking for a phone he could use. He found one. Because he wasn't sure who to trust back at the Station, he put in a call to the Emergency Services, telling them that there had been a huge accident at Monkey Beach on Cat's Cradle Island, that an illegal mine had collapsed and that there were lots of dead and injured.

He gave directions to the Presbytery and then he rang off. He tried Pete Wilson and was relieved when his friend answered. He asked to be picked up at the wharf as soon as possible and Pete told him he was already on his way. When he had finished, he wiped his prints off the cellphone, dropped it on the rocks and crushed it under his heel. No sense, for the moment, leaving evidence on the SIM that he had been there.

Outside, light was showing in the east. He set out down the slope towards the Beach, followed the old track that wound like a pale, broad, wavering scar through dew-soaked and overgrown fields. He went carefully, alive to the possibility of attack, relieved that his wounds had stopped hurting. He passed among the old buildings, indistinct shadows in the half-light of morning.

He went with heightened purpose. He thought about what had happened to him, what he had witnessed in the Pavilion of Stars, about Patsy. He was so focussed that he didn't hear his attacker come up behind him, slipping out from behind an old house. He also didn't see the overgrown drainage ditch at his feet. He felt the push, lost his balance and dropped hard. He must have struck his head on the way down because the last thing he remembered before he blacked out was the feel of damp earth against his cheek.

CHAPTER 40

Archie struggled back to consciousness. He entertained and rejected different theories about where and what he was until, at last, it clicked in and he remembered that he was a police detective in a ditch. His head hurt and he was cold, wet, and muddy. He got to his knees, found his bearings, assessed the walls of the ditch, stood up and looked around for his pistol. When he couldn't find it near him, he grasped the long grass at the edge of ditch and boosted himself out. As he dragged himself up onto the wet verge, he heard a voice, turned his head, saw Streya Wainright sitting on a fallen log six feet away. Her red hair hung limp in the damp air and her eyes were crazy-wild. She hefted the SIG Sauer he had brought from the cave, pointed it and peered at him over the sights. She laughed, cold as the morning.

"Are you okay, poor, poor, Detective Stevens?"

And then — angrily.

"My love, my betrayer — I hate you," she said.

He held up a hand as if in surrender, shook his head to clear it and stood up. He knew that it was she who had pushed him. He wasn't sure how he should handle the situation. She might decide to shoot him on the spot — or do something completely unexpected.

"What's up, Streya?" he asked

"You for one. I've been waiting for you to wake up. I sat here for over an hour, waiting and waiting. Your buddies are already in the cove, you sleepy head."

"Do you mind if I have a look, Streya?

"You can look, lover."

He turned and watched Pete Wilson's boat, Cherish, edging up to the wharf. Streya rose from the log where she had been sitting, pushed her damp hair back with one hand, kept the pistol pointed at him. He felt sorry for her. And he was worried for her too; he told her so. She giggled, hid her mouth behind the gun hand and then became serious.

"I've got a proposition for you, Archie."

He brushed some dirt off his bloody T-shirt, grimaced at the pain in his side and shivered. Streya looked like death warmed over but he didn't think he should tell her that. He figured that he probably looked worse anyway.

"What do you propose?" he asked.

"Here's the pro-po-sal. I think you'll agree to it. I'll take you to find your Patsy. I'll help you get her away from Brother Emile. After that, I go away and you come with me. Do you like the plan?"

He could see the madness in her eyes, hurt and betrayal, a confusion of emotions. He had no choice but to agree to do as she asked and to hope he would find a way to both help her and to get Patsy back too.

"Tell me where Emile and the others are and I'll come back for you, I promise."

She laughed.

"That's not the way it's going to be. I'll be with you the whole way."

He nodded, said, "Okay." He promised he would do what she wanted. Then he decided that he had nothing to lose by asking for the gun back. She hesitated but then she walked it over to him, reversed the butt and put it into his hand. He let her kiss him on the lips and take his hand. Together, they walked down to meet a surprised Pete and Walter. Archie turned to Streya.

"I have to go talk to them. I won't leave you behind."

"I know. I trust you."

She turned away from him, sat down on the ground looking back towards New Jerusalem. Archie walked along the dock to where the Cherish was now moored, and to Pete and Walter. Pete waited until Archie was close before he spoke.

"What the fuck, Archie?"

Pete was angry and he wasn't trying to hide the fact. Walter just shook his head in disbelief.

"You wouldn't believe me if I told you. I've got to get off this island and find Patsy. Streya's necessary for that. It's not ideal, I grant you."

"Not ideal is putting it mildly."

"Look, Pete. I need your help. Are you going to help me or not?"

Pete screwed up his face.

"Of course — whatever you need, you've got."

"Streya has to come along."

Walter looked at Pete and laughed.

"Next time he comes to the Long House, let's pretend we're not around."

"You talked me into it," Pete replied. To Archie, he said. "You and your spooky lady friend better get aboard before I come to my senses."

Archie called to Streya, now looking forlorn and distracted. She rose and walked to the boat, her hands jammed into her pockets. She had tears in her eyes.

CHAPTER 41

Patsy Kydd tucked up her legs, pulled herself into a new position and made herself as comfortable as space permitted. She was tied and gagged, squeezed into the tiny space under the forecastle where Emile Pared had put her. Some light came through the edges around the locked cuddy-cabin doors. That helped a little — at least she wasn't in total darkness. She could feel the muffled throb of the engines of the boat through the floorboards.

After her capture, she'd been scared but the fear had passed. Now she was just mad, at Stone, at Pared, at herself for being stupid. She had no idea where the other Children were. She worried about what they might have done to Archie and vowed to herself that she would somehow get free and find him. Pared had surprised her; she wasn't even sure who he was until he told her. He was obviously in charge. At intervals, she heard Lisa Wainright's voice in the pilothouse above her and guessed that she was driving the boat. That surprised her.

Her thoughts turned again to Archie, wondered where he was, wondering if he'd escaped from Chad Reddin, wondering if he was safe and unhurt. Somehow she sensed that he was okay. Maybe he was even now searching for her. The thought gave her hope.

Eventually, the boat slowed. She felt it bump into something and then the engine noise and vibration stopped and all was quiet. After a little time had passed, she heard the sounds of cargo being unloaded and then nothing. She realized that she was alone on the boat, with only the sounds of water and the hollow thump of the hull hitting the dock to keep her company, and wondered if there might be some way she could escape. She hadn't eaten for hours and she was fiercely thirsty. She mumbled some spit into her mouth and tried to turn her thoughts away from food and fear.

After some time had passed, someone unlatched the doors to her prison. Emile Pared grinned at her. Outside it had grown dark. He hauled her out, pulled her gag off, gave her water from a plastic bottle. She gagged and water spilled down her shirtfront.

"You look rough," Pared said. "Lucky I didn't forget you."

Patsy glared at him, mumbled a swear word. He grinned at her, held the water up in front of her.

"If you want to be treated right, you have to be a good girl."

He cut the ropes binding her legs and pulled her to her feet.

"No time to play now. I have things to do."

She stood up slowly, defiantly, her legs stiff and uncooperative.

"I'm not going with you," she said.

"You think you have a choice?"

He put his face a few inches from hers, put a powerful hand on her shoulder and squeezed. Patsy winced in pain, twisted against his crushing grasp.

"I'll keep pressing until I bust up all the muscle in your shoulder," he said. "You'll never be able to use your arm again. Is that what you want?"

The pain from his grip was unbearable, a practiced unrelenting pressure on the nerve. She had tears in her eyes from it. She shook her head.

"No, it's not what I want," she said. "I'll come along with you. I don't want to stay in this cabin anyway."

"You are going to be a good girl after all. That's good."

He took his hand off Patsy's shoulder slowly and pointed to the way out.

"You go ahead of me."

He pushed her up the steps and out onto the deck. She saw that the boat was moored to a dock in a small cove; an old farmhouse stood nearby, fronted by overgrown fields.

"What is this place?"

"A farm — a property owned by my father, a place I use from time to time," Pared said.

Patsy turned to face him.

"Is Lisa Wainright the leader? She was driving the boat."

Pared laughed.

"My sister? We're equals — in theory. But I run things. I sent the others away for awhile, so you and I could be alone."

He looked at her intently and she shivered involuntarily. For a moment, she felt close to panic. Pared seemed to enjoy frightening her.

"Don't worry — nothing's going to happen right now because the planets have to be in the right place for certain things. You've got a few days yet."

He frog-marched her up to the house and then to a side door into the basement. He pushed her inside. In the innermost room, he used a leg iron and chain to secure her to a post. Then he cut the ropes off her arms and left her alone. She rubbed the circulation back into her limbs, sat herself up. When she saw the plastic sheeting hanging everywhere, and guessed what it was for, she almost panicked. She struggled against the chain but the metal bit hard into her flesh and drew blood. Half an hour or so later, Pared returned with food and water in plastic containers. An hour or so after that, he came back for the dishes. Roughly, he bound and gagged her again before he turned off the light and left her alone in the dark.

CHAPTER 42

Archie sat at the cabin table. Streya sat across from him and watched everything he did. The tears were gone and now her eyes were like those of a very young girl, innocent and curious. She seemed to want to act something out, to pretend that she and Archie were on an outing together, like in the old days. She talked about inconsequential things. The light tone of her conversation unnerved Archie more than anything else that had happened. She watched Walter and Pete bicker.

"Do they always talk to each other like that?" she asked.

Archie didn't bother lowering his voice.

"It's been like this since we were kids. Now they're like a couple of old ravens arguing over a dead fish."

Pete looked back over his shoulder, played along.

"Both of us had our hands full trying to keep Archie out of trouble."

Walter laughed — a short, powerful exhalation that sounded like "hoh" that summarized his agreement.

"This is a Harbercraft we're looking for, isn't it?" Pete asked.

"Yes. It may already be at the farm," Streya said. "Can't you tell from the radar?"

She stood, made her way over the heaving floor to stand beside Pete. Every time she saw a blip on the radar, she asked if it was her brother's boat.

"There are way too many boats out in the Strait." Pete said. "There's no way you could tell one from the other on the basis of a radar contact."

She shrugged and sat back down, stared out the window into the grey; Archie knew that her mood had shifted again. They ran on until they were close to where Streya said the farm was located. Suddenly, a handheld warning horn sounded close by on the water. A boat was following them, trying to catch up. Walter eased up on the throttle.

"They're trying to signal," Pete said. "I'd better throttle down."

Streya stood up abruptly, her hands made into fists.

"No, no, no, no — we can't stop now," she said.

Walter looked to Archie, who nodded. Walter shrugged, held position, nudging throttle and wheel at intervals.

The horn sounded again in the mist, closer this time. They heard the outboard motor of a small boat as it came speeding towards them, off to starboard. Archie and Pete went out on deck. They watched as the boat came up. Archie had the SIG Sauer ready in his hand.

The runabout had a big motor, which was why it had caught them so easily. John Robbie was at the helm. Archie grabbed the painter Robbie threw to him and made it fast. Moments later, Robbie was aboard. Archie covered him with the SIG Sauer, spun the little man around and pulled a cheap-looking pistol out of his belt. He passed it to Pete. Robbie asked if they'd caught Pared and the others. Archie answered in the negative.

"Not yet. Plus you're under arrest."

Robbie shook his head.

"For what?"

"For Bonnie Tran's murder, or Nick Donaldson's — or both. And then there's what happened back in the cave."

"I never ever killed nobody except in self-defence. Nick found the Eli coins and told me.

He'd been helping Tran with dope and other stuff and then he found the place where Brother Eli had scuttled his yacht years ago. He started to put things together, collected information, tried to do a little blackmail. I figured he was playing with fire and told him so. The night he died I went back to his shop to have it out with him, saw his body and freaked. I turned him over, got blood all over me, cleaned up as best I could and then I ran like hell. I abandoned my truck and trailer even. Then, Bonnie died. I saw what had happened to her and had to figure out what to do."

"That was you on the dirt bike in the rain, wasn't it? Why did you run?"

"You know why, Archie. I had no chance. I had to take off."

"You should have come to me."

"Maybe — look, I cared about her, Archie. I knew it was the Children that done it so I figured Lars would help me get close enough to get them. I figured wrong. I had to go to Tran for safety and then got dragged along on his stupid attack. I saw them get killed in the caves. You know that Emile killed Bonnie and the others. After what happened, I escaped. I used Tran's boat and came after you."

"Why did you do that? You ran from me before, John. You steal my car, escape custody and now you show up out of nowhere after all that's happened and you want me to be cool about it?"

"Sorry about that but I want Pared same as you. I got to see him dead for what he done to Bonnie."

"You're still under arrest."

"So, I'm under arrest. I'm coming with you though."

Streya came out on the deck. She looked confused again. She saw John Robbie and said, "I don't like him." He looked at her, obviously surprised to see her there.

She screamed something at him in Finn — repeating Emile's name three or four times. Archie went to her and tried to calm her. She seemed to like the closeness of him and switched to English. The important thing, she said, was that Emile would rape and kill Patsy Kydd and that Archie wouldn't want her after that. Then she told Archie not to let John Robbie or anybody else divert him from his purpose.

She looked up at him and tears started in her eyes again. He began to guess what Pared had done to her. He felt a deep pity for her and put his arms around her and told her softly that they would do as she asked. Then he guided her back into the cabin. When he had settled her in the bunk, he came back into the pilothouse.

"Let's go."

Pete, who had taken the tiller, said, "Aye, Aye, Captain," slapped the wheel over and pulled back on the throttles. They were getting close. Walter already had the twelve gauge out. He ratcheted a shell into the chamber, waved Robbie to a seat with the barrel. Cherish picked up speed, running on through the mist towards the headlands marking the location of the farm, which was now less than a mile away.

Pete brought Cherish into the first of two small bays at the edge of the property. He idled the engine and let his boat drift on the brow of the tide past the rocky point. The dock with the Harbercraft moored to it was just visible behind a low broom-covered bluff. Archie was on deck, looking, without success, for the farmhouse, maybe a quarter of a mile away. He asked Streya about the house.

"You can't see it from the sea anymore. The trees have grown up too much. It's a copy of the Presbytery on Cat's Cradle Island. The layout is much the same as the one at New Jerusalem. Emile doesn't use the main floors much; he uses the basement for his amusements."

She emphasized the word "amusements" and her eyes grew troubled. Archie wanted to ask her more but hesitated. Pete had brought Cherish into the bay and eased up to the moorage, just behind the Harbercraft. Walter, armed with the Remington, jumped down onto the dock and tied the gill-netter off. Archie stepped over the side rail onto the damp wood of the float and then, pistol ready, he almost ran to the other craft. He jumped the rail and went inside. Finding no one board, he returned to Cherish to plan his next move. John Robbie, out on deck and obviously ready to go, looked his question at Archie. Because, Archie didn't want to give Pete and Walter the responsibility of holding him, Archie gave his okay. Robbie jumped down onto the float and stood beside him.

Before he went looking, Archie asked Pete to take the boat away from the moorage, out to the bay where it couldn't be seen from shore. He also asked his friends to radio Cal Fricke for help. At first they protested, insisting that they'd be better off backing him up but Archie persisted. If something happened to him, he said, somebody would have to rescue Patsy and bring in more help.

"Alright," Pete said. "We'll do it your way."

Archie planned to watch Robbie closely but that didn't happen. When Archie turned to look to Streya, Robbie jumped off the side of the wharf and dashed into a thicket of alders. Before Archie could stop him, he had disappeared from view. Archie swore, shook his head. Robbie on the loose was a complication he didn't need.

Head down, he started up towards the farm-house with Streya half-running alongside him. She caught his irritation, grabbed his arm and slowed his pace.

"We don't want him helping anyway."

"That's not the point."

She made some odd signs with her hands. Then she led him up into an overgrown orchard some distance from where the house ought to be. He wondered why they weren't going direct-ly and asked her.

"It's best not to go that way," she said.

She continued on through the orchard, made a wide circuit through an abandoned garden and brought him to some outbuildings. The night had been dark but now moonlight again illuminated the gravel road out of the property. Archie saw the shape of the house. A pickup truck was parked close by.

Archie turned to ask Streya about it but, sud-denly, she was no longer with him. He didn't go looking for her — no point now. Expecting a trap, he moved through the shadows of the outbuild-ings. He unholstered the SIG and made sure that there was a bullet into the chamber.

The house was quiet, a dark mass against a moon-lit sky. As he crept closer, he heard a sound off to his right. He turned to see a man and a woman walking down the road. They started arguing and he recognized the voices of Lisa Wainright and Wes Means. They didn't seem to see him standing there.

"I'm trying my best to follow orders," Means said. "I don't like the way Emile is acting."

"He just wants to make sure Stevens is dead. That's why we're waiting. You should have stayed at New Jerusalem."

"We were chasing some fishermen. I'm still feeling that gunshot wound I got at Donaldson's, so I'm slower than usual. They picked up somebody and took off in a boat. What was I supposed to do? Then I had to get rid of Troy. I dumped the body in the usual place."

"Anyway — Emile told you to wait. You should have waited."

"I wasn't going to stay just because Chad was late. He can handle himself."

They came within a few feet of Archie. He stepped out of the shadow and aimed his pistol at Mean's head.

"That's far enough."

Lisa, startled, slapped her brother hard across the chest and swore at him. Means cringed. Even in the semi-darkness, Archie could see the fierce look of abrogation on Lisa's toad-like face.

"It'd be better if you put that gun to your own head and pulled the trigger," she said.

"Emile will make you wish you'd never been born."

"Both of you — lie face down on the ground," Archie said.

They hesitated. He wasn't sure how he was going to immobilize them and keep them quiet. He might have been able to use Robbie's help after all. He aimed the pistol at the bridge of Mean's nose.

"I'd just as soon shoot the both of you — I'm that pissed off."

They grumbled and argued, went down to their knees. Lisa cursed, told Archie again that he was going to regret what he was doing. Then, suddenly, she stopped talking. Archie read the meaning in that but reacted too late. He turned at a touch. Pared held a short, black H&K automatic rifle; he jammed the barrel into Archie's ribs.

"So nice to see you again, Detective. Stand away. And get up the pair of you," Pared said.

"I told you, Stevens — I pity you," Lisa said.

She almost jumped up off the ground; her brother picked himself up more slowly. Archie, sensing some confusion, tried to turn, to get better position. The swinging barrel of the gun caught him across the chin, causing his teeth to slam together. He reeled and almost fell. Pared brought the barrel of the H&K down hard on his wrist and knocked his pistol out of his hand. Archie moved his jaws to try to ease them; his fingers were numb from the blow to his wrist. He turned to face Pared.

"God, you're lucky," Pared said. "You should be dead."

"I'm not."

"Maybe I'll keep you alive until Chad gets here. He'd like that."

The idea that Archie had killed Reddin obviously hadn't occurred to Pared, or any of the others. Archie thought it best to keep his mouth shut about it.

Pared motioned Archie towards the porch of the farmhouse with the barrel of the gun. As they neared the steps to the porch, the front door opened and Streya walked out. She smiled at him — mischief or cruelty in her eyes, he couldn't tell. He realized how stupid he had been and knew that his own idiotic self-importance, the idea that she really did need him, had screwed him. Pared prodded him with the barrel of the H&K; Archie resisted. The next nudge hurt and he half turned, his hand raised.

"The gun's got a hair trigger, Archie," Pared waned. "I don't want to kill you just yet. Plus I really would like to know how you got away from Chad."

Archie shrugged and moved forward.

"He's not with me; that's all I can say."

"I can see that, smart guy. Where is he?"

"Fuck off."

Pared punched the gun barrel into the back of Archie's skull. Archie swore again.

"Smarten up and get going," Pared said. "You'll save yourself a lot of grief."

Archie looked towards Streya who was watching everything, her hands to her mouth, wide-eyed. He saw again the craziness in those eyes, her confusion obvious even from a couple of dozen feet away. She brushed back her unbound hair, came down off the porch and stood close to her siblings, the four lined up in front of their father's house. They were very different in appearance, but the same somehow. Pared pushed Archie on and the siblings parted to let him pass. Then they followed him up the steps onto the porch and into the old house.

CHAPTER 43

John Robbie watched the farmhouse from the bushes where he had concealed himself. He studied the interaction between Archie Stevens and the others, he saw Pared come out of the house, and then Streya Wainright. He knew the trouble Archie was in but he couldn't do anything about that; besides it did give him the diversion needed to get into the building.

He had spied out the basement door as he passed by the house. Now, he went to it quickly and silently, keeping to the shadows. He expertly picked the lock. He had decided that he was going to kill Emile Pared to make him pay for Nick and Bonnie. He even had a message memorized to whisper in Pared's ear as he finished him off. After that, who knew, maybe he'd even get some of Brother Eli's gold, not that he would have wagered much on his chances of getting out of the house alive once his job was done.

He entered a storage area and then crossed to a locked and sealed door. He saw evidence of soundproofing and wondered at it. To Robbie, no door was a barrier. He had it unlocked in fifteen seconds. He went into the room.

Patsy Kydd was in the center of the room tied with hands tied above her head, ready like a beef waiting to be butchered. Her surprise at seeing him was evident in her wide-eyed look of sudden hope. She grunted something through her gag. Robbie glanced at the walls. They were hung with plastic sheeting, the purpose of which was evident. It reminded Robbie of what he had heard and read about the activities of Foster, the serial killer, who had been caught fifteen years ago.

Hurriedly he cut Patsy down, helped her take the gag out of her mouth. He put his finger to his lips and shushed her before she could speak, said he had done all he could for her, whispered to her that she should leave immediately — if she knew what was good for her. He indicated the way he had just come. Keeping her voice low. she asked about Archie. Robbie told her what he had seen in front of the house moments before.

She looked worried. She stood a few seconds as if she were thinking about what to do. Then she rolled the stiffness out of her shoulders and massaged her wrists. She picked up a claw hammer from the tool bench and said, "Let's go."

Robbie shook his head emphatically. He pointed again to the door out said, "Get out now, for God's sake. Pete Wilson and Walter George have a boat close by. You can signal them and get help."

She hesitated. He thought that he had convinced her. He left her, went to the other door — the one that led upstairs and into the house. He unlocked it and opened it slowly, quietly. He didn't look back, certain that Patsy would make the right choice and get out like a sensible person. But she didn't do what he expected. Instead, she pushed past him, slid through the door he had just unlocked, and closed it behind her. Alone in the room, he rethought his options.

She had had the hammer ready in her hand and he knew that she was heading directly upstairs to try to rescue Archie. That was stupid. He swore under his breath. Now he would have to wait for a new opportunity. He found a place in a storage room where the joists were exposed, concealed himself and listened for sounds above his head. He heard people moving on the wood floors, deliberate, unhurried movements. He guessed Patsy was waiting, still hidden near the top of the stairs, undiscovered. She would make her move soon. At least, he thought, she could confuse things, do something that he could exploit, something that would help him get to Pared.

CHAPTER 44

The house seemed ordinary in every way. Not that Archie was paying much attention to the décor. He was handcuffed to a straight-backed chair and his complete attention was focussed on Streya who, when she spoke to him, seemed apologetic one minute and psychotically fixated on humiliating him the next.

Emile Pared concentrated on his sister. Sometimes, he stood close beside her, ran his fingers through her long, red hair and, when he did so, he whispered in her ear and she blushed. Lisa Wainright and Wes Means seemed interested only in Archie, openly discussing his grim, likely future. Archie, who was still trying to come to terms with what had transpired, had refused to respond to the siblings. He kept silent. He wondered what they were waiting for.

"You don't have all night, Emile," Lisa said.

Pared removed his hand from Streya's hair and walked over to Archie. He knelt down and looked directly into Archie's face.

"We do have all night, Detective, and more."

"I'll make you pay for this, Emile," Archie said.

His words seemed hollow and desperate. Pared laughed coldly.

"Do you think I came here without help on the way?"

"I'm not stupid," Pared said. "You came in a fishboat and you knew how to get here because Streya told you. Where is that boat now, sister?"

"It's gone, Emile," Streya said. "It's gone — back to Harsley. It was so that Archie and I could be alone. I told them that that was what Archie wanted and they believed me."

"You're sure they believed you?"

"Of course they believed me. They know Archie loves me and would do anything in the world for me."

"There you see — you have no hope, Detective."

He rose and returned to talk to Means and Lisa, to discuss logistics.

Archie tried to figure Streya out. She could have told her brother everything, about John Robbie, about Walter and Pete, about his instructions to them, but it seemed that she hadn't. She was lying to her brother. Maybe she hadn't made up her mind yet about what to do. He caught her eyes and he could see the confusion there, that she was mostly controlled by her brother, but that there was a part of her that struggled against that control.

Pared said something under his breath about getting to work. He turned back to Archie who was now the focus of attention. At Pared's word, Lisa produced a long, carved staff and handed it to her brother. He hefted it and then, without warning, he swung it hard across Archie's shins. Archie stifled a cry of pain. He told himself that he had had worse in hockey games and that helped. Pretending you weren't hurt when you were had been part of his youth. The difference was that — in sport at least — he could retaliate. Not here. Pared grinned.

"How'd you like that one, Detective?"

Archie glared at him, but said nothing.

"I want you to tell me everything you know, from Donaldson on. Be a good boy and we'll kill you quickly. We also want to know about Chad, about how you escaped from him."

"Go away, Emile," Archie said. "My advice is that you get out while you still can."

Pared grunted, reversed the staff and then drove the metal-shod end into Archie's midriff. Archie twisted, trying to dodge the main force of the thrust, but winced as the steel point raked his wounded rib cage. He could feel the blood oozing out of his wounds again. Streya saw the dark stain, stepped in between Archie and her brother, pushed Emile back.

"Leave him alone, brother," she said. "You promised to let me decide what happens to him."

Emile nodded, lowered the staff and took a step back. Streya knelt, put her hands on Archie's hands and squeezed them gently. She looked over her shoulder at Emile.

"He's bleeding, Emile. He can't take much more."

"I didn't make him bleed and I didn't promise not to punish him."

Streya had a short conversation with herself; it was as if she was two distinct people, or had two distinct personalities. Then she started to sing one of her Finnish songs. If she intended to soothe Archie with the song, she failed. He knew she was close to madness — or already mad. Everything she did now made him more apprehensive. She bent down beside him, put her hands on his wounded side and gently lifted his torn shirt. She peeled back the bloody T-shirt and then slowly and carefully she unwrapped the bandage. Emile Pared moved closer to have a look.

"Those are bullet wounds."

Lisa Wainright said, "Ask him how he got those, Emile."

"You heard the question, Stevens."

Archie laughed.

"Your brother shot me just before I killed him."

Streya screamed; her features contorted bizarrely. She slapped Archie's wound as hard as she could. Then she stood up and started to weep. Lisa moaned, a terrible sound that made Archie's hair stand up on the back of his neck. She pushed Streya aside and attacked Archie, slapping at his face, swearing curses at him. Archie could do nothing to protect himself. Finally, Pared and Means pulled her off. Means took the staff from Pared, and took a swing at Archie with it.

Archie twisted in the chair and the head of the staff mostly missed, just glanced off his temple. Even so, the blow half-stunned him. He shook his head, tried to clear it. Pared moved in. He instructed Means to calm Lisa, said that they would find out about their brother later and that Archie was obviously lying. He told them to go to the cache and to start loading the gold and drugs. The two hesitated; Lisa had settled down but she was still incandescent with rage. Means and Pared had to guide her out.

When they had gone, Archie tried reasoning with Streya. He insisted that things had gone wrong, that Reddin was probably still alive. She seemed out of it, barely registering what he said to her. He promised he would help her if he could and tried to soothe her with soft words. He said he understood her and that he wanted help her. If he could make her think that he was on her side, then she might indeed help him. Otherwise, he had little hope he would live through the rest of the night.

But Streya stayed confused, like she couldn't find her bearings. She ignored Archie. Pared returned. Streya asked her brother how it was possible that Chad could be dead since they were all immortal. Pared dismissed her questions.

"Didn't you hear me, Streya? He's not dead. You can't believe Stevens. Chad will come like he promised. He hasn't had a chance to call in, that's all. We'll load the gold, take it south, and he'll meet us where we planned."

She smiled, said, "I guess that's right," and then, "You still love me, don't you?"

Pared winked at Archie.

"Nobody else — beautiful girl. It's always been you and only you."

"You wouldn't keep any secrets from me, would you?"

"Never — I love you same as always, just like father wanted."

Streya seemed happy with that. She turned, smiled at Archie. It was a triumphant smile like he was a lover who had jilted her but now she had someone better.

"I'll be back for you, Archie," Pared said.

Then he put his arm around his sister and led her out the back door. She looked back at Archie over her shoulder, and winked at him.

Archie, still handcuffed, looked around for a means of escape. At that moment, Patsy Kydd came through the door from the basement and entered the room. She saw him and hurried to him, reached and touched the wound on his head, saw his bloodied side and made a sympathetic sound.

"You're a mess," she said.

"You're not exactly ready for downtown yourself."

She shook her head at that, found her own handcuff key in the coin pocket of her jeans, and set him loose.

Archie stood, wobbled. Patsy put her arm around his waist to help support him while he recovered his balance. Neither heard Emile Pared re-enter the room or come up behind them. Archie sensed his presence but turned too late. Pared put the muzzle of his weapon to the

back of Patsy's head. He motioned Archie back
with his other hand. Then, laughing, he grabbed
Patsy by the hair and pulled her to him. He put
his lips close to her ear.

"Here's the deal — I'm going to kill Stevens
and then you're going back to the dungeon. We
haven't had our fun and games yet. Streya
doesn't know about you and me, about how I
amuse myself."

Patsy turned her head and spat at him. He
laughed, grabbed her hair and pulled back her
head.

"That's okay, you know. I like it when you
fight back."

She kicked at his shins with her heel,
fighting against his grip and the pistol still
jammed behind her ear. He shuffled his feet,
stumbled backwards over a turned carpet edge.
Momentarily, he lost his grip on her and the pistol moved away. Archie saw his chance. Pared
anticipated Archie and reacted. He hit Patsy
hard with his fist and knocked her to the floor.
Archie threw himself into Pared. Pared half-
turned to avoid the worst of it and somehow
kept his balance. He still had the Glock and he
swung it at Archie like a club. Archie ducked,
slipped and stumbled to his feet, too weak from
loss of blood. Pared raised the Glock and fired.

Archie felt the hammer blow of the bullet and then his legs gave way beneath him. He tried in vain to get up. Pared switched his attention to Patsy, now getting to her feet. When she was standing, he motioned her to come to him.

"That Indian just keeps going and going, like the battery bunny."

Then he laughed. Archie rolled over and got to his knees. Patsy moved quickly. She shielded him with her body, said, "Leave him alone."

Pared's expression changed, like he had a job to do, and didn't have much time to do it.

"You have to be put back where you belong before she comes back."

"She — you mean Streya?"

Then Patsy figured it out.

"Streya's jealous, isn't that right? You want to avoid that — what has been going on here?"

Pared shrugged. He paused, as if in thought. Archie, watching, tried to rally his remaining strength.

"Too bad. I wanted to have fun with you, Patsy. Now, I think it's better I look elsewhere."

He crossed the few feet of floor and put the muzzle of the Glock in the center of her chest. She froze. He pushed her back towards a couch. He nodded, a little smile on his lips, said, "Of course, she's jealous. Why wouldn't she be? We're bonded, blessed by the Prophet."

He put his hand to her cheek and stroked it. Patsy recoiled from his hand. Pared swore at her, jammed the pistol hard into her chest. He brought his face close up to hers, his breath in her nostrils.

"But she doesn't understand that I need lots of women. I deserve them. I use them, like I was going to use you. It doesn't mean anything. I let Streya be when she wanted to be with Stevens, didn't I? That was fair."

And then he was gone from in front of her. Archie grabbed him by the back of the shirt and yanked him back. He had the staff that Pared had used to thrash his shins and he used it as a prop. He felt superhuman, knew that was adrenalin and that he had better do what he had to do quickly. He had no feeling in his wounded leg at all. He had Pared off balance and he spun him around, hoping that he could get his hands on the Glock. But Pared kept his gun arm safe. He twisted out of Archie's grasp, hit the floor and rolled away. Archie's wounded leg cramped up on him and he stumbled. He tried to work it, to loosen the muscle. Before he could move forward, Pared had him covered once again.

"Boy, you are something else, Detective," he said. "You've been shot at least three times and you're still fighting. I admire that. I'm still going to kill you and cut your head off but I admire your spirit."

And then Archie saw that Streya standing in the shadowed hallway and knew she had watched everything. Pared caught his look, turned his head to look; he saw her too. A look of worry or guilt crossed his face, as with a small boy caught lying. But she smiled at Pared as if nothing was wrong; she walked across the room, took her place by his side. She touched his face, so tenderly. Pared, smiling now, brushed her hair with his hand. She took the hand and used it to lead herself around, like a dancer so that she faced him. Suddenly and without warning, she slapped his face hard and shouted at him in Finn. Archie saw that she had a small nickel-plated automatic in her left hand. He recognized the gun; she had showed it to him once and told him it had been a gift from a brother. She raised it, pointed it at Pared and told him to drop the Glock.

Pared's eyes registered surprise, then hurt, then worry, then cunning.

He shrugged.

"Okay, baby. Whatever you say."

He bent down and placed the pistol on the floor. The gun was close enough for Archie to grab. He moved a little. Streya turned and fired a shot into the floor near his feet. She motioned him back with her free hand as her attention switched back to her brother. Archie stayed where he was.

"If you only knew," she said. "The terrible things I have done for this person. I never failed him, not ever, ever. But he has failed me. "

She was very angry and she voiced feelings obviously suppressed for years. She scolded Pared, told him how much she hated him, how much she hated their father and mother, how much she longed to leave the Children of Eli. Her tone was strident and her voice rose and fell. Her voice changed too — two people in one. Then she stopped, seemingly exhausted. She raised her gun and pointed it at Pared's heart, ready to fire, hesitated and began to weep. Pared, watching her intently, seemed ready to exploit any vulnerable moment.

"I made a mistake, baby sister. Let me make it up to you. The Kydd woman means nothing to me. I just use women like her for fun, and then they're gone. I make them disappear. I can change my ways. Whatever you want, I'll do."

For a moment, Archie thought that Pared might get his way. But Streya surprised him.

"You betrayed me," she said. "You lied to me, older brother — lover."

She reset her stance, pointed her gun at Pared's head. Her shoulders were shaking and she mouthed incoherent words. Her eyes closed; she pulled the trigger. Even with the small gun, the sound of the shot in that confined space was deafening. The room filled with smoke. But her brother was not where the bullet went. He had dodged to one side and she had missed. The echoes from the shot subsided. Pared tried to get the pistol from her but she held onto it.

"It's time we were gone, baby," he said. "It's not safe here anymore. It will be all right, I promise."

She was crying. She moved in to him and put her head on his chest. Archie, watching, felt light-headed. He eased toward the Glock, trying to keep his mind focussed, trying to keep his leg from seizing up. He saw Patsy shift position, ready to back him up. The siblings seemed completely focussed on each other, on what had just happened. Pared whispered some endearment, perhaps, in Streya's ear.

Suddenly, she shifted her position very slightly, stepped back, raised her automatic and fired two shots into him. Pared stopped, a look of surprise on his face. He looked down at the spreading pattern on the front of his shirt. Angrily, he tried to brush off the blood. Then he wavered.

"Damn you, Streya," he said. "I had plans for you and me. We would rule a new star kingdom with new disciples. You've ruined it, you stupid girl. Your jealousy has destroyed us."

Then he sighed and dropped to his knees. Streya, tears streaming down her face, bent down and brushed her brother's face with her fingers. And then her mood shifted. She pointed her gun at Archie and Patsy and motioned them out of the room with it.

"Get out of here — now!" she said. "I have things to do."

"Wait, Streya," Archie said, his lips barely able to form the words.

"Leave or I'll kill you, both of you."

She pointed the pistol at him. He stumbled and Patsy caught him, helped him stay on his feet. Suddenly, John Robbie appeared in the doorway. He looked at Streya and at the pistol in her hand; he even nodded a greeting to her. Streya seemed surprised to see him and swung the automatic to point in his direction. For a moment, it seemed certain that she would pull the trigger.

"We're going, Streya," Robbie said. "We're going."

She was on the verge of a breakdown. She waved them all away, shooing them out. Archie pulled away from Patsy and tried to cross the floor to Streya but John Robbie grabbed him and held him back. In his weakened state, Archie couldn't resist. Together Robbie and Patsy dragged him out through the front door and out. Archie couldn't seem to do anything to stop them; to go back into the house and help Streya seemed impossible.

They were just off the porch when search-lights snapped on. Police cars roared and skid-ded down the access road and into the parking area — a half dozen or more of them. Lights flashed from the seaside too, illuminating the house from every angle. A SWAT team captain appeared and yelled out orders. Black-clad of-ficers forced Archie and Patsy to the ground; others took up positions around the house, pointing their weapons at windows and doors. Fricke appeared out of the bright lights. Through dimming eyes, Archie saw other Hars-ley cops. Fricke shot John Robbie a fearsome look but then he shrugged. He waved the SWAT officers away.

"These are my detectives," he said. "I'm tak-ing command here."

With Fricke's help, Archie found his feet, his attention again on the house. He heard crashing sounds coming from inside as if someone was moving furniture and then he saw the flickering of flames through the windows. The front door opened. Streya stood framed by the sash and silhouetted by the fire that was rapidly claiming the building. Flames punched out windows and raced up the sides of the building. Desperately, Archie called to Streya, tried to go to her but his weakness, and his friends, would not allow it.

Streya looked his way, complete madness in that look. She put her fingers to her lips as if telling Archie to stay quiet. He watched her hair smolder and catch fire. She did not seem to notice. She waved, turned away from him, walked back into the house and closed the door behind her. Archie tried to struggle against Fricke and the others but they held him fast. It was too late anyway. Flames blew out the front windows and shot out from under the roof beams. A few minutes later, the whole structure collapsed.

CHAPTER 45

Archie had made a promise that he had been reluctant to keep. He was still having nightmares, after all. He had said he would give Lee his first-hand account of the Brother Eli matter and the time had come. Both men were still recovering from gunshot wounds too — Archie at home and Lee up in Rochville. But things were getting better. When Lee called and asked Archie to set a date, Archie picked one. They went to the Weather Glass, a popular pub near the waterfront, which was Lee's choice.

Archie parked Lee's wheelchair close to the fire, hung up Lee's coat and creaked his own way into a chair. He ordered fish and chips for himself. Lee got a specialized concoction that seemed to consist entirely of leaves and shrimp. Lee, still pale, was in good spirits and happy to be out of his convalescence imprisonment — as he called it. They talked about many things but

Archie postponed their discussion of the case as long as he could. Lee seemed very much at ease. He wore a new mauve blazer he'd just bought and seemed to like the attention they received. Many people waved or nodded in a friendly way in their direction.

Archie was less happy. For one thing, he wasn't comfortable being out in public, not with the attention he'd recently got from the media over the case. Still, Thomas Lee was good company and Archie had spent far too much time in his condo. Besides, Archie had healed faster than he had thought he would and no infection had set in — that seemed remarkable to him. But he still had many sleepless nights over Streya, tormented by visions of her turning back into the flames.

With effort he pushed the terrible image from his mind. He had avoided the Weather Glass in the past; he hadn't felt comfortable there. Now he felt more at ease. He ordered another diet cola from the waitress and another pint of craft beer for Lee.

Lee was entertaining him with a funny story about a holiday he and Philip had made to Key West when Archie saw Patsy Kydd arrive. She was with the young cop, Tracy Gillot. Archie wondered at that. In spite of his advice, Gillot had gone for the gold ring and his confidence had obviously paid off. Archie felt a twinge of disappointment, not sure why. Patsy saw them, waved in their direction and smiled, and then she and Gillot went to a table in a corner on the other side of the busy room.

Lee saw Archie's look, Archie's eyes following the couple. Lee harrumphed, said something like "all wrong for her." Then he asked Archie if he'd read the article about the Children of Eli in the daily paper.

"If you mean the thing in the Coast Pilot and Guardian, then I did."

"What did you think?"

"It was okay. They left my heritage out of it this time."

"I don't know what you mean. You've got nothing but good press since the event."

"I guess so, but sometimes it seems patronizing to me."

"You're too sensitive, my friend."

"Maybe, I am. It's too hard to tell what people really think."

But it was true that the press had been kind to him. Surprisingly, Jameson had called him to ask how he was and had seemed genuinely concerned.

Since the destruction at the farm, Archie had had to fend off questions about the escape of Wes Means and Lisa Wainright. The press focussed on the fact that Brother Eli's gold had not been recovered. The death of Jim Stone was treated as an unsolved murder relating, the department speculated, to Stoney's involvement with the criminal activities of the Children. Archie did not disabuse them. He had faced some probing questions from Cal Fricke, but Fricke had not pursued the matter too far. The important thing, he said, was that Archie had done his job; he had destroyed a group of serial killing drug runners and had shattered their criminal conspiracy.

Archie's attention drifted to Patsy Kydd across the room, still deep in conversation with Gillot.

"John Robbie?"

Lee's voice interrupted Archie's reverie. He turned to see Lee looking at him, a query there that Archie had missed. Lee had finished his meal and had the look of a sleek, if somewhat pale, cat that had just eaten a particularly plump canary.

"Pardon?"

"When did you stop thinking that John Robbie murdered Nick Donaldson?"

"That happened right away," Archie said. "I knew Robbie from the old days and I couldn't imagine a circumstance in which he would cut his partner's throat that way. He wouldn't have snuck up on him for one thing. Robbie's the kind of guy who loses his temper but wants to have it out with whoever he's got a beef with face to face. They would have had a fight and Donaldson's face would have registered that — Robbie's more so. And Donaldson would have won a fight. And then there was the whole business with the computer. Why would Robbie take Nick's computer and why would he have taken the trouble to erase the hard drive? Like I say — I know the guy. He can hardly turn on a computer. So I more or less eliminated Robbie from the start."

"How did you figure out Tran was involved?"

"I thought about it. I figured Nick had to be involved with dealing drugs. I'd heard stories. Tran was the obvious first place to look. Nick owed money but nothing that would get his throat cut, not like that anyway. That wasn't Tran's style. Tran had visited Nick that night. His boys beat Nick up and recovered their cocaine but somebody else killed him."

"So you figured it was the Children of Eli."

"Not right away, but I came round to the idea. I thought that maybe they still met, a headhunting cult, almost extinct — like a bunch of homicidal Elks. Then I wondered how they made a living. After that it all seemed almost obvious. I figured that they saw Nick diving near Cat's Cradle Island and got worried about that. I didn't know for sure about Pared being Eli's son until I found your tablet. Stoney and Means were both complete surprises. I know now that they had all been fostered out to others in the cult, to the less important members, and changed their names as kids, as you discovered at the archives. The old lady was always a presence. I guess Emile saw an opportunity to make a break with the original group. The siblings were going to take the gold and set up a new Temple."

"So you figured out what Emile intended?"

"Not right away. Not until later. It started with a hunch. But then again I'm probably just flattering myself. Robbie was the wild card in all this."

Lee was obviously pleased that Archie acknowledged his contribution.

"And so Pared killed Bonnie Tran to motivate Bill Tran to attack the cult members while they were meeting."

"Maybe — but Pared, or maybe Lisa, thought Robbie had told Bonnie about the coins Nick had found. Nick had found the wreck of the yacht Brother Eli had pretended to escape on. The Children decided to eliminate him. They also wanted to get rid of Tran, a major competitor. Plus they wanted the old guard of the Children gone. The siblings set the whole thing up.

Most of the ritual murders were group projects, except for what Emile did on the side."

"Then there was the whole incest thing."

Archie didn't say anything to that, just shrugged. Across the room, Patsy was standing. She seemed to be upset with Gillot. Gillot seemed to be trying to convince her of something. After a moment or two, she sat back down.

"They tell me that Patsy did well."

"She did good work and she saved my life. I owe her a lot and I owe John Robbie too. He got to Pete and Walter and they called in the troops."

"It still freaks me out how much a part of the town these people were, and for so long too."

"That was the strategy from the beginning. Eli infiltrated the police force and the local government back when. He would have gone on from there if he hadn't been arrested. He pretended to escape on his yacht but scuttled her. After that he ruled from hiding — ran an empire based on bootleg booze, cigarettes, then drugs."

"So they mummified him when he died and kept up their sacrifices."

Archie nodded. He took a drink from his diet cola. A band called the Pickled Walnuts was setting up their equipment. Their leader, String Johansen, arrived, his mane of hair jammed into his fedora. He was an old acquaintance of Archie's. He saw Archie, raised his hat as if in homage and bowed; his hair blossomed out like an exotic weed. Archie grinned, bowed his head in return.

But he was ready to go, to get out of the Glass before more people arrived. His attention drifted back to Patsy and Gillot; he saw her saying something to him, animated and intense. Gillot said something in turn, but then he seemed distracted by the pretty barmaid who was hovering near their table. Archie inwardly shrugged, decided to let it go. What Patsy did on her time was her own business. He let Thomas know that he wanted to get out of there.

"I'm tired. Plus I've got a year or two's worth of paperwork and trials ahead of us, plus the half dozen unsolved homicides we think the Children of Eli were responsible for. Anyway — I think I'm going to head out.

Lee nodded. Across the room, Tracy Gillot stood up and threw some bills on the table; Patsy stayed seated. Archie felt a moment of something like relief but then Patsy got up like she was ready to leave with Gillot after all. Archie forced himself to look somewhere else, to the band setting up. Lee had been watching him. Archie tried to ignore him.

"What do you really think?" Lee said.

"About what?"

"You know about what."

"She's got her own life. If she wants to try to spend time with a kid like Gillot, it's no business of mine."

"You should be honest with her."

"And where would that get me? It's impossible, Thomas. I'm her boss — a good, professional, working relationship is the best I can get from this."

"Uh-huh."

Archie wanted to change the subject, to get out of the place. When the waitress came by, he ordered a round of Winter Ale for the band. When they had been delivered, String lifted his glass in Archie's direction. Archie responded by raising his cola.

"I owed them that. I lost a bet with String — bet on the Canucks because of Walter George."

"She likes you," Lee said. He wasn't about to let it go.

"What do you want me to say, Thomas? That I'm jealous?"

"Are you?"

"I'd rather that she was with me instead of Gillot — maybe."

"I knew it."

"Let's drop it. I'm not going to do anything about it and, obviously, neither is she. We should get going. I'm done here."

Lee shrugged and settled back into his wheelchair.

"I'll just say that he who hesitates, loses. If you want her, let her know. Also, I'd like to stay a little while longer."

Archie resigned himself to more society than he felt like.

"I don't expect you to stick around, Archie."

"You'll need a ride home."

"Not me — first time I've been out, really out, for weeks. Philip is coming to take me home."

Seeing Patsy with Gillot had unsettled Archie more than he liked to admit.

"Then I'll be gone, Thomas. I'm glad you're on the mend."

Lee nodded. Then he leaned back in his chair, watching Archie grimace his way to his feet, and smiled.

"Ditto."

Archie nodded, gritted his teeth and shrugged on his jacket. The Walnuts were warming up with "Five Long Years". Archie lifted a hand in a wave as he went by the stage. The Walnuts raised their glasses again. Outside, the night was clear and cold, and stars had started to come out. Across the harbour, Galliano Street was busy with shoppers taking advantage of late opening hours.

Archie looked down the street and then cursed his sense of timing. A hundred yards away, Patsy and Tracy Gillot were standing by her car talking, their heads close together. He couldn't tear his gaze away. He saw Gillot move to kiss her. Archie held his breath until he saw her turn her head away. He wanted to be any-place else but where he was — at the same time, he was morbidly fascinated. He could hear their voices.

"How about coming to my place?" Gillot said.

She hesitated, looked like she was going to accept his invitation.

"Not tonight, Tracy."

"You don't have to stay late."

"Not tonight. Thanks for dinner."

Gillot shrugged and walked away down the street. Patsy got into her car and started the en-gine. Archie felt a huge sense of relief and was surprised by it. He tried to back away, tried his damnedest to make himself invisible but she saw him and smiled warmly. Then she waved, ground the shifter into gear and drove off.

Archie remained where he was. Inside the Weather Glass, the music was getting louder. Cars pulled into the parking lot; people got out and went inside. It was definitely time to go. He pulled his collar up and looked down the road.

Her taillights had long since disappeared into the distance.

He turned and limped towards the harbour and went out to the end of the dock. His wounds were starting to bother him. He leaned on the rail and looked out across the cold, moon-lit sea, saw Cat's Cradle Island, deserted once again, as a darker smudge on the horizon. As he watched, he thought he saw a pinprick of light where the old cult settlement was at Monkey Beach, like someone had built a fire there.

The wind was rising and he felt the chill. The slap of waves was loud against the pilings and the ozone bite of the sea in the air told him that bad weather was on its way. He was pushing it and he knew it — his healing wounds had started to hurt like hell.

As he limped back along the dock towards his car, a chant his uncle had taught him popped into his head. He started to hum the tune. He looked back to the Strait. The pinprick of light at Monkey Beach was larger and redder and he thought he could smell smoke on the wind. He took his cellphone from his pocket and made the call.

-The End-